CW00469382

Lots of love

Sandra x

Sandra Antwis is a survivor of years of working in the Social Care and Charity sectors.

She was born and raised in Kent and moved to the north of England after some years on a smallholding in Wales.

This is her debut novel.

Dear Jack

A novel

By Sandra Antwis

ISBN 978-1-80049-972-0

eISBN 978-1-80049-971-3

For
John
Matthew
Alex
With love.

With thanks to Lucy Antwis for the wonderful cover art.

Chapter 1

When Eileen Gilbert won the EuroMillions Lottery, she was not particularly surprised. Rather, she felt that it was about time. Jack's belief that they would win had always been absolute. As she believed in him, so she too had come to believe.

Their plans for the money had been so finely tuned, over so many years, that there was little to do bar putting them into action, but when she finally got the letter that told her the money was actually hers, she stood for a long time screwing and picking at it, alone in her little living room, at a loss.

Finally, she laid the letter on the table, smoothing it flat and turned away. She took a deep breath, dropped her shoulders and closed her eyes for a long moment.

Suddenly purposeful, she tried to drag the sofa away from the wall. It refused to budge. Cursing with frustration, she sat on the floor, braced her feet against the wall and dragged at the sofa. It gave an inch or two and she reached behind to haul out a large art folder which she lifted onto the table, showering an age of dust into the air. She hesitated and stepped back as it settled around her, then walked slowly to the kitchen to fetch spray and cloths. Gently, her hands shaking, she wiped the folder and table until they were absolutely clean. She returned to the kitchen and carefully washed her hands.

There being no more reason to delay, Eileen untied the tapes, opened the folder and studied the large painting inside. A wide, red brick mansion on the side of a hill, viewed from the valley below. A road, a river and a park in the foreground. A wildflower meadow sweeping up to the house. A large wood to the left. A walled garden to the right. Trees on the skyline behind the house.

She moved the painting aside to reveal another. The same house, viewed from the top of the hill. A garden running down to the front of the house. Large French windows, a patio, a porched front door, dormer windows in the roof. Outbuildings in the same red brick ran away from its left-hand end. In the far background the river, the park, the road, a pub on the other side. A hint of a village away to the left.

This time she didn't linger —she moved the painting away to see the next. A view along the front of the house revealing a cobbled yard at the end surrounded by outbuildings and cottages. Behind the cottages a paddock with barns and stables. A driveway snaked away into the distance to a gatehouse.

The next was a drawing – a view of the whole, from above. Neat notes covered every inch. 'Nature reserve…park…football pitches…' Arrows pointed to the house – 'refectory…offices…workroom...apartments…' Little people populated every scene. Children playing in the park; families around picnic tables; teams playing football; people with binoculars and cameras around the woods; faces glimpsed through the house windows; women gossiping in the yard; a man waving up to a woman in a cottage window; a smiling group around a barbeque in the garden.

Eileen sat down, tears dribbling unheeded through the dust on her face, and stared from one to the next, to the next and the next. Dozens of sheets of sketches and notes covered the table. She stroked them with something like reverence. She then moved them to clear a space and, after fetching a sheet of paper from a drawer and a mug of pens, returned to sit at the table.

Dear Jack,
Well, my darling, you were right – £158 million, the biggest UK win ever.
Now what we imagined can be real.

2

We somehow always knew it would happen – it was too real not to. I didn't expect to be forty-eight by the time it did, mind you, and you long gone.

It frightens me, Jack. How can I do it without you? I don't think I can, I am not strong enough. I can't be the public face of it, obviously. You said you were my consigliere, do you remember? I will have to find someone else to help me. It can't be you, I know that.

Then I will need to find Gilbert House. I am just looking at your plans and pictures so I know exactly what to look for.

I will do it all, Jack, I promise, just like we planned.

And I promise you that I will find a way to punish…however many years have gone by, that anger still burns. They say "Revenge is a dish best served cold" and I will relish every mouthful.

I love you.

She folded the letter and put it in an envelope, carefully writing his name and the date on the front. Then she opened the drawer, slipped it in with all the others and closed the drawer again.

Chapter 2

Eileen approached a firm of discreet head-hunters and was clear about her requirements. She interviewed whizz-kids and smart alecs; sharp business people and do-gooders. She lost patience and her temper with the agency, who seemed incapable of understanding what she was looking for.

'This is a charity! Find me someone charitable!'

On a clear October day, Eileen stood in the window of her suite in the country hotel that she used for these frustrating interviews, watching a man walk up the long driveway, a small white dog trotting at his heel. He was wearing an old felt hat, so she couldn't see his face. He didn't seem to be in a hurry, yet his progress was purposeful. As he reached the courtyard, he pulled off the hat and stuffed it in his pocket, lifting his head and surveying the building as if considering if it was worth his while entering.

'He needs a haircut,' Eileen thought.

She studied him as he came into the room – late thirties; tall and lean; dark curly hair; clear, intelligent blue eyes; a rather weather-beaten man wearing a beautifully tailored, grey greatcoat which he slipped off and dumped on a chair, to reveal chinos, slightly scuffed brogues and a soft shirt. He did indeed need a haircut.

A dog is a useful ice-breaker. After politely greeting Eileen, Tilda settled herself under his chair.

'Tell me about yourself,' Eileen said, having already read Richard Aubrey's dossier from the agency. This told her about the candidate – she wanted to meet the man.

'Rather lefty parents – Irish mother, English father. No wife, no children. State school, Law school, the Bar. Defence mostly,' he said simply. 'I have never knowingly defended a guilty person. I made it a rule. Even so, I have had enough of the law for now. Too grubby, too much

4

politics. Some people I trust told me that a new charitable foundation was looking for a director, suggested they put my name forward. The suggestion was short on detail, but I was sufficiently intrigued to take it further.'

Eileen had, for the first time, to lay her vision before a stranger.

'Have you ever read or heard or seen a story about a handful of ordinary people who are trying to help others but are having to fight against injustice or the system or money? The media likes to call them "unsung heroes" but I rather like "champions." Have you ever imagined the kick you would get from just walking in there and saying "There you go – problem solved?" That's what we would do – you and me and our team – finding them and stepping in. Imagine the fun we would have blowing their minds!' Her rather ordinary face was full of mischief. 'We would be the ones with the power for a change. We could do it all our own way.

To survive in the modern world, many large charities have had to become soulless, corporate entities – demanding that their staff meet the needs of others while meeting none of their own. They have to have the same ruthless ethos as you see in big business. The overworked, under-valued staff get minimum wages and lousy terms and conditions. Volunteers are expected to put up with being treated as unpaid skivvies. The Gilbert foundation will be different. It will reflect everything we want to give our champions – first class working conditions and amenities. A park…a nature reserve…we will practice what we preach so our people will have the first-hand experience to offer advice and guidance to our champions.

Out there are thousands of ordinary individuals and small charities who devote their lives to helping others, because they care. Those are the quiet champions that we will find and support. We will actively seek them out. There will be no 'bidding process'. We won't expect them to fill in round after round of forms and climb over endless hurdles. We will take the support to them. As well as money, we will provide experts and professionals to give them such things as legal, fundraising or financial advice. We will work with them, listen to them, give them what they know they need, not what some committee decides they need.'

She stopped, suddenly aware that she was on her feet and striding up and down the room. She returned to her seat and took several deep breaths.

'Where would this foundation be based?' Richard asked, intrigued by the transformation.

'I have a clear picture of the property, so we would need to be prepared to go anywhere in the country to find it,' she replied.

Richard listened patiently as she described Gilbert House.

'You are very particular in your requirements.'

'I have had a long time to plan it, while waiting for the money,' she replied.

Richard regarded her thoughtfully. 'How much money? Enough to do it properly?'

Eileen laughed. 'Oh yes!'

'Sounds interesting. I would be up for that,' Richard said.

'Good. That's settled then.'

Dear Jack,

Well, I have found my consigliere. His name is Richard Aubrey. He reminds me of you a bit. Not physically – he is dark-haired and older than you, late thirties. But he has the same open, intelligent expression. It won't be the same as you and me, Jack, but I think he will do.

Chapter 3

Eileen had assumed that unlimited money would open doors previously closed to her, but she was taken aback at how wide.

Within days, every property agent in the country had their best people on it. It is not every day that multi-million-pound properties are sought by cash buyers and every salesman wanted to be the one who found it. Even with Richard's help it seemed almost impossible.

'It doesn't have a big enough room for the refectory,' or 'It doesn't have a stream,' or any one of a dozen other features that it absolutely had to have.

The small, urban, northern agents, who rarely handled a property like this, were the most dedicated hunters. The sales commission on such a property was worth chasing and it was one of these who, to the surprise of everyone involved – except possibly Eileen – found a property remarkably like the one she described. It was not for sale – the hunters had long since given up on that and widened their search to include every property throughout the country. The owners were an elderly couple: the Rt.Hon. William and Mrs. Edith Champley.

'Let's go and have a look!' Eileen said.

'We can't just barge in there,' Richard replied.

'Oh, I wasn't thinking of knocking on the door!' Eileen said gleefully. 'I have always wanted to go up in a helicopter!'

Clattering above the frozen Yorkshire countryside, a wide, shallow valley opened before them. Apart from a few cattle standing up to their ankles in mud beside the stream, there was little sign of life on the snow dusted land below. On the gentle hillside the great house was sagging and neglected. The roof of the old coach house had collapsed and the gardens were overgrown. Old farm machinery, covered in brambles, rotted in the paddock and an ancient dog barked up at them from the yard.

'There it is, Jack,' she whispered. 'Gilbert House.'

*

Richard wrote, explaining that he represented a charitable foundation and requesting a meeting. Intrigued, yet suspicious, the owners called their solicitor.

'Richard Aubrey QC, eh? I will check him out.'

The solicitor's enquiries revealed an honest, reputable man; highly thought of in his profession. 'Nothing to fear there. Go ahead and find out what he wants,' was his advice.

Spring was beginning to soften the starkness of the old house when Eileen and Richard arrived in the courtyard. A curtain twitched in a window of the mews, though they didn't notice – they were too busy drinking in their first impressions. The borders of the old garden were overgrown, but daffodils could just be seen coming through and the grass had been mowed and the rose bushes pruned. Ivy and clematis smothered every inch of the old coach house and grass was pushing up through the cobbles. Eileen was reduced almost to tears by the warm red brick mansion; so close to the vision she had carried in her heart for so long.

The door opened and a dignified couple in their seventies stood regarding them with friendly curiosity. The old dog emerged to give them a cursory sniff before turning her attention to Richard's little dog, who sat at his feet, watching it with disdain.

'Do come in,' Edith Champley said.

'May we bring Tilda?'

'Of course.'

Eileen's eyes were roaming everywhere. The sweep of the great hall leading to the old mahogany staircase which rose before them; doors on every side, all closed. There was no smell of damp, only dog.

They were taken into a faded drawing room and settled in dusty armchairs. Tea things were waiting on a table before an unlit fire. Eileen was glad she was wearing winter clothes.

'Good afternoon,' Richard said. 'Thank you for agreeing to see us. I am Richard Aubrey, this is Eileen Gilbert. We represent a new charitable foundation which is looking for a home. We have searched the length and breadth of the UK looking for the perfect place. To put it simply, Mrs. Gilbert would like to buy Cheppingham Manor.'

There was a stunned silence.

'Buy The Manor?' William Champley echoed. 'But it is not for sale!'

'What exactly would you do with it?' Edith Champley asked, ignoring him.

Eileen leant forward and addressed her directly. 'We would restore your estate to its former glory. The buildings would look much as they did in their heyday, though the inside may have to be remodeled. I would try to keep it as near to the original as possible. Then my Foundation would employ local people in its beautiful surroundings. They would devote their working lives to supporting small charities across the land. We would also create a park and a nature reserve for the town. It is my dream and here, on this lovely old estate, it could become reality.'

Edith smiled and turned to her husband who, after a moment's hesitation, smiled back.

'This place got beyond us years ago, but we couldn't allow it to be torn down or turned into exclusive retirement apartments. Would you want all of it?' Right Hon William asked.

'All of it?'

'Well, most of the land is let out to neighbouring farmers but we still have the Home Farm House, though it has been empty for some years. There are quite a few farmworkers' cottages – a couple are still occupied by retired workers…and then there is the walled garden, and the gatehouse, of course…'

'I suppose we should have checked out the extent of the Estate instead of just rushing in,' Eileen said, laughing, 'but it was so much like I imagined Gilbert House, that I was rather impulsive.'

'Gilbert House? Is that what it would be called?' Edith asked rather sadly.

Eileen wavered briefly, but then regained her resolve. 'Yes,' she said, 'it must be Gilbert House. As to the rest of the estate, well, of course we want it all if you want to sell it. If there is any part you want to keep, that would be fine, too.'

'No,' William said firmly, 'whatever would we do with it? We have long wanted to retire down into the town. The Old Rectory has been for sale for some time: too big for most buyers. It needs a bit of work, but it would suit us in our retirement.'

'That is settled then,' Eileen said.

'But what about George and Susan?' Rt Hon William asked.

Edith turned her gaze on Eileen. 'Where would they go?' she said. 'They have been with us so for long, we couldn't turn them out now.'

'George and Susan?' Eileen asked gently.

'They live in the old mews. George looks after the grounds and Susan helps in the house.'

Eileen smiled with relief, trying not to let her horror show that people actually lived in the teetering ruin in the yard. 'They sound exactly what we need. Do you think they would be willing to stay on? We hope to convert the old coach houses to three or four cottages. Would they move into one, do you think, or would that be too much upheaval for them?'

'Well, we can ask them,' Edith said, going along with Eileen's fiction that George and Susan would be doing her a favour by agreeing.

'Well, we had better show you around. You can't buy the place without seeing it,' Edith said, getting to her feet.

Standing in the great entrance hall, she said, 'There are four floors altogether and four staircases. Below us are the cellars. Because the House is built on a slope, they are underground at the front, but at the back, they are almost above ground, so there are windows and doors to the outside. Shall we start there and work up?' She led them behind the great staircase to some pokey stone steps going down.

'This was the servants' staircase – there is another in the middle and one at the far end of the house. They would not have been allowed to use the great staircase, of course – not fitting at all.'

By the light of a dim bulb, they descended into another world. Here was a big stone-flagged kitchen; a servants' hall; a butler's pantry; a wine cellar; a cold room and storerooms. Grimy, cobwebbed windows let in a little light. Mr. Champley wrestled with rusty bolts and hauled a protesting door open. A shallow step up and they found themselves on a paved area, looking down the valley.

Eileen stood transfixed, devouring the view. Away to her left was a walled garden and off to the right was a large wood. Between them was the meadow, rolling away down to a wide brook and a road. She smiled to see that it even had a small hotel on the other side. She turned and looked up at the house towering above her, lost for words.

William Champley said, 'When I was a child, there was a small army of servants and farm workers – labour was cheap. So many war widows… people would work for little more than their keep. Then the Second World War came, and the men all went off to fight again. So many never came back and things were different then. Folks wanted more for themselves and their children. And so they should, of course. Why should one family have it all while others waited upon them, eh? Shall we go back upstairs?'

They wandered from room to room – lady's writing room; gentleman's study; dining room; library; music room; drawing room; morning room; rooms without any discernible purpose, until finally Mrs. Champley flung open a door and stood back. A great ballroom stretched away from them and Eileen gasped. Mrs. Champley laughed.

'I just knew you would love this room – everyone does. It has a sprung floor, you know, so they could dance all night without getting aching feet!'

Eileen wandered the echoing space, picturing the refectory that it would become.

'At one time, that door led to a conservatory – that is why it is quite small – to keep the damp and heat out of the ballroom. The conservatory is long gone – it was finally demolished over twenty years ago,' Edith Champley said. 'It was very sad, but it would have cost too much to repair. We thought it would break George's heart.'

Back in the grand hall, wide, creaking mahogany steps took them up to a half landing where the staircase split into two. Up they went to the bedrooms with their dressing rooms and bathrooms. Everything was dust-laden and musty, but surprisingly dry.

'The one thing we never stinted on was the roof,' William Champley said, as if reading their thoughts. 'We made sure it was always maintained. Nothing worse than damp for doing damage, eh?'

On up they went again to the vast attics. They were divided into small and large rooms, a dormitory for the lower maids, separate rooms for the more senior servants.

'The cook, housekeeper and butler had their quarters in the cellar, so they could keep an eye on things. Can't have the minions getting in the wine cellars and pantries now, can we?' Mr. Champley said with a chortle. 'Being above ground like it is, they had natural light and could sit outside on their days off.'

They descended via another endless narrow servants' stairwell – down and down to a vestibule. By this time, they were completely disorientated and surprised to find themselves at a door to the far end of the ballroom. Opposite that was a door to a large gunroom with coat hooks and boot racks. Yet another door would have taken them outside.

'Well, that's about it,' Edith said, 'unless you want to explore the outbuildings.'

'I think we'll save that for another day,' Eileen laughed, 'when we have an Estate Manager who knows what he is looking at!'

'An Estate Manager…' William Champley said wistfully. 'It will be like when I was a boy…' He squared his shoulders. 'Did you have anyone in mind?'

Eileen shook her head. 'It's not something we know much about.'

'I just might be able to help you there,' William said. 'My second cousin has just had to let his estate go to one of those property developers. They are turning the house into a Health Spa and the land will be sold off. They have an excellent Estate Manager, John Hardy, who will be out on his ear. Shall I get him to come and see you? No obligation, of course. I don't mean to interfere.'

'Please do, thank you.'

'I would be interested to see the old place when you have restored it.'

'But I'm counting on you to help me.' Eileen said, 'You know this building inside out. How would I manage without you to advise me?'

The Right Honorable William studied her face for patronising signs. He saw none and smiled. 'It would be a pleasure, my dear.'

My dearest Jack,

I have found Gilbert House!

It is just as we imagined – a rambling red-brick mansion on the side of a hill.

The village is actually a small market town and the river is just a beck – much more sensible if children are to play around it.

It even has a ballroom where we can have our refectory. When did we start calling it that? Ah, I remember, it was when we went to Aylesford Priory to feed the ducks, though you were too old for that sort of thing by then really – they had one and you said that if we could find a house with a grand enough room, we would have one and it would be your kingdom.

Chapter 4

John Hardy slid from his battered Land Rover and looked slowly around the courtyard of Cheppingham Manor. He made his way across to the coach house, his two border collies hugging his heels, and hauled open one of its great wooden doors. Inside was gloomy but he could just see a pony trap. He opened the door wider to let in the light, ran his hand over the gleaming, sea-green varnish of the old carriage and smiled at its canary yellow wheels and shafts. Opening its little door, he stroked the rich, leather interior.

'Pretty little thing, isn't it?' a voice said behind him. 'I like to keep it nice, though it's long since we had anything to pull it.'

John turned to see a weather-beaten man in his fifties, his kindly face creased in a sad little smile.

'George Sanders, general dogsbody,' he said, thrusting out his hand. 'You'll be John Hardy – come about the Estate Manager's job. Don't worry about treading on my toes – I don't want it. Gardening's more my thing.'

John shook his hand.

'They're expecting you,' George said. 'They reckon they're going to restore the house and the estate. A nature reserve, a park. They want me to stay on. It would be good to see the old place come back.'

'I've come from Norwood, a big estate in the Borders. It's been sold to a property developer. Nobody can afford the upkeep of these places any more. Property rich and cash poor, eh? Most were torn down in the Fifties. I've had a drive round already, got the lie of the land.'

'I'll take you across then,' George said.

Eileen and Richard were waiting outside the front door with the Right Hons and Eileen studied his honest face with its bright, intelligent blue eyes and laughter lines, liking what she saw. He was younger than she expected, no more than thirty-five, though why she had thought he would be older, she couldn't say. He hadn't dressed for the interview, she noticed, though his country clothes were at least clean.

John carefully assessed Eileen and Richard with a long look, then smiled widely and thrust out his hand.

I've seen your plans. I'll be responsible for all of the estate?' he asked, before they could invite him in. 'Free hand to do it properly? No penny pinching?'

'Absolutely,' Eileen said, her eyes dancing.

'And I'll be living in the coach-house conversion, is that right?'

'Yes, four cottages altogether.'

He nodded. 'When do you want me to start?'

'Did we interview him, or did he interview us?' Richard asked, laughing, as John drove away.

Chapter 5

Richard learnt, during those first months, that while Eileen required, and had, a detailed and comprehensive overview of every aspect of the project, she refused to be the public face of it. Her insistence on anonymity was absolute: Richard was to be her representative in all things. He had almost complete authority, but nothing was to be done without her knowledge. She would go to extraordinary lengths to be involved while maintaining this anonymity and was adept at inserting herself into proceedings – a favourite role was posing as Richard's Personal Assistant –taking notes and making coffee. He never introduced her, and no-one ever asked.

Though puzzled, the Right Hon Champleys agreed to Eileen's insistence on absolute anonymity and respected it entirely. Their son quietly withdrew his objections when he totted up the inheritance that would eventually come his way with very little inconvenience to himself. His wife had always refused to countenance living in the desolate north anyway, much preferring her Cotswold cottage and London flat.

My dearest Jack,

Richard has taken on all the boring stuff – the Councils, Authorities and Planning Committees.

As you can imagine, their interest quickened noticeably when he described the plans for Beckside Park! There is already a small tractor bridge, across the beck, onto the meadow below the house. Local people regularly trespass on the meadow, walking their dogs. As the Champleys aged and the property began to fall into disrepair, this trespass became bolder. Locals took to picnicking beside the beck, lighting barbecues and holding family parties.

Tales were spreading that we would forbid this: that the meadow would be ploughed, fenced off or even, horrified rumour had it, built on. The locals were gearing themselves up for a fight to protect their rural idyll, so we called a public meeting in the Memorial Hall, which is falling down. Shall I blow their minds?

Large detailed plans were pinned to boards and a model was laid on trestle tables.

There would be a car park; a cafe booth with outside seating; a children's play area; cricket nets; a football pitch; a tennis court; a bowls court; a pavilion. A warden would be on duty and groundsmen would keep it trim.

Wild flower meadows would sweep away up the hill to The House and a Nature Reserve would be created in the woods.

The hall was packed. As I lurked, listening to the chatter, I could see that the local barrack room lawyers, ready to give battle, were disarmed and had to hastily regroup to look for the flaws in the project. Most people were simply mind blown.

Richard eventually asked people to be seated.

'Ladies and gentlemen,' he began, 'thank you all for coming. As you are no doubt aware, the Great Estate has been sold.'

He smiled across at the Right Hons who were seated in the crowd. They nodded graciously in his direction, and I felt some of the suspicion in the crowd soften.

'It has been bought by The Gilbert Charitable Foundation. My name is Richard Aubrey – I am the Director. On the stage with me are representatives of your Councils and Local Authorities, and the Estate Manager, John Hardy. He will oversee the project and will be your first point of contact. Tonight, I wish to lay before you some possible plans for the meadow beside the beck and for a nature reserve. As you can see, it is our wish that these areas become amenities for the free use of the Community.'

Eyebrows were raised, glances were exchanged: 'Free?'

'What do you mean by free?' someone called.

'There will be no charge for the use of the amenities.'

There was a buzz of surprise.

'People will come from all over! It will be bedlam!'

'We would like to work with you to decide how this will be managed. Perhaps we could have a system of passes for the park? We wouldn't want to stop you bringing your friends and relations...visiting teams…we would need to work out the detail of this, of course. However, we would prefer that the nature reserve have unrestricted entry. It is far enough away from the town for visitors to have little impact.'

'This nature reserve…can you tell us some more about it?'

The Councillor, on Richard's left, murmured

'Dean Magson, Chair of local Wildlife and Environment Groups.'

'It will encompass the existing woodland which will be managed and expanded. We hope to create pools and boggy areas within it using the flow of the beck. We'll have paths that run through it, leading to hides and we will plant native trees and other plants to create habitat. John Hardy has a wealth of knowledge of these things. However, we are aware that there are people locally with a real understanding of the area and we would very much welcome their input. I hope very much that we can work with local groups and volunteers to create and run it. We need your expertise.'

Dean sat down, apparently satisfied, but I noticed that he puffed out his chest and tried to look unconvinced. A man used to his own way is my guess, a big fish in a little pool.

'This cafe in the park…is it going to be doing meals?'

'Simon Hance, Beckside Hotel,' murmured the Councillor.

'No, we intend that it will just be a booth, serving drinks and ice creams. We hope that visitors will bring increased trade to your local cafes and hotels.'

Simon Hance sat down with an expression of intense satisfaction. He will have already calculated that the new carpark would encourage customers –- his tiny carpark and the narrow roads will have limited the number.

Families…nature lovers…bird watchers...he will have visions of his tatty hotel, just across the road from the new park, becoming a lucrative business at last.

'What plans do you have for the old walled garden?'

'Jane Rawlings - Cheppingham In Bloom,' came the murmur.

Richard was nonplussed, 'We have none, at present, why?'

Jane smiled wistfully, 'Well, we have often dreamt of being able to restore it.'

Richard shook his head in mock horror,

'So, a park and nature reserve are not enough, eh? You want our walled garden as well!' Jane blushed as laughter ran around the room. Richard met my eye and I gave an exaggerated shrug and joined in the laughter.

'You had better put together a proposal and take it to John,' he said and there was a buzz of delight.

Oh, you would have loved it, Jack!

After the meeting, progress was amazingly swift. The Council and the locals had no problems with the alterations to the Great House itself. Councillors quietly instructed Planning Committees and Building Regulations Officers to prioritise the project. The transformation of the run-down estate and the Beckside area were the source of constant interest and excitement. The local Environment and Wildlife Groups became passionately involved in the creation and maintenance of the nature reserve. Dean Magson was summarily outvoted whenever he became awkward and decided, eventually, that if he was to maintain his position, he would just have to work with the Estate, though he remained a source of some vexation to John Hardy.

Throughout that first winter, John was a constant presence. To the relief of the locals he didn't roar about on one of those noisy, four-wheeled quad bikes, but got around on a stout pony which sometimes pulled a cart, accompanied by his two good-natured, enthusiastic, but incredibly obedient collie dogs. He quickly appointed the first Ranger – Harry – and a crew of groundsmen. His energy seemed boundless and he appeared able to be in several places at once, supervising the working parties. The nature reserve, park, sports fields, wildflower meadow and carpark, were all appearing as promised.

My dearest Jack,

Dear God, it's been a brutally cold winter, but we didn't let it stop us.

Roofers and plumbers; plasterers and decorators; electricians and landscapers swarm in and over the buildings and grounds, spurred on by the promises of bonuses if targets are met.

The Right Hons flit around, poking into everything; offering advice and often in the way, but always welcome. I had said that they were welcome any time, and they have taken me at my word!

They are relieved that many of the original features have been preserved but fled when the great French doors were driven through the wall of the old ballroom, and the dormer windows through the roof. When they returned, they were delighted that the features looked as if they had always been there. Mouldering carpets have been torn up and the old ballroom floor sanded and waxed to return it to its former magnificence. The dingy floor of the great entrance hall has been stripped and buffed, revealing a complex pattern of ruby and white tiles that gleams in the wintry light.

George stomped about, seeing off curious locals who came too near, and picking holes in the workers' efforts. He insisted that most of the old gardening equipment had plenty of life left in it and tucked it back in the barn as soon as the men left for the night.

John appealed desperately to me to get him out from under their feet. I suggested to George that the Right Hons would no doubt appreciate some help settling in to The Old Rectory. George cursed himself for being so thoughtless and whisked Susan off first thing every morning. I assured the Champleys that not only could I spare them, but that they would be doing me a favour! George would be a valued employee once the building work was done but right now, he was just upsetting himself over all the changes. Nicely done, don't you think?

Chapter 6

The sports teams, the Scouts, Beavers and Guides, the Photographic, History and Archaeological Societies and every interest group, however tiny and obscure welcomed an influx of new members as their contributions were sought by The Gilbert.

The Garden Society consumed a great deal of wine and nibbles as they researched old photographs of the walled garden and argued over the restoration plans. Not knowing how much money, if any, The Gilbert might contribute did not dampen their enthusiasm. The tiny Museum, in a back room of the Memorial Hall, took delivery of every bit of broken pot, green encrusted coin and possibly ancient tool. Sadly, nothing of any great interest was found.

Cheppingham had never had any great claim to fame. Dickens had never lived there; Queen Elizabeth the First had somehow failed to sleep the night in the area; no famous, or infamous politician, actor, sports star, or TV chef had grown up there. History had somehow passed them by.

Some residents resented the excitement and activity but, as it was not directly affecting the town centre, were content to pretend that it was not happening. Too many of their fellow residents welcomed it to be worth objecting and besides, the system of passes should ensure that their town would not become the destination for hordes of outsiders.

The Memorial Hall Committee was moved to delighted hugging and back-slapping by the size of the donation to the renovation fund. Volunteers turned out to begin the work, having long lost hope that it would ever actually happen. Any dissenting voices fell silent as the people began to believe that a genuinely benevolent force was at work in their community.

There was a continuous stream of news for the local paper to report. Circulation increased as everyone wanted to keep up with the latest developments when it became apparent that The Gilbert was to have no social media accounts, though there was much discussion on the pages of every local Interest Group.

There was a lot of gossip, of course, about the nature and purpose of this Foundation. Where was the money coming from? Who was behind it? Theories and rumours abounded. It was a local lad made good. It was a pop or sports star with local roots. It was a rich American whose ancestors had once owned the Estate. It was a Government initiative. It was a research project.

That it was a lottery winner was, of course, the obvious answer, but why here? Why this town? It was a local, of course! Someone in their midst was the benefactor, keeping very quiet. Any purchase of a new car, an unexpected foreign holiday or a new extension caused nods and winks. More than one unwitting resident was tipped as the benefactor, before being dismissed as unlikely or, hearing the rumours about themselves, hastily disabused the gossips of the idea.

My dearest Jack,

I moved into one of the old farm workers cottages and in theory, Richard, John and I share it.

In practice, we have more or less lived in Gilbert House from the very beginning.

It has been a strange experience. Many is the night we sleep in our clothes, too tired to care. Some nights I go back and bank up the fire in the cottage and they fall in through the door, filthy and frozen, with fragrant fish and chips. By the time they're eaten, the water is hot and we take it in turns to bathe. We have forgotten that they are men and I'm a woman – it just doesn't come into it, somehow. They have become my family, Jack – and they are all the family I have in the world except you, thanks to that woman. There will always be a raw wound where you should be, and it will never heal until I find you. Even if I do find you, I know I can never bring you home, but at least I could keep you safe.

The first thing I did when I got the money was hire a private detective. He didn't hold out much hope; told me it could take years and a small army to pick up your trail. I told him he'd better recruit his army then and get on with it.

My dearest boy, do you have any idea of the hours, days, weeks and years that I tramped the streets looking for you? You would be just around the next corner...that huddled bundle in the shop doorway would turn and look at me and it would be you. Every time I dropped a coin into a cup on the ground it was for you. Every plateful I served up in the shelter was feeding you.

Believe it or not, I actually caught a glimpse of you once, on the telly. That hateful bitch was smugly justifying cutting a shelter's funding, to the TV reporter. I recognised her immediately, of course, and was so transfixed that I nearly missed you, slipping away in the background.

By the time I got there you were gone, of course. Oh, my darling boy...where are you now?

Leaving our old home is hard, Jack. I'm not going to sell it. All my best memories are there, along with the worst, of course. But what are we if not our memories? They make and shape us, good and bad – we carry them with us wherever we go.

I cannot be in this house without remembering that last, terrible night –those memories I am glad to leave behind. I am giving it over to an abused women's charity. They can use it as they wish and they know where to find me.

Eileen folded the letter and slid it into the envelope with photos and plans of The Gilbert.

She lifted the bundle of letters from the drawer and packed them into a metal box with Jack's childhood drawings, her photo albums and all those precious things which would be the first that most of us would grab if there was a fire. Closing the lid, she locked it and put the key on the chain around her neck. Closing the front door for the last time, she carried the box to her car and, without looking back, took the long road to the north.

Chapter 7

At the end of the busy days, exhaustion ensured Richard's sleep was instant and deep but, his first night in his new apartment, he was awake with the first light of the day. He had thought this pattern, so familiar in London, was behind him.

Pulling on some clothes, he fetched his greatcoat from the cupboard and went outside. The battered felt hat, long unworn, was folded in the pocket. He regarded it for a moment, punched it out and pulled it on. His hands in his pockets, his shoulders down, he set off across the lawn towards the sunrise, he and Tilda's footsteps leaving a bright green trail in the heavy, silver dew.

He had loved her so. She had stopped loving him and he had not noticed. Why hadn't he noticed? It was the loneliness, she had said, being so much alone – he at his Chambers or in his study. She had to leave. No, there was no-one else. She would go to her sister's in New York. She must go now, tonight. She could not bear his pain, or her own. Tilda's anxious eyes. It was too much. She had gone there and then: leaving him wordless, stupid, utterly bereft. Emails and phone messages were ignored. Friends' efforts on his behalf were rebuffed.

The hurt, profound, had shredded his soul. And now the spiked ball of pain in his chest was back, doubling him up, hunching his shoulders. He walked and walked, away across the fields, towards the dawn, in a great circle and, finally, back to the Reserve. Everything was grey, the cloud low over the hills, rolling down into the valley. He rested a while on the bench outside the new workshop, staring across the meadow as the sun rose behind him, burning off the mists.

It was time to let go– he would sell the London flat. He must let her know – some of her things were still there.

He trudged back along the lane behind The Gilbert, his shadow leading him home.

Chapter 8

A grand opening ceremony took place on the Park just in time for the school holidays in July, though there was still much work to be done on Gilbert House. The mayor cut a ribbon, and children poured in to clamber on the play equipment and splash about in the beck, while their parents sipped wine and carried away platefuls of food from the barbecues and pig-roast.

Eileen and John sat behind the house in the sunshine, drinking champagne and watching as Richard and the local worthies mingled with the crowds in the valley below.

'Rather him than me,' John said.

Eileen laughed. 'He loves it, really.'

'And you?' John replied. 'Don't you mind him getting all the attention?'

'The less attention I get, the happier I am.'

John regarded her curiously. 'I've noticed. Why is that?'

'I don't think that's any of your business, John. You don't have much grasp of boundaries, do you?'

'Good god, woman – boundaries? We've scratched along like rats together in this place for months, sleeping on floors, huddled together for warmth. I've seen the state of your socks…dammit, I think I've *worn* your socks. I like your new red hair, by the way. It matches your trousers.'

Eileen shook her head at his cheek as he roared with laughter.

*

Eventually, as the developments neared completion, Richard began the staff interviews. He had watched with interest as discrete surveillance systems were installed throughout the building so that Eileen could watch the meetings and consultations that went on between himself and the contractors. He was, frankly, taken aback when he was asked to wear an earpiece so that she could suggest supplementary questions for him to ask during the staff interviews. He was generally amused by her dual need to be involved in every small detail while remaining unknown. He was, of course, curious to know why this absolute privacy was necessary, but eventually had to conclude that she was just a person who did not relish the limelight. Though they lived and worked so closely together, she guarded her private self and he lacked John's courage to ask her outright.

My dearest Jack,
You would love the refectory.
Tables and chairs line the room. Across its width is a long chiller carousel. At the far end are comfortable, squishy sofas and armchairs, grouped around coffee tables. The huge French doors open onto the garden and the room is full of light.
The new head chef is called James Connor.
Finding him was easier than we expected. There was no shortage of enthusiastic, mostly single, men and women – the hospitality trade has brutally anti-social hours – who realised that their own kingdom was theirs if they could just grasp it.
He is a cheerful lad, in his late twenties. He was excited at the prospect of this new project and delighted that he was to be trusted with a scarily large budget and a decent-sized team. He was impressed with his private apartments in the cellar and the labyrinth of pantries and wine cellars. But far and away the best feature, in his opinion, was the old dumb waiter, which actually works.
It is difficult telling you all this. It should be you. I think you would approve of my choice though, Jack. I do hope so. He reminds me a little of you, of course.

We have two sisters, Jo and Amy, sharing the housekeeper job. One has a little boy, Paul. Seeing him toddling about pulls at my heart.

The old coach house has been converted to four cottages. They have one. John Hardy, George and Susan, and a Ranger, Harry, and his partner Annie have the others.

Now we must find our support and project workers and then the real work of The Gilbert Foundation can begin.

I love you. I miss you.

                                      *

Richard read the email again, more slowly,

'I returned to London a month ago. Friends tell me you have moved away, but no-one seems to know where. Or if they do, they are not telling me. You have given up the law, they say. How sad it is that that you would not do it for me, things might have been so different. I do still miss you. Our ending was so brutal. Where are you?

I have been to the flat. There was very little that I wanted. Give Tilda a kiss from me.'

He stared out of the window, imagining Sophie here, with him. How would that be? She was a creature of the city. What would she do? He couldn't imagine her becoming part of The Gilbert. This was no place for designer shoes and fear of the dark.

He had changed, though. Why shouldn't she? He snapped his laptop shut. He would reply later.

Chapter 9

The Support Staff came from the town, intrigued and excited to see the inside of Gilbert House. They were not disappointed, either by the facilities or by the employment package. The Project Workers were the heart of The Gilbert Foundation. First, second and sometimes third interviews were conducted by Richard, with Eileen following and, too often, intervening through the earpiece, from the adjoining room. They disagreed constantly. Promising candidates were rejected for the most random of reasons.

'She is a Lady Bountiful, I cannot abide a Lady Bountiful!'

Richard lost count of the number of applicants and interviews.

But, at last, it was done: The Gilbert was fully staffed.

*

As the weeks went by, the new team quickly developed a sharp eye for the true champions out there and the charlatans looking for free money. Richard and Eileen began to relax as trust grew. It helped, of course, that the purpose of their work was so joyous. Who does not like being able to help good people do good deeds, especially at no cost to themselves and in such congenial surroundings?

Everyone at The Gilbert now knew Mrs. Gilbert, but their loyalty to the project was already such that, at home, no-one mentioned her. The staff got used to her suddenly appearing at their shoulder, smiling and apparently approving of everything she saw. New gadgets and pieces of equipment appeared without anyone remembering mentioning that they would be useful. She was, it seemed, a mind reader.

Chapter 10

My dearest Jack,

You were found and now you are lost again.

When the investigator told me they had finally traced you to a hotel in Leeds, my heart leapt. I know that sounds corny, but it was true - it actually leapt up in my chest. One of the staff remembered the manager finding you huddled in the doorway and taking you in. He told you he would feed you in exchange for scrubbing the pans in the kitchen. They thought he was mad – that you would rob them all blind then take off, but you didn't. You got your head down and worked for your dinner, then quietly disappeared. But the next day, and every day, you were there, sitting on the back steps. You never complained, however rubbish the work was – you would do anything he asked of you. In the end he put a camp bed in the old boot room, found you some clean clothes. He let you use the shower in his quarters and took you to the barber. He taught you the trade from top to bottom. You stayed until the manager moved on. The day he left, you did too.

Where did you go, Jack?

The staff member told him where the manager had moved to and he went straight to him, but the man said you had made him promise never to give anyone your address and he would not break that promise. He said he would forward a letter and that you are well and settled.

The investigator said he could try to trace your address but I said no. If you want me to have it, you will give it to me yourself. It must be enough for me that you are safe.

I love you.

Chapter 11

As the evenings lengthened into summer, Eileen would often appear at the stable behind John Hardy's cottage and politely request that the pony and trap be made ready. She usually took the gravel drive that ran behind Gilbert House, sometimes turning off down the hill to the Nature Reserve. Leaving the pony tied to the bench in the parking area, outside the new workshop, she would wander in through the young trees, around the paths that skirted the ponds.

Late one evening, she startled Dean Magson as he came away from a hide.

'The Reserve is closed for the night, Madam,' he said pompously.

'I was not aware that The Reserve had opening hours,' she replied, mildly.

'We can't have people wandering in and out when they please. Disturbs the wildlife, you know. Do you have a pass?'

Eileen smiled to herself. 'I don't, I'm afraid. I didn't think that I needed one for The Reserve.'

'Are you local? I don't know your face. I know all the locals. This is a facility for locals and proper groups, you know. There is a lot of important work going on here. I am a Ranger.'

Eileen raised her eyebrows and held up her hand, still smiling. 'Thank you, Mr. Magson. I am familiar with the remit of The Reserve. Next time I will bring a pass.'

Dean, suddenly unsure of this woman who somehow knew his name, though he did not know hers, followed her out of The Reserve. He recognised the pony, of course, and remembered his boasting and hard words with uncomfortable feelings. She had laughed at him, hadn't she? Who was she to laugh at him?

One of the other volunteers came up behind him.

'Who's that in John Hardy's pony and trap?'

Dean jumped. 'How should I know, Rob? Prowling around here at this time of night. A visitor to the House, I guess. Snooty baggage. I shall have to have words with John about strangers randomly wandering in and out. Richard even.'

'Well, it's their Reserve. They can come and go as they like.'

'Who puts all the work in, eh? Us volunteers, that's who.'

'Nobody makes you, Dean,' the volunteer replied as he got into his car and drove off.

*

Dean realised as he parked in the courtyard, that he had never been invited to Gilbert House. For the first time, the omission registered, and it irked him. He had always met John Hardy, and sometimes Richard, down at the workshop, never here. He wanted to poke about – peer in windows; explore the garden he could see beyond the cottages; see what was behind the big French windows, open in the sunshine – but he didn't quite dare, though there was no-one around. Someone might see him from an upstairs window. He looked up, but the glass was dark and blank.

Eileen observed him from her window as he surveyed his surroundings and smiled quietly to herself. She watched as he squared his shoulders and marched purposefully towards the entrance. A young woman rose from her desk and came to the wide reception hatch.

'Good morning, Dean. How are you today?'

'I am here to see Richard Aubrey, Magda,' he stated, maintaining his dignity.

'Is he expecting you?' she asked, all smiles and politeness.

'No, but it is important,' he replied, firmly.

'Of course, I'll ring up to him.'

'Mr. Dean Magson is down in reception. He would like to speak to Richard…. yes…certainly I will. Thank you.'

'Richard will be down shortly, Dean. He's just finishing a meeting. Perhaps you would like to wait in The Refectory. It's just behind you. I will take you in.'

She appeared through a door that he had not noticed and escorted him across the foyer.

As they came into the room, Dean's curiosity about what lay behind the French windows was satisfied. James came forward.

'Dean is waiting to see Richard, James. James will look after you, Dean.'

She disappeared and James, smiling, said, 'Please do sit down. Inside or out. There is a drinks menu on the table and there are pastries and things on the carousel. Just help yourself.'

Dean was, frankly, flummoxed. Feeling rather self-conscious, though the room was empty, he wandered over to the long, narrow carousel which spanned the room. The spotless shelves contained an array of lidded jugs of soft drinks, meticulously labelled, with glasses alongside. He couldn't remember seeing home-made lemonade since his childhood. Re-useable plastic boxes contained an assortment of sandwiches, also carefully labelled. Bread rolls and mini-loaves waited on lidded platters. Pretty china plates were neatly stacked. Cold meat and cheeses and bowls of salads of every sort were below, flanked by dinner plates in the same pattern. His eyes led him along the length, round the corner, up the other side. Here were cakes, pastries, pies, bowls of fruit and fruit salad, a large glass jug of cream.

'The hot lunch is not yet ready, but you are welcome to help yourself from the cold carousel,' James said quietly, behind him.

Dean turned and stared at him, bemused at the quality and quantity of the cornucopia before him. Living as he did, alone and in some squalor, subsisting on shop-bought pasties and fish and chips, this was temptation indeed.

He hastily picked up a plate and, almost without looking, took a pastry. He sat himself at a table and stared out at the gardens. Seeing James approach out of the corner of his eye, he grabbed the drinks menu. James waited patiently, smiling, while he made his choice.

'Coffee,' he said.

'Milk or cream?'

'Milk, please.'

It occurred to him to wonder how much this was going to cost, but it was too late now, and there were no prices on the menu. The coffee was hot and strong and delicious. The pastry was some sort of ingenious turnover affair. He recognised plum in there but failed to identify any of the other flavours. It was so good, though, that he was contemplating slipping over for another when Richard came in, his little dog, as always, at his side. He jumped to his feet as Richard greeted him.

'Tea, please, James. Will you have anything else, Dean?'

A combination of trying to maintain his umbrage, and concern over the lack of any meaningful cash about his person, stopped Dean.

'How can I help, Dean? Are you happy to talk here or would you rather go to a private office?'

'Here will do.'

Richard relaxed back into his chair and, idly stirring his tea, waited for Dean.

'It's about The Reserve. I was down there late last night. There was someone in there without a pass. A woman. She had John's pony and cart. How she came by that, goodness only knows, but I supposed she was a visitor to the house, else I would have called the police. I think we need to talk about the security of the place. We can't have strangers wandering in and out whenever it suits them.'

Richard kept his face impassive as Dean leant forward, waiting to be told who the mysterious woman was.

'Was there any damage done?' Richard asked as the silence lengthened.

'Who knows what might happen down there when I'm not around to protect the place,' Dean said. 'We could get druggies and all sorts, tearaways on motorbikes. Doesn't bear thinking about.'

Richard appeared to give the matter serious consideration. 'We very much appreciate the work that you and the other volunteers put in. Your contribution is vital. We do have the Rangers, under John Hardy, though. They keep an eye day and night, as you know, and there has never been a hint of trouble there, or in the Park. The Reserve is not closed at any time, nor do people need a pass.'

Dean's unsuccessful application for a Ranger's job hung between them. Dean stood up.

'Well, you have been warned. How do I pay my bill?'

'There is no charge, Dean.'

'I prefer to pay my way.'

'There's no charge to anyone in The Refectory. It is free, like the Park and The Nature Reserve.'

Dean took his leave, reflecting that if he had known it was free, he would have filled his pockets while he had the chance. 'Free! Whatever next? Who's paying for it, I'd like to know. And who was that woman? He never did tell me. Bloody funny goings-on if you ask me. Where's the money coming from for all this? Nobody honest has that kind of money. It'll be money laundering. Yes, that's it, money laundering.'

As Dean drove away, he thought he caught a glimpse of the woman, going in through the French windows.

*

'Well-handled,' Eileen said to Richard. 'Silly little man'

'I'll have a chat with John Hardy, get a feel for the situation,' he replied. 'Are we about to have our first dissenting voice? Trouble in Paradise?'

'You are my consigliere,' she laughed, 'I am sure you can get the problem resolved.'

She met his gaze, hard-eyed, shrugged and went back out into the garden. Richard watched her leave, reflecting that, for a woman devoted to charity, she had a distinctly uncharitable streak.

He met John returning to his cottage at the end of the day, with Harry.

'Dean Magson came to see me today, John. What do you make of him?'

'Come inside, Richard, have a brew with me. Join us, Harry, if you don't mind.'

Once they were settled, with the dogs stretched out, cooling on the stone flags, John said, 'He's harmless enough. Likes to toppit the nob.' Seeing Richard's baffled look, he added,

'He likes to pretend he runs the show. He takes visitors in hand, directing them to the best places; pointing things out; showing off his knowledge. He avoids the Big-Lens Boys, of course! Sticks with the people who know nowt. A lot of people quite like that though – he makes sure they see things, identifies birds and suchlike for them. Mixed blessing. Why, is there a problem? What did he want?'

'He bumped into Eileen the other night down there. Virtually threw her out.'

The men's eyes met, and they snorted with laughter.

'Oh, my days!' John said. 'I would like to have seen that. I'm guessing he didn't know who she is….'

'She had your pony and trap. That spooked him a bit, when he saw it, but by then it was too late. He had said he was a Ranger and the place was closed. Demanded to see her pass!'

John's great laugh filled the room. The dogs lifted their heads. Were there games to be had?

'I think he scared himself and came up to get his word in. He went on about the risks to security of having strangers coming and going at will. I was as tactful as I could be, but he wasn't much happier when he went.'

'There is no way we want the place closed off at night,' John said. 'There are often people down there spotting owls and bats. The Rangers do keep an eye, making sure people don't disturb the wildlife, and we haven't had any bother, have we, Harry?'

Harry shook his head. 'We keep people straight.'

'Do you think we could?' Richard asked. 'Badger baiters, druggies, that sort of thing?'

'You are more likely to get scallywags down on the Park at night than in The Reserve. Too far for them to walk! We keep an eye down there too, though. I have a Ranger around at night, and they know it.'

'It sounds to me like you have it all in hand, John, Harry, as I guessed. What do we do about Dean?'

'Nothing, is my advice,' John said. 'From what you tell me, he seems to know he might have made a bit of a fool of himself. If you rub it in, he could turn into a right ugly bugger. I was already thinking the Rangers and volunteers should have badges or something, so people know who to ask. What about some T-shirts, with "Volunteer" on them? That'll check his delusions of grandeur. Ha ha!'

Richard agreed with him, approved the T-shirts, suggested fleeces as well and decided that should do it. Dean would hopefully see a 'uniform' as a confirmation of his position rather than a put-down.

Harry was glad to get away. Annie had booked a meal down at The Beckside Hotel and now he was late. She would not be pleased, though why she wanted to go there, when James cooked the best food in the district was beyond him.

'We never get away from this place. You're forever at work and then your idea of a night out is to eat in the canteen. I want a change. There is another world, different people who don't work for The Gilbert down in the town. Perhaps we can talk about something else but your work!'

'People will pick my brains about what goes on up here, ask me if I can put in a word for them about this or that job,' he replied. 'Better to go to Leeds if you want to get away from it. And I would have thought you would have wanted a real change. You work at The Beckside!'

'My friends and family are down there! You might not be a local, but I am, and I want to go to The Beckside,' she retorted.

So, The Beckside it had to be.

*

All of the local interest groups had been offered the free use of the large workshop in the car parking area of The Reserve for their meetings and many were glad to take it up. James always sent down a picnic basket for them and, on pleasant evenings they sat outside at the tables.

Once a month, the rangers and volunteers met there. In September, Harry brought samples of the new forest-green T-shirts and sweat shirts. "The Gilbert Nature Reserve. Volunteer" was prominently embroidered in gold on the chest.

'We thought it would be useful if visitors could identify you,' he said.

Dean studied them with interest. Peeling off his own T-shirt, he selected his size and pulled it on. 'How many do we get?' he asked.

'Four T-shirts and two sweat shirts, for now. We have arranged with the Country Store in town to supply them and also waterproof jackets – you can go in there any time.'

Dean preened, well pleased. It was about time The Gilbert recognised their contribution. He would wear it around the town.

A golf cart appeared down the lane, bringing their picnic basket, distracting him from reflecting on the fact that it said 'Volunteer' rather than his preferred title of 'Ranger' on his uniform.

Chapter 12

'Good afternoon. Thank you for agreeing to see me, Ms. Marsh, gentlemen,' Richard said to the group in the tatty classroom. The room was a paint-spattered, glorious jumble of easels and half-finished paintings and sketches. It looked chaotic, but each easel had its own formica table with its share of paints and brushes, water-pots and mixing dishes. He noticed that the windows were clean so that the room was full of light. The woman looked anxious and uncertain and her students collected protectively around her.

'Do sit down,' she said.

'Thank you,' Richard said, perching himself on a plastic, paint-smeared chair. 'My name is Richard Aubrey. This is Gemma. We're from the Gilbert Foundation. I apologise for interrupting your session. We saw the feature about your work on the local news programme recently and gather you are having problems with regard to these premises, and with funds. Have you had a positive response following the programme?'

Forgetting for a moment that she had no idea who Richard was, Mrs. Marsh exclaimed,

'People have been so kind, so generous. We've had so many donations! Art materials, money. Hundreds of pounds! We have not solved the problem of where we will go, sadly, but we will keep trying.'

'This Adult Education Centre is to be closed, I gather,' Richard said. 'You will be faced with finding somewhere to hire…that you would have to pay for...'

'Yes, and here we have the room to ourselves, so we can leave all our materials out and the lads can come any time that the Centre is open. We do rather live here!'

Richard looked around at the group of "lads", who ranged from teens to elderly. He reflected that "lads" was a useful collective term: that men remained, at heart, lads all their lives.

'Will you tell me about yourselves?' he asked

'Who are we telling it to?' one of the men demanded

'My apologies. As I said, we are from The Gilbert Foundation. It is a Charitable Foundation which attempts to support small charities and individuals. We are hoping we might be able to help.' He passed cards across, which were examined by the all men in turn, and then passed to Mrs. Marsh.

'The Gilbert Foundation. Gilbert House, Cheppingham, Yorkshire…Supporting The People Who Help Others… Richard Aubrey, Director…an email address…a phone number,' one of the men read out.

'For the benefit of those that cannot read?' Richard wondered to himself.

'You're a long way from home,' the man stated.

'We are a national organisation. We hope that you will visit Gilbert House in the future. It's in a particularly pretty area. You would be very welcome.'.

The man nodded and sat down, suspicious but satisfied, for now.

'We're all ex-cons, but, if you saw the programme, you already know that. We've all got what they call "mental health issues". We come to Mrs. Marsh's Art Group. It helps. People in the group don't generally re-offend. What else do you want to know?'

Richard smiled. This was his favourite part of his job. He could have let the Project Workers deal with this on their own. It could have been done quietly and low key. But he never tired of the kick he got from telling people they could stop worrying about bloody money and get on with what mattered to them.

'The Foundation does what it says on the card. All we ask is that we remain anonymous. What do you and the lads need?'

'Well, we need a home for the group, but I really don't know how that can be. We have tried the Council, the Probation People, oh, you know, all the official bodies.'

'Does it need to be here?'

'I suppose it doesn't have to be, but it needs to be on a bus route. Some of the lads have to come quite a way, though some are homeless, sadly.'

'There are a number of empty shop premises in the pedestrian precinct, near the Bus Station,' Richard suggested. 'If you were a registered charity, you might get some relief from business rates. We could help you with that.'

'Oh, if only! That would be so perfect. There are some quite big shops there. We could have a little sales and exhibition area at the front and the studio at the back...but it's quite out of our reach. We could never afford it.' Tears brimmed in her eyes. The lads glared reproachfully at him for upsetting her.

'A visit to the precinct, then, to see if it might suit. I think the Foundation could run to a long lease on a shop there and running costs. We have people who could apply for grants for you as well. We have an expert for everything! Oh, and some fittings and materials.' Richard said, standing up. 'Now? I have rather cheekily already been in touch with the property agents etc. They have made themselves available this morning. Our legal people would deal with all that sort of stuff when you have found what you need. But, of course, if it doesn't suit, or you find somewhere better, just say and we will follow your lead.'

They stared at him.

'No time like the present!' Richard said gleefully.

*

After a decent lunch, during which Gemma's excitement at being out in the field had bubbled over in endless chatter, their next call was a squat nearby.

A group of activists had taken possession of an empty office block that was being refurbished, moving homeless people in off the streets. An appeal had gone out on social media for bedding, clothing, equipment and food, and the response had been magnificent. He was not sure what more the Foundation could offer, but there was no harm in finding out. They had made an appointment and there was a small crowd waiting for them, led by two sensible women. A lone, bored policeman stood outside the door.

'Get out the way. Let them in,' said one of the men, who they recognised from the Art Group.

The policeman shrugged. Outnumbered and probably sympathetic, he stood aside.

Gemma had studied the press photographs carefully to check that the building had disabled access. Her first task for Mrs. Gilbert had been to delight a charity which provided people with tailor-made wheelchairs, and they had repaid her with a state-of-the-art electric model. However, the entrance had been partially demolished by the builders and with dismay she realised she couldn't get in.

'You hang on there, miss,' one of the lads said. He nudged his friend. 'Give us a hand, mate.'

They disappeared inside, reappearing with a battered door, which they laid down. They all regarded it for a moment.

'You drive it to the edge, miss.'

The lads manhandled the front wheels onto the door.

'Easy does it…. take it forward…no, stop, stop! Left hand down a bit. That's it. On you go…mind the gap!' And she was in, to cheers and laughter.

The policeman, unnoticed, removed his foot from among the others that had been steadying the door.

'Go to it, Gemma,' Richard said, quietly. 'You found them, now you get to follow it through.'

There was an air of excitement. The Lads had obviously told the group what The Foundation was about. Gemma took a deep breath,

'I expect you know why we are here,' she grinned at the Art Group Lads and they grinned back. 'You have had a great response from the local people. This is how it should be – a community helping their own. We absolutely don't want to take over here. We just want to know if there is anything we can do to help. Our only condition is that we remain anonymous. The Foundation offers money, of course, but we also provide support and advice. That may be legal, property, admin, whatever you need. We will work with you and be guided by you.'

'Legal sounds good,' one of the women said. 'The owners of the property can afford the big boys. We have diddly squat.' There was laughter at the unintended pun.

'Do you have someone in mind?'

'No. We're winging it a bit here. We have worked on the streets for years, trying to feed and support our homeless friends. Jumping in here was a spur of the moment thing. The people refurbishing it left it insecure and we just took our chance. It was a bloody cold night.'

'We can put you on to a firm that specialises in this sort of thing,' Gemma replied, 'set up meetings with the owners, try to reach an arrangement, talk to the Council…. We will stay with you and support you as things develop. The Foundation will cover the costs. Is that OK?'

Richard and Gemma stayed with the group for the afternoon, listening to their views; assessing needs; planning; making phone calls; setting up meetings. Eventually, they emerged into the evening light. Gemma was glowing.

'What a brilliant session,' she said, 'such good people…'

'I know exactly how you are feeling, Gemma. And you will stay with this project. You'll see it through. What better way to earn a living is there than this?'

George was waiting outside with the minibus. Richard sat next to Gemma's wheelchair in the back and they headed for Cheppingham.

'One thing that really puzzles me is Mrs. Gilbert,' Gemma said in the darkness. 'She created the Foundation. It is her dream becoming reality. You would think that she would want to be involved in all this, to get something out of it, like we do.'

'I have often wondered the same, Gemma. I have no satisfactory answer to that question.'

Gemma fell silent, and was asleep within minutes, Tilda stretched out on her lap.

Chapter 13

My dearest Jack,

We have been so busy these last months that I have hardly had a moment to stop and think.

Now that we are up and running, I do, but I wish that I did not. Succeeding in creating The Gilbert has made me look back at the sad creature that I was. How did she get so ground down that she put up with it, Jack? I pity her but I can't help being angry with her. She should have simply walked away. You would be here with me if she had.

I am angry with her, but I am even more angry with them, and that anger grows and festers.

There can be no grand gestures of revenge, because it is not in my nature, nor would I wish it to be, but I find myself planning petty acts of spite; imagining scenarios where I humiliate and demean. I am not proud of these thoughts, but I am only human.

*

Richard was deep in spreadsheets when Eileen came into his room. She had a habit of doing this: not knocking, appearing from nowhere. She went to the window and stared down the valley. Richard tried to carry on with his work, but he knew she would require his attention eventually.

'I was thinking, Richard, of appointing a Deputy.'

Richard was suddenly listening. He swivelled his chair to face her. 'Deputy what?' he asked.

'Director,' she replied.

'I don't need a Deputy. Do *you* think I need one?'

'I think that I want you to have one. Though General Manager might be a better title, maybe' She sat herself down opposite him.

'The Foundation is up and running. All of the hard work is done. I have the time and resources to run it. We are already over-staffed. What would this General Manager do?'

'Organise staff training…'

'The Section Heads do that. They are always getting together and cooking up some new training that everyone must have. We have the best-trained workforce in the sector!'

'Staff Welfare.'

'Section Heads.'

'Building Maintenance.'

'John Hardy, George, Jo… and me.'

'Recruitment.'

'Section Heads…and me.'

'Financial Management.'

'The Admin Team…and me.'

'And that is my point, Richard, you are wasted on all this day-to-day stuff. We could look at research and development if you were not taken up with all that sort of thing.'

Richard sat back in his chair and studied her ingenuous expression.

'What sort of research and development?'

'New roles for the Foundation, maybe. We could specialise…go into more depth in some areas…I have been on to the people who found you for me. They have identified some possible candidates. We will invite them here for several days. They'll stay in the mews and you will interview them. I will observe from my office. We'll put them through their paces, see what they are made of.'

Richard could not help reflecting back to his own interview which had lasted no more than an hour.

'Eileen, may I ask a question?'

'Of course, Richard. You ask me questions all the time.'

'This is a little different, personal…why do you remain in the background? Why must nobody outside know your face? The staff all know you now. What difference can it make that others know you? Interacting with our champions is hugely rewarding. Don't you want to be part of that?'

She was not expecting the question – he could tell by her expression. She stood up and turned back to the window. There was a long silence.

'When I won the money, I was scared of the media. It was one of the biggest UK wins ever. They did their damndest to find me. I had opted for anonymity, so they didn't know my name, thank goodness. Can you imagine the thousands of begging letters if they had? The Foundation has been able to follow its own path; define its remit; choose its beneficiaries; remain autonomous. Would that have been possible if I had been its public face?' she said without turning.

Richard studied her rigid back, her hands gripping the window sill. 'Eileen,' he said gently. 'What is it really? You can trust me, surely?'

Her head dropped, she relaxed her hands and leant on the sill as if exhausted. After a long moment she straightened and turned. She deliberately sat herself facing him.

'I have an ex-husband, Richard. He was a nasty, abusive bully and womanizer who made my life a misery. I should have left him the minute I realised what he was. Why do women do that – convince themselves that that is the best they deserve? I put up with it, thinking I could change him.' She snorted in derision at her own naivety. 'He left in the end, anyway. I have reverted to my maiden name but if he sees my picture in the paper and finds out I've got money he'll be back to cash in'

'You are not the timid woman you were when I first met you, Eileen, and you are safe here. We would soon see him off,' Richard said gently.

Eileen stood up, her face twisted with irritation. 'I have given you my explanation, Richard. That should be enough, even for you. How I choose to behave is my business.' Seeing his shocked face, she took a breath and deliberately softened her stance. 'Perhaps I might make the occasional field trip. You do rather seem to have fun on those. After these interviews, though. I don't want these candidates to meet me. I will leave you to make arrangements. Here are the details. We'll meet again to plan the interviews,' she said firmly, and left.

Richard stared at the closed door, baffled.

*

There were three people's details in the folder. Two women, one man. None of these people had seen an advertisement or filled in an application form. That was not how the Head Hunters worked. Their ways were many and mysterious. They found people; people did not find them. Once approved by the client, these candidates would be approached, told that their excellent record had attracted the attention of a top-class employer, and invite them to be considered. That was how it had happened with Richard. He began to read.

Chris Turpin was a man in his forties. His background was in hospitality. He had managed golf clubs, hotels and conference centres. His experience and qualifications were relevant and appropriate.

Jasmine Gwembe, 42, had risen from care worker to manager of an elderly care home. She had NVQ and Registered Manager Qualifications and steady, sound experience.

Jennie Green, 38, had a work record in Further Education and in social care training and charity. Her last post had been a manager with a private elderly care group. She had various rather random qualifications including a Distance Learning Degree from a private college.

What immediately struck him was that the longest she had ever stayed in a post was two years. She had hopped from job to job, each a little higher up the career ladder. Some were temporary posts – fair enough – but most were not. She had stayed just long enough to throw everything up in the air, but not long enough to catch it as it all came down again.

Whatever did this person have that had prompted Eileen to include her?

Chapter 14

A car crept slowly along the back lane behind The Gilbert, its wheels scrunching on the gravel. It stopped behind the house and a woman got out, looking up at the windows. She turned and walked on ahead, the car creeping along behind her. As they reached the end of the mews, she pointed, and the driver pulled over, parking his car as far onto the verge as possible.

The pair made their way up the steps beside the mews and emerged into the courtyard. Two dogs bounded from a cottage and the pair froze. A man emerged and smiled a welcome.

'Daft buggers might lick you to death,' he warned.

'Is this The Gilbert?' the woman asked hesitantly.

'It is. What can we do for you?'

'We have just been to your Reserve. We saw it on social media and thought we would come and have a look. It's wonderful. People down there said it belonged to The Gilbert and sort of waved in this direction. We have left our car on the lane behind the house. I hope that is alright. We were hoping for some advice...'

'You've come to the right place, then. Your car will probably be fine where it is, but I can have it brought up here for you if you give me the keys.'

He banged on the next cottage door and George emerged.

'You got a minute, George? These lovely people have left their car behind the house. Fetch it up here for them, will you?'

'Be happy to,' George said and held his hand out for the keys. Too surprised to question, the man handed them over.

'I will take them into The Refectory,' John called to George's retreating back.

'Righto!' George called back.

'You realise you may never see your car again, don't you?' John said and winked.

They smiled nervously, not wanting to admit that they had been thinking exactly that.

'Come in, come in,' John said and led the way along the patio.

The pair paused and looked up at the garden, full of colour in its summer clothes.

'At its best at this time of year,' John said. 'Our George has the greenest fingers of anyone I know.'

He led the way inside, where they were greeted by James. A few people were dotted about, and all said hello.

'Are you hungry?' John asked. 'I am going to have something. We have missed lunch, but there's always cold. Will you join me?' He took them over to the carousel and began to systematically load a plate with meat, cheese, salads and bread. 'Don't worry, there's no charge,' he said, 'dig in.'

The pair looked at one another with barely concealed surprise mixed with some suspicion, but followed John's lead, albeit with much more restraint.

John led them to a table out on the patio where James took their drink order.

'Right then,' John said. 'What sort of advice were you looking for?'

'Well,' the woman said. 'We come from a small market town over near the coast. We run the environmental group there. What we want to do is to try to make the whole town more wildlife friendly. Most of the houses have gardens but they are mostly neat and tidy and not ideal for wildlife. We have an idea for a scheme to plant at least one British native tree or bush or perennial in every garden in the town, to try to create sort of wildlife corridors. Some people have come on board already, but they are mostly the people who're already into feeding the birds and putting up bug hotels and so on. What we want is to get everyone involved, but people are busy working and raising families, and can't really afford the time or money. Others are elderly and can't do much with their gardens even if they wanted to. We are quite a big group – we have about twenty members – and most are willing to go into the gardens and plant a tree or bush, but we don't have the money for an advertising campaign or to buy plants and there are just too many gardens. We were hoping you might have some advice on how to get it off the ground.'

John sat back and regarded them.

'What a clever idea!' he said. 'So simple! One in every front and back garden, a few dotted around in parks and so on. People plant fancy foreign things then wonder why they get no birds and bees and butterflies. It is understandable, of course, our schools don't teach the useful things. People don't know about ecosystems. You could put hedgehog tunnels in between the gardens, too…very labour intensive, though. You would need some manpower to get one in every garden! You would need low maintenance ones ideally, for the busy people…a publicity campaign… the local council on board… Is there a tree nursery anywhere near?'

'Yes, there's one about twelve miles outside the town.'

'Excellent. I'm John Hardy, the Estate Manager. How much time have you got? 'Do you want to get started now?'

The bemused couple said that they had plenty of time.

'Right then, let's get this clever scheme under way.'

Chapter 15

All three of the manager candidates accepted the approach from the Head Hunters, flattered to be so singled out. They were required to sign a confidentiality agreement and to be discreet about who they informed. They were told that the interviews were to be held at the headquarters of the charitable organisation concerned and that they would be required over a maximum four-day block. There would be no formal interviews on day one: just a chance to get a feel for the layout and facilities and to meet the Director. They were asked to arrive at 3pm. Internet would be available, and they were to bring a laptop or tablet as some written work would be required of them.

None had ever heard of The Gilbert Foundation. Internet search engines produced nothing except a single page website, though it was registered with the Charity Commission.

Intrigued but a little suspicious, all refused the offer of a chauffeured car to transport them from the station. They preferred to have their own cars to hand to make a quick getaway should this mysterious Foundation prove to be unpalatable.

Jennie Green was the first to arrive. She turned off the road into a drive at a discreet sign, 'Gilbert House,' but there was no other notice – nothing advertising that this was, she had been informed, a Foundation with 40 permanent staff and a multi-million-pound budget.

Parking her sporty little car in the courtyard, she got out and looked around her.

'Impressive,' she thought.

The main door opened, and a woman approached.

'Ms. Green? Welcome to The Gilbert. Please come with me. Bring your bags and we will get you settled in. If you give me your car keys, our man George will park your car round the back of the cottages, if that is OK with you?'

To Jennie's surprise she did not take her in through the main door, but up a little ramp to a sliding door in the long conservatory that ran along the front of the building which stood to one side of it. She saw that these were cottage apartments that had no doubt been converted from mews.

The woman ushered Jennie inside, passing the key to her. Jennie dumped her bags down.

'This is where you will stay. There are very basic provisions in the fridge and cupboards but there is also a Refectory which you will see shortly. If you wish to cater for yourself, or have special dietary needs, they will tailor your provisions to suit you. The bedrooms are upstairs. I will leave you to get your bearings. I'm sure you'll need a little while to recover from your journey. At four o'clock, if you follow the conservatory veranda along, there is a door which will take you into the foyer where the reception staff will welcome you. Is there anything more I can do for you now? No? I will leave you then. I'm sure we will meet again.'

Jennie explored the big room. Beautifully appointed to the highest standard, it had everything she could need. She had assumed that she would be in a hotel somewhere nearby. Was this better? It was luxurious, certainly, but here she could be observed day and night if they chose.

She put the kettle on to boil and found a selection of teas and coffees and a cafetiere. There were several types of milk and juices in the fridge along with a selection of fruit and some butter and cheese.

She rooted in the cupboards. Little rolls and mini-loaves…cereals…little cakes and pastries…biscuits. All obviously hand-made.

Taking her coffee and her case, she climbed the stairs. She explored the bedrooms linked by a bathroom. She chose the back one, away from any watching eyes in the courtyard, where she unpacked her bag. Hearing the sound of a car she slipped into the front bedroom and twitched aside the curtain.

A woman. Tall, beautiful, dressed in soft, flowing clothes and wearing flat shoes.

'Damn!' Jennie muttered. 'A black woman. Let's hope they don't have some ethnicity quota to fill.'

Jennie listened as she was taken into another cottage. A third car arrived, and Jennie watched a man emerge. Smart suit, polished shoes, well-groomed. He was taken into the third cottage.

Jennie stood, thoughtful, working out her strategy. Should she be the first to go along to reception? Would that give her a head start? Or should she play it cool, let someone else possibly appear pushy?

She watched with interest as a handsome, dark-haired, young man came out of the cottage opposite and disappeared down a snicket.

'Now then, Jennie,' she scolded, 'behave! You could be his boss in a few weeks. It wouldn't do to fraternise with the staff.'

She went downstairs and carried her coffee out onto the rear balcony, just as the other woman did the same.

'Hello, I'm Jasmine Gwembe. Are you here for the interviews?'

'Yes, I'm Jennie Green.'

The man had heard them and emerged too.

'Chris Turpin,' he said. 'Is this all of us, do you think?'

They were peering at each other through the trellis that divided them, and Jennie thought that it wouldn't hurt to get the measure of the opposition.

'Do you want to come round while you drink your coffee? We have time,' she asked.

They nodded their agreement, no doubt as curious as she, so Jennie disappeared inside to open her door to them.

At the turn of the stairs from the foyer of Gilbert House, there was a window in the side wall through which the balconies of the mews could just be seen below. Eileen stood at this window, watching. She saw the candidates speak briefly then disappear. She was about to move on, when all three appeared on the end balcony. She smiled to herself, imagining them sizing each other up.

Richard came down the stairs. He looked over her shoulder to see what was so interesting. She grinned sheepishly, and shrugged, but made no effort to leave.

The three rivals did not have time to learn much about each other, just enough to realise that they were probably all serious contenders. They were, however, in agreement that their situation was unusual and intriguing. With an eye on the time, they hurried off to prepare themselves.

Returning to her bedroom Jennie stood for a while, surveying herself in the long wall mirror. She yanked her tight skirt down a little. Was it too short? Too tight? She twisted this way and that. She had been aiming for a business-like look but with hints of sexiness, a bit of allure, so she had chosen a dark suit but one with a short, tight skirt. The blouse showed some cleavage. The Director was a man, wasn't he? Men liked a bit of cleavage and a tight skirt, in her experience. Suddenly she doubted – what if they were lefty types – all cheese-cloth and sandals? Never mind, she had brought several alternative outfits. She peered closer, at her make-up. That was fine –subtle but effective. She ran a brush over her hair, refreshed her lipstick and perfume. Glancing at her watch, she saw that it was ten-to-four.

Gulping down the last of her coffee, she grabbed her handbag and her iPad and headed out. The conservatory veranda ended at a door. Opening it she found herself in a corridor which led her to the foyer. Here, the walls swept away up through the full height of the building, to white plaster and great rafters. A staircase twisted away left and right. There must be windows up there, as the area was flooded with light. She was startled by a voice beside her.

'Good afternoon. Ms. Green? Ah, I see you are all here now. Welcome Ms. Gwembe, Mr. Turpin. I will bring Mr. Aubrey down to meet you. If you will follow me, I'll take you through to the Refectory. The staff there will look after you while you wait.'

They followed Magda into the lovely room, bathed in sunlight, the garden stretching away to their right, glimpsed through the open French windows, where they were greeted by a cheerful woman, shown the carousel, invited to help themselves, asked what they would like to drink. The Refectory never failed to impress. Jennie did not know what she was expecting, but not this! Every feature of Gilbert House was beautiful and elegant, yet homely and welcoming. If the rest was like this, she wanted it to be her kingdom.

Chapter 16

Quentin Rivers was a man who took great pleasure in nursing a grudge. And he had a right to, by his calculation. Every time he thought he had it made, some bugger would bring him down. After four years in the freelance wilderness, he had finally landed a job on a paper again. It was only a piddling local, The Cheppingham Argos, but it was a start. He would soon impress them, find something to interest the Big Boys and move back to the Nationals.

And what had happened?

'It'll be a year this July since The Gilbert opened Beckside Park. Time to do a bit of a celebratory piece. You won't get anything up at the House - they don't do interviews, but you might get something from the workers and the locals will be happy to talk to you. They love their Gilbert,' his editor, Eddie Mason, had said on his first day.

Quentin looked blank. 'The Gilbert?'

'There's plenty in the archives. Get genned up. And don't upset them, eh?'

What was the first name that jumped out of those archives? Richard bloody Aubrey. Photos confirmed that it was, of course, the same Richard Aubrey. Just his luck.

Later, he sat brooding in the bar of The Beckside Hotel, staring out of the window at the house on the hill. Beside him sat a sweet-faced, very young woman, clutching a camera. Not only had he got Saint Richard Aubrey, but they'd landed him with a damned apprentice to drag around.

'So, what's with this Gilbert outfit, then?' he asked her. 'Where's the dirt? What was your name again?'

She stared at him, confused. 'Laura…. I don't think there is any dirt, Mr. Rivers. They have given us Beckside Park and the Nature Reserve and the walled garden. Lots of local people work up at the House. They have been good for the town.'

He sighed. 'Where's the money coming from, though? Who's financing it all? Come on, if you are going to be a photo-journalist, you have to find an angle. Sweetness and light are all very well, but it doesn't get you noticed. What about this Richard Aubrey?'

'He's the Director.'

'I know that! But it won't be his money, will it? We're talking millions here, is my guess. They don't ask for donations or do fundraisers, they have no proper website. Could be something dodgy. Money laundering, a tax fiddle.'

The more he thought about it, the more he convinced himself that this could be the Big Story that would get him back onto the Nationals. If he could take Aubrey down at the same time, it would be all the sweeter.

'I need to get on it,' he said. 'Have a poke about. Who do you know that works up there?'

'I can't tell you that, Mr. Rivers,' Laura said, wretchedly. 'They are not supposed to talk to the Press, and they won't. It's a good place to work. You won't hear anything bad from the staff.'

'Then I need to get up there myself,' he said. 'You will come with me and get some pictures. Come on.'

Standing in the courtyard of Gilbert House, Rivers had a good look round, appraising the set-up. He walked to the edge of the gardens, noting the faces of the three people sitting on the patio. Possible sources of info? He went to the apartments, but the conservatory veranda obscured his view. He crossed to the Cottages, hoping to peer in but backed off as a barking dog appeared at the window, closely followed by a man at the door.

'Can I help you?' he asked, politely.

'I'm looking for reception.'

'Just behind you, sir.'

Rivers made a mental note of his face.

He and Laura came in through the front door just as Richard came down the stairs to meet the manager candidates.

'Photos!' Quentin hissed.

Richard moved fast. He put his hand over the lens just as Laura raised the camera, and firmly took it from her.

'You may NOT take pictures in here,' Richard stated, his voice icy. 'This is private property. You will leave now.'

He looked at Quentin with distaste. Everything about Rivers was sharp, from his carefully spiked hair, thin face and skimpy suit to his pointed, patent shoes.

'We are from the Argos,' Quentin said pompously. 'We are doing a Gilbert birthday celebratory piece. Perhaps you could give us an interview? I'm sure you wouldn't want to block your local paper from celebrating your involvement in our town.' He managed to make it sound like a threat.

Richard studied him coolly for a few moments.

'I will be happy to do an interview for the Argos, of course. But they will need to make an appointment. I am otherwise engaged right now. But there will be no photographs in or around Gilbert House.' He handed the camera back to Laura.

By now, several staff members had anxiously collected in the foyer, unused to raised voices. Eileen stood on the half-landing of the stairs, her face hard.

Magda touched Quentin's arm.

'I will let the Argos know when it is convenient for Mr. Aubrey to meet with you. I think you need to go now.'

Laura, near to tears, met Magda's eye. The older woman smiled reassuringly at her.

'I told him not to come, Magda!' she said.

Turning, Quentin threw her a look which promised retribution. Shoving his card into Magda's hand, he stalked out, Laura scurrying after him.

'Got an interview, didn't I?' he crowed.

Richard took a moment to collect his thoughts before going into the Refectory. That man had been familiar, but he couldn't quite place him. He was glad to see that the three candidates were sitting out on the patio, so had been unlikely to have heard anything.

'Welcome,' Richard said as he joined them. 'Thank you for coming. I hope you will find the accommodation comfortable. Please let us know if there is anything further you need. If you have forgotten your toothpaste, just shout!'

He took them across the Refectory to a door which led to a corridor, lined with offices. Choosing the largest, he led them inside.

'I am aware that we have chosen you for interview, but that you have not chosen us. We know enough about you to have made that choice. I will spend an hour or so giving you enough information to decide if you want to proceed. After that you will be free until tomorrow. A hot meal is served in the refectory from 5.30. Cold food is always available from the carousel. You may eat in your apartments if you prefer. James is happy to do room service and the meal times are not part of the selection process! Feel free to explore the downstairs rooms, gardens and grounds. Please don't be offended if you are not engaged by the staff. We have asked that they give you time to observe and relax. '

Richard described the remit and the workings of the Foundation, giving just enough detail for them to understand the scope of the manager's role.

Then he said, 'The itinerary is as follows. The Gilbert has a public park and nature reserve as you now know. Tomorrow, you will be given a tour of those and the house. I want you to take careful note of what you see and write a brief report. What do you make of what you see? Could the running be improved? What, if anything would you change? How does the private part of The Gilbert compare with the public part. Have we got the balance right? What did you like? How could we improve?

You won't have enough information for a detailed analysis, of course. We are interested in your ideas, the kind of thoughts you might have in your first days in the manager's role, how you think you might make a difference to The Gilbert.

This will take up most of the day.

On the morning of day three, we will meet again as a group and you will share your reports. The afternoon will be taken up with the first individual interviews. Second interviews, if required, will take place on the morning of day four.

We will try to remain as informal and relaxed as possible as we believe that will give us all the best insights into each other. You may withdraw from the selection process at any point, of course. I will let you go now. Talk to the Refectory staff at any time about your food requirements. Relax, as far as that is possible! And good luck.'

*

Richard sat in his office, supposedly considering his first impressions but actually trying to remember the reporter's name. He rang through to Reception.

'That reporter left a card. What was his name?'

'Quentin Rivers. Do you want me to arrange an appointment?'

'No, he can wait.'

After a few moments thought, he rang Eileen's mobile.

'I need a word if you are free,' he said

'I'm in my apartment,' she replied. 'Come up.'

*

'Come in,' she said. 'Tea? Sit down. Is there a problem?'

'Thank you,' he replied.

'I know that reporter who came this afternoon. It was one of the last cases I dealt with in court. I don't usually do libel, but this was a friend of mine. A politician; a good, decent woman. She was becoming influential – possible leadership material. She was the wrong sex, wrong colour, and the wrong party for The Daily World. That reporter, Quentin Rivers is his name, he was on the World, did a nasty and prolonged hatchet job on her. Lies, but they don't give a stuff. Print now, retract later, on page 94 in tiny font, that's their view.' He paused, thinking of Eileen's confession of her fear of the media. 'Anyway, she sued. I was her barrister, and we thrashed them. Huge libel payout. All over the media. You might remember it.'

'I do indeed. She is a Shadow Minister now.'

'Rivers took the fall. The World very publicly blamed it all on him. They sacked him there and then. No other paper would touch him. I don't know where he has been since but the Cheppingham Argos will be a real come-down in his eyes. He'll come after me and The Gilbert. Invent some dirt and run with it. If he can get the Nationals interested, it could be his ticket back.'

Richard watched for her reaction.

She was silent for a while, frowning as she stared out of her window.

'Can we trust the staff not to talk about me?' she asked, a note of anxiety in her voice.

'But why?' Richard asked. 'It's only a local paper.'

'I don't want some nosey reporter poking about in my private life. Is that so strange? I am a private person, Richard. Give him his interview if you must but leave me out of it.'

*

All three of the candidates stayed in the Refectory to eat. They wanted to get the measure of each other and the place. Jennie spoke little but listened as the other two compared notes on what they had learnt so far, except to probe for information to assess the threat level from them. It was obvious neither intended to drop out.

Jasmine was still puzzled as to why she was here. Chris and Jennie seemed so confident, had such a wealth of experience. Jennie was apparently so innovative and pioneering, Chris a strong, firm leader. She, on the other hand, had just plodded and worked and studied and made her way step by step.

Having eaten, they were glad to get back to their apartments and relax.

Chris avoided the balcony. He didn't want to meet that pushy Jennie woman again.

He knew why he had been chosen. He was a man of strength and character. He should have been a politician, of course. His eye for detail, love of procedure, prodigious memory, and ability to do what needed doing would have been ideal. Qualities equally important in a managerial role, however. He was the Prime Minister, naturally. His Team Leaders were his cabinet, his staff were the backbenchers. The guests were the constituents. He enjoyed elaborating on this fantasy in his head after the day's work was done, in his rooms in the hotel complex. Scrupulous fairness; the permitting of some debate; the allowance of a level of democracy, and the occasional use of the whip ensured everyone felt valued and secure and remained loyal, but in their place.

Checking his appearance in the mirror, he headed outside. He noted with satisfaction that the place was tidy and well-maintained.

He wandered through the gardens, past the Refectory windows, to the far end of the building. The countryside stretched away before him and he wondered how far the land extended. He re-crossed the gardens and went round the back of the cottages. He could hear a child playing behind a fence. Here was a paddock with three grazing ponies; a car park; stables; barns with several cars, a minibus and a pony trap inside.

'Ponies?' he thought, puzzled.

Seeing a man appear he slipped away and returned to the courtyard.

He studied the upper storeys of the main house. No mention had been made of what went on up there – maybe they would find out tomorrow. Remembering that he would have reports to write, he returned to his apartment. Removing his jacket and tie, pulling a pad and pen from his briefcase, he settled on the sofa to think. Occasionally he jotted a phrase on the pad.

But what was it all for? Surely not just for the staff who worked here. Who and where were the 'constituents'?

*

Jasmine kicked off her shoes and put the kettle on. Peeping to check that the other balconies were empty, she went outside. Standing at the rail, looking down the gentle hill, she was struck by how beautiful and peaceful it was. The flower meadow was a mass of colour and she could hear birds all around. Beyond, she could see families, the children playing in the beck and on the swings, though their voices did not carry this far. Tears came to her eyes. This would be a new start, far away from the mess of her broken relationship. He would never find her here. It would be hard to leave the Home, though; she had worked there for so long. But it had not been the same since it passed out of Council control. The new regime was harsh, heartless, money orientated. It was all about efficiencies and contracts, an endless battle for staff and resources. She had stayed and fought for the staff and residents, but she was so aware that she was exhausted. It might be good to work for a charity. If the Refectory was anything to go by, they knew how to look after their workers. Little had been said about what they actually did, apart from the Park and Reserve, or where the money was coming from. Perhaps they would learn more tomorrow. But how could she possibly compete against the other two? Sighing, she stood for a long time, lost in thought as the kettle cooled.

*

Jennie was brimming with restless energy. Unable to settle, she changed into smart trousers and flat shoes and set off out. She turned right, along the drive and back to the road she had come in from. Looking down, she could see a pub or hotel, no more than half-a-mile away. She could use a drink – there was no bar in the Refectory – and there were bound to be locals there whose brains she could pick. That could give her the edge! Congratulating herself on her cleverness, she marched away down the hill.

The Beckside Hotel was quiet. The afternoon family crowd had gone. A few people were eating but the evening punters were yet to arrive. She bought herself a gin and sat in the window, looking up at Gilbert House.

Quentin Rivers, forced to stay at the Hotel until he could find his own billet, saw her the moment he came down the stairs. Pretty, blonde woman. Nice figure. Fit. About his age. On her own. Where had he seen her before? At The Gilbert, this afternoon, of course! Never forgot a face. Good observational skills, good memory – essential in this game.

He sat behind her, on a bar stool, ordered a pint and waited to see if anyone would join her. When no-one did, he approached.

'Hi, Quentin Rivers, Cheppingham Argos. I saw you up at The Gilbert this afternoon, I believe. I am doing a birthday spread about it for the paper.'

Jennie looked up at him. She was about to give him the cold brush-off but checked herself. A local reporter – he could know more than most about the place.

'Will you join me?' she asked, sweetly.

Unfortunately, it took them little time to discover that neither knew very much of interest about the place.

Alarmed by his insistent probing and mindful of her Confidentially Agreement, Jennie lied – they had merely been visiting, passing through. She was disappointed, eager to get away and talk to someone who did know, but not able to think of a good excuse.

Quentin decided he might as well chat her up.

After a wasted half-hour fending him off, Jennie finished her drink and left him sitting, just as he thought he was getting into his stride.

She stood outside, undecided, unsure what to do. She was reluctant to give up her plan. She wandered along towards the Park where there were still a few people enjoying the late spring evening. She was mortified to be politely asked for a pass at the gate. 'Are you staying at The Beckside Hotel? They will have passes that you can use. We will be closing in a couple of hours, anyway. Do come back tomorrow. So sorry…'

Deciding to let it go, she gave up and set off back to The Gilbert. In the courtyard, she met the same handsome young man that she had seen earlier. By this time, she was too cross to do more than exchange pleasantries with him.

*

Richard and Eileen sat in his office, dossiers open.

The candidates would have been surprised and possibly disturbed to learn how much detail there was about them in those dossiers.

'I can understand why Jasmine Gwembe is on the list,' Richard said. 'A good old-fashioned social care manager. Competent, decent and ethical. Brave. A bit of a dinosaur in the modern corporate world, but probably a good fit here. Hmm…that's odd…her home address is given as care of the head hunters…'

'That's because she is currently living in a women's refuge. I was working there before I came here and have continued to support it. I met her when I visited recently,' Eileen said, matter-of-factly.

Richard smiled and continued

'If you want a tight ship, everything as it should be, all the ropes coiled down and every man to his duty, Chris Turpin is your man. It is Jennie Green's inclusion that I don't understand. What has she got to offer The Gilbert?'

'She has a complete lack of sentimentality. If you want a work-place sorting out, rationalising, she will do it, without compunction,' Eileen said.

'But we don't need sorting out and rationalising, do we?' Richard replied.

'Well, she would ensure not a penny was wasted, get rid of any dead wood.'

Richard was taken aback.

'Is there a problem with money? Dead wood?'

'No, but if we did have, she would wield the axe with relish! The other two are the safe candidates. They would be competent and sure, but would they be innovative? Bold? Pioneering? Jennie has edge, confidence, drive. Let's see how it goes. Make them sweat for it. I am going to enjoy this.'

'There it is again – that little ruthless streak,' Richard thought.

As Richard made his way back through the Refectory, he met Gemma.

'I was just coming to find you!' she said. 'Excellent news from the squatter project. You know, the one where they put a door down to get me in?'

'Ah, yes, that was a good day.'

'Well, there has been the best possible outcome. The company that owns the office building were converting it into low-cost student lets. They have several similar properties on the go in the town. They have agreed with the local housing association to lease a small one to them for social housing instead, and our homeless people are to be offered some of them. Once they have an address, they will be able to claim job-seekers and suchlike and hopefully will be able to get back on their feet. Isn't that great news?'

'It certainly is, Gemma. Well done!'

Chapter 17

The following day was dull and cloudy after overnight rain, but thankfully it stayed dry until the afternoon. The three candidates found themselves sitting facing one another in a pony trap, of all things. The handsome dark-haired young man, who said his name was Harry, was driving. Jennie studied his back and allowed herself a few unworthy thoughts before pulling her attention back to the surroundings. This was rather fun.

Chris looked uncomfortable in his rather unsuitable formal suit. He did think that it was exceedingly unfair that he had not been warned that they would be tramping about the countryside. He had perfectly suitable smart-casual clothes he could have brought, if he had known. He sourly regarded Jasmine and Jennie in their tailored trousers and flat shoes. It was alright for women, they always had trousers in their wardrobes – perfectly acceptable, even for an interview if they were formal enough. He had learnt not to mark down job applicants if they wore trousers to interviews – even lady Cabinet Ministers wore trousers nowadays.

Jasmine was a little afraid of horses, never having had much to do with them, but this one seemed friendly enough and the journey was soon over.

'As long as they don't expect me to drive!' she thought.

Harry took them into the workshop where John Hardy was waiting.

'Good morning, everyone. I am John Hardy, the Estate Manager. You have met Harry, our Ranger. I have outdoor coats, jumpers and wellies here for you. It is a bit muddy out there after last night's rain. Please do help yourself while I put the kettle on.'

Three sets of clothes, on hangers, hung from hooks and Wellington boots stood below.

'They certainly look clean enough,' Chris thought. 'Like new, in fact.'

He picked up the sweatshirt, surreptitiously sniffing it to check it was clean. He was more reluctant about the Wellies – you could catch things from other people's feet. But they too looked new and were exactly his size. The waterproof coat was too.

The first session was spent in the workshop. John explained the history and remit of the Reserve; their plans to create habitats for rare creatures. Chris was fascinated and took copious notes. The man certainly knew his stuff. Jasmine, too, listened rapt. Jennie was, she had to admit to herself, rather bored and passed most of this time admiring the physique of young Harry.

She became more interested when John described the running of the Reserve as he took them round it. She asked detailed questions about the number of staff and volunteers; whether there was any income to offset the costs; what the exact policy was on the use of the workshop. Did they do lectures, tours, school visits? All the time, she took notes. Chris and Jasmine found most of their questions answered without having to open their mouths.

They were introduced to several of the volunteers.

'Close your mouth, Dean. And don't stare, it's bad manners,' Rob muttered in Dean's ear.

Dean hastily occupied himself with an imaginary problem on the ground. He slid his gaze sideways though, to covertly study the blonde woman. Dean had never been smitten before. If asked, he would have scoffed at the idea. But she was stunning. Sleek blonde hair, baby blue eyes…like one of those dolls his sister used to have when they were kids. And she smelt divine. She caught his gaze and smiled at him and he was lost. He stood and gazed after her as John led her away.

Chris raised the issues of health and safety and Insurance and was gratified to learn that all the staff and volunteers had done training in Health and Safety and First Aid and that there was full public liability insurance. John added that they had also all done courses on orienteering, wildlife, conservation and a range of other relevant subjects.

Jennie raised her eyebrows and made more notes.

They emerged through a gate into the Park. This was a shorter visit, many of the issues being covered by previous questions. They noted the man in his little hut at the gate, keeping an eye on the visitors and examining passes; the little cafe booth with its tables outside; the group of school children studying the wildflower meadow; the groundsman mowing the grass and weeding the beds; the school teams on the football pitch and in the cricket nets.

The pony-and-trap was waiting to whisk them back to Gilbert House. They were given time to change and freshen up before meeting back in the foyer at 12 o'clock.

Table service in the Refectory was maintained, which made for a hectic period for the kitchen and serving staff. The food was, as always, of the highest quality and offered a meat or a vegan dish, with a pick and mix choice of salads and hot vegetables.

Richard sat with them over lunch, answering their many questions.

This was when the candidates got a feel for how many people The Gilbert employed. They recognised John Hardy and Harry but there were about thirty others, all chattering and cheerful, coming and going. A few they had seen before but the others presumably came from upstairs. Would they learn more about them?

'It is very hectic over the lunch period,' Jasmine said thoughtfully and made a few notes.

Jennie wondered what was in her mind – she wanted to be the one who came up with ideas.

Chris was impressed with the service, the food and the hygiene. Staff morale seemed high and the servers showed exactly the right level of attentiveness. This was his area, of course, and he could not fault it.

Their next visit was to the offices. Jo was in her office with two housekeeping assistants, having already eaten.

'My sister is the other housekeeper,' Jo told them. 'We live in a cottage in the courtyard. There are two assistants who do all the cleaning and maintenance. Some work to fit in with school hours, others do the later shifts, maintaining upstairs and Reception, when their staff have gone. Rotas can be a bit of a nightmare, especially upstairs – I sometimes wonder if they ever go home! We are pretty flexible, though, and work it out between us.'

Chris and Jasmine reflected on how difficult it was for them to recruit and keep workers. Low pay, early mornings and late nights put people off, but they seemed to have no problem here.

'This place must employ half the town!' Jennie thought.

She thought that it seemed no better in the Reception Office. The atmosphere in there was relaxed, too. Several people were at desks, chatting and enjoying their lunch break. She discovered that one person did wages and accounts. Another did general admin. One person arranged and coordinated training. They all attended to the Reception hatch, but it was hardly busy: she had yet to see anyone visit the place.

She studied the training calendar, pinned to the wall alongside the leave calendar.

'No wonder they need so many staff,' she thought. 'Half of them are out on training!'

Richard took them to the office corridor behind the Refectory, where he had first met with them. The offices were empty, their purpose unclear. As they stood in the corridor, two people came in from the foyer. They recognised one from the Admin Office. Giving the visitors a cheerful greeting, they disappeared into an office.

'Our final visit will be to the workroom upstairs,' he said.

'At last!' was the first thought of all three.

There was a lift in the foyer, but Richard took them up the wide staircase. There were windows at every turn.

They paused at the door to the workroom.

'This is where the work of the Foundation happens. As you know, the Foundation supports people who help others.

The Project Workers facilitate and coordinate this work. Please remember that you have signed a confidentiality agreement.'

Opening the door, Richard ushered them inside.

The large, light room had big windows running along the wall, overlooking the valley and was full of activity. People sat at computer desks, studying their screens, or talking on phones. Twos and threes were gathered round tables. Two people were scrawling on a large white board, obviously in a brainstorming session. People looked up and smiled a greeting, then went back to their work. They showed no curiosity, nor attempted to speak to the visitors.

'There are fifteen full-time Project Workers and six part-time, at present,' Richard said. 'Three of them are Team Leaders, elected by their peers. They work here or in the offices off this room or below us. Sometimes they work in the garden. They have the option of working flexitime. They interact with the Foundation's beneficiaries, here and out in the field.'

'Who are the beneficiaries?' Jasmine asked.

'We support people who help others,' Richard replied, his expression inscrutable.

'How does someone become a beneficiary?' Chris asked.

'By various means. However, we will be interested to hear any suggestions for the selection process in your reports.'

They absorbed that remark, guessing that for "interested" they should read "expecting."

'What are your funding sources?' Jennie asked.

Richard looked vaguely out of the window as if considering his reply.

'Confidential, but what I will say is that all our funding comes only from private wealth. Donors who wish to remain anonymous.'

To their disappointment, he did not take them on into the room, but turned and led them back on to the landing and on to a pleasant, large room above the foyer.

'This is our Training Room. We will use it to share our reports. There is the usual equipment in here, should you require it. You may share your report in any way you want to. There is no right or wrong way. You are free, now, to work on your reports. However, I will be in my office downstairs on the back corridor. You may come and interview me at any time. Or not, as you wish. The Refectory is open for hot food until 7.'

*

Jasmine stared at her laptop screen.

What was she to say?

'I think it is wonderful – the Reserve is beautiful; the park is pretty; the building is stunning; the staff are busy; the food is superb; morale is high. Apart from one or two really minor details I would not change a thing until I had been here long enough to know what I was doing. It would be a pleasure and a privilege to work here. Thank you. End of report.'

Hardly!

Chris was confused. What was it all for – the Reserve, the Park, all those staff?

Who were the 'constituents' here? The Project Workers upstairs? The beneficiaries of the Foundation? The townsfolk?

Jennie was buzzing. So much potential! So many changes she could make that would get the place moving, noticed, renowned. So many efficiencies to be made. All those staff, for a start! What were they thinking of?

Grabbing a pad, she started to write lists of figures:

Office staff.... ancillary...housekeeper ...chef... kitchen/servers .... Rangers .... Estate Manager.... groundsmen ...fifteen Project Workers, plus six part-timers...Richard. Plus on-costs...she totted it up.

'Good god! This place must be costing a million a year just for staffing!'

Chris decided he would just have to go and ask. He slipped out of his front door. Deciding not to go past the others, he gently slid a conservatory door open and stepped down into the courtyard, just as Jasmine did the same. Startled, they looked a little sheepishly at one another. Jasmine smiled and, as if by agreement, they walked together across to the patio and in through a Refectory French door. They settled themselves in a corner with coffee and cake.

Chris regarded Jasmine –

'She is one of those people that are immediately liked and trusted,' he reflected. He had often wished he was one of those people. He knew he was respected by his staff; that they appreciated the order and certainty; that he was considered fair and competent, but he doubted that they actually liked him.

'I am going to see Richard,' Jasmine said. 'I just feel I don't know enough about what goes on upstairs…'

'So am I!' Chris replied. 'I understand the confidentiality aspect, of course, but without more detail, I don't feel I can make informed judgements and so forth.'

'We could go in together,' Jasmine suggested tentatively – they were rivals, after all.

'I think that makes sense,' Chris said, decisively. 'If we are both going to ask the same question, why not?'

Richard was leaning back in his chair, his feet on another, looking down the valley; Tilda asleep along his lap.

'Come in,' he replied to the knock on the door behind him.

As they came into view, his face registered some mild surprise that the two had come together and he noted that Jennie was not with them.

Tilda jumped down and approached daintily to be petted, then settled on her bed under the desk.

'Pull up some chairs,' Richard said, swinging his legs down. 'How can I help?'

'We understand the confidential nature of the work of the Foundation, of course, and will respect that,' Chris said, rather formally. 'However, it is difficult to get a picture of the balance between the public and the private aspects of the

Foundation without more information on its remit and methods.'

'Its ethos, its philosophy…' Jasmine added.

Richard appeared to consider, though it was no surprise and he had always been ready to answer this question, to those that asked.

'The Project Workers are, if you like, at the centre of a web. They seek out small charities and individuals who help others and support them by any means that they need. That could be just money, but it could also be expert input and advice on everything from legal aspects to property issues to fundraising. They work here and out in the field. The rest of the staff deal with the day to day running of Gilbert House, but they are also experts in various fields such as benefits, IT, personnel and legal matters. They support and advise the Project Workers. The Outdoor Team can also be involved, working with environmental projects; play areas; town farms and so on. The Catering Team and Housekeepers might be involved with homeless meal providers, for example.

So, a single project might involve all the staff from all the teams. With their help, the Project Workers put together a plan of action and are responsible for seeing it through. And we usually remain involved – few cases are ever closed,' he added ruefully.

Richard saw light dawn on their faces.

'Are you planning expansion?' Chris asked

'Oh, it is like Topsy,' Richard said. 'It just grows and grows.'

*

Jennie had reached an impasse. She had analysed the staffing and the training; facilities and equipment, but it just did not add up. Why did twenty or so Project Workers need so many support staff? And the Nature Reserve and Park – they were all very nice, but what were they for?

She was missing something. She should go and interview Richard, but they needed to be intelligent questions. He must be impressed by her grasp, her insight. She glanced at her watch. Four o'clock already! She would go and have a good poke round, clear her head, then see Richard.

She stepped out into the courtyard just as Chris and Jasmine returned. Together! They greeted her cheerfully and disappeared into their cottages. Suspicious, she watched them go.

The day was dull, the light poor, but at least the rain had stopped.

As Jennie turned towards the garden, she saw a woman walking on the patio who paused, regarding Jennie for a long moment before disappearing in through the French doors.

The woman was familiar, but from another context. Jennie was sure she had not seen her here before. Suddenly unsettled, she hurried in through the foyer, glanced up the staircase, almost ran into the Refectory. There were people dotted about but she was not there.

Feeling a little foolish, Jennie helped herself to a pastry, ordered coffee and sat herself where she could see the room.

The woman did not reappear. Jennie searched her mind, trying to place her, without success. The light was poor, she had been there only a few moments. She was imagining things. Why should seeing the woman throw her like that? It was ridiculous. But the combination of seeing Chris and Jasmine together – in cahoots? – and the familiar woman, had broken Jennie's equilibrium. She went back outside just as the rain came on again. Cursing to herself, she fled back to her cottage.

Jennie had that enviable quality of unshakeable self-confidence, however, which enabled her to push over and through obstacles. It had served her well –hadn't she got almost every job she had pursued? She shook off her doubts and settled to her notes and her laptop. How she wanted this job, though! What a kingdom to rule! This was a new feeling, an uncomfortable one. She was driven by ambition, always had been, but this was different. She could build an empire here. There were no irritating outside influences – no Government regulations telling her she could not do this or that, no contractual constraints by fund holders or unions, no shareholders to consider. No Boards of Trustees or Directors. No damned committees! There was Richard, though… he was difficult to read, and he was king here. King to her Queen! What a team they would make, eh?

Chapter !8

Breakfast was a stilted, awkward affair that morning – no-one wished to converse but felt it would be rude to sit alone. At 9.30 they made their way up to the Training Room where Richard was waiting for them. The room was informally arranged, Richard welcoming and relaxed in his usual chinos and soft shirt.

'Does anyone want to start?' he asked.

Jennie had thought about this. If she went first, the others could seem to be just echoing or copying her thoughts, but then they could steal some of her ideas. And what if they had thought of a point she had missed? Best not to go first, on balance.

No-one spoke.

'We will go alphabetically, then,' Richard said. 'You can start us off, Jennie. OK?'

Jennie's presentation was an impressive lesson in professional analysis. PowerPoint slides illustrated her bullet points as she described the merits of the outdoor areas and her ideas for educational courses in the Reserve and Workshop. These would be charged for, of course. Links could be made to a college or university – teaching students could be used as free facilitators.

The Reserve and Beckside Park were great facilities for the locals, of course. However, as The Gilbert had no need to keep the locals onside, offering, as it did, good employment to so many, she felt it was reasonable to expect that there should be an admission charge. The Park and the Reserve could be developed as tourist attractions, bringing money into the Foundation.

Moving on to the house, she analysed the staffing ratios, implying that the support side was overstaffed. She suggested economies and job merges. She also addressed the training regime – this was her area of expertise, after all. Professional development of the staff was laudable, of course, but was it really necessary for everyone to do almost everything? The more advanced diplomas and suchlike were a luxury, not a legal requirement, so could be scrapped.

The Gilbert could offer courses, too. The mews could be used to accommodate visiting speakers – such good facilities would mean they could charge top rates to students.

The selection process for beneficiaries seemed a little random: a comprehensive application process with strict criteria would weed out the amateurs. Current funding came from private donors, but they would want to see that their money was spent well and that every penny of their largesse counted.

Her conclusion was that the Nature Reserve, the Park, and the Refectory were unnecessary luxuries. If The Gilbert was leaner it would be fitter and could take its place with the top charitable organisations, leading the way in research and development, attracting government funding and commissioning.

Chris and Jasmine were awed by Jennie's grasp of the way in which modern charity and social enterprise works.

Chris had never worked for a charity. He understood balancing the books; staffing efficiency; mandatory training; diversification – the hotel's wedding licence had been his idea after all, and a profitable one it had proved to be. But he had no grasp of commissioning …Government funding…if this was what The Gilbert was looking for, he had no chance.

Jasmine's report had a completely different tone.

She described the outdoor and indoor facilities in positive terms – workers appreciated good working conditions and lifted their performance accordingly. Being trusted encouraged workers to be trustworthy. Local people, appreciating what The Gilbert had done for their town, were eager to work there and came with a positive attitude.

The whole slant of her conclusions was about integration; co-reliance; the sharing of expertise. She described how the personal and professional development, combined with the excellent facilities, had led to an overriding impression of harmony and job-satisfaction. The Gilbert was still quite new but the policy of involving all of the different teams in the action plans drawn up by the Project Workers was creating an atmosphere of co-operation and teamwork. Everyone felt equal and valued. The opportunity for everyone to work both in-house and out in the field, using their strengths with the Foundation's beneficiaries, seeing the results of their work, ensured there was no 'them and us', no jealousy.

From that sound base, it was possible to make changes if their value could be seen. If The Gilbert needed to make economies the teams, loyal and committed, would endeavour to ensure its survival by co-operating. Strong leadership was essential, of course - someone had to take ultimate responsibility and the ordinary worker just wanted to get on with their work. However, when goodwill and morale were high, willingness to adapt was usually high too. For example, she felt that the cleaning staff could well be open to acting as servers during the mad lunchtime rush in the Refectory.

She finished by saying that it was incumbent on any new employee, particularly in a managerial role, to avoid a 'new broom' mentality. Watching, listening and learning was essential during the first weeks – building trust, looking objectively at every aspect, consulting. Only then could, and should, any changes be attempted.

She sat down, shaking and sweating.

Jennie stared at her. What was all that about the support staff working with the Project Workers? Where had she got that from? She began to panic and then thought that probably Jasmine had seen something that was not actually there. Even, so, it might be a good idea. She would work on that, bring it into her interview.

Chris was near to panic- so much of his presentation echoed Jasmine's, but without the passion. However, he collected himself and stood up. He straightened his jacket, adjusted his tie and began.

Feeling utterly unoriginal, he described the various areas he had seen in positive terms.

He went on to commend the system of utilising and developing the expertise of the different departments and teams to inform and guide the work of the Project Workers. He commented on the resultant high morale and efficacy this engendered.

However, he began to realise with some satisfaction, his conclusions were a little different.

'This establishment, with its various permutations and combinations, operates in a complex web of interdependent threads. If one snaps or tangles, chaos can ensue.

As the work of the Foundation grows and develops, these threads will be pulled ever thinner and tighter, the knots and patterns becoming ever more complex.'

He realised that he was off-script, but that he was enjoying the direction this was taking him. He had known what he wanted to say, but his script had been dry and dull. Like his Houses of Parliament analogy, his meaning was clarifying and developing as he spoke.

'The role of a manager in this situation is like a captain on the quarter deck of a great sailing ship of the line, his eye on every team. He must consider all of the factors at play – the wind, the tide, the weather, the direction of travel, the strengths of the crew, even, heaven forbid, the enemy. He must study the ropes and the sails. He must ensure that there is sufficient canvas, that it is not holed or set incorrectly. That the ropes – I believe they are called sheets – are all as they should be, not tangled or crossed or frayed. He must provide certainty for his crew. He must think fast, order adjustments – the taking in of one sail, the unfurling of another. He must trust his officers, of course, to send the men up the right masts, but must facilitate their work. He must engender trust – that what is needed will be provided.

Above all, as the vessel, or even the fleet, gains speed across the ocean, he must ensure that it has sufficient materials and men with the right skills, to take the ship steady away into the fray.'

He suddenly became aware that the room was silent, that every eye was on him and he faltered.

'People need to feel safe,' he said. 'They need to know that the operational running is taken care of, that they do not need to concern themselves with trivialities. That, as the Foundation expands, so does its sound operational base.'

He sat down, hard.

Richard stood up.

'Well done to you all. I am impressed with the level of thought and commitment that you have given to your reports. Does anyone have any questions or comments?' He paused. 'No? Then I think you deserve some down-time. We will start the individual interviews at one in my office. I will send word who we want to see first. Until then, take a well-earned break. Thank you,' he said and left.

'Well done. You were inspired,' Jasmine whispered to Chris.

'Oh, and you too, you too!' he replied.

Jennie stormed into her cottage and hurled her bag at the settee, followed by her laptop, which bounced and hung in mid-air, before slapping back onto the cushions.

She cursed and cursed, angry and bewildered, marching up and down the room.

She simply did not understand what had just happened. The first job she had ever really, really wanted! Almost every job she had ever gone for, she had picked like a ripe fruit. She had been clever, resourceful, done her homework, sparkled, shone.

This time she had been too cocky, too damned clever to just go and talk to Richard, as those two had so obviously done. It had been a bloody test.

"You may come and interview me at any time" she parroted. And she had missed it! She had been going to and then she saw those two all cosy, cosy and that damned ghost woman on the patio and she had lost her grip. She never lost her grip! She dropped onto the settee. Her laptop slid gently to the floor.

Chapter 19

Quentin River's day was not going well either.

'You, in here!' had been his editor's first words that morning.

'I told you not to upset them!'

'His lordship been complaining, has he?'

'He has not. I have heard about it from every gossip and busybody in the bloody town. What the hell were you thinking of?'

'This is downright feudal! Does that place own this piddling town?'

The editor stared at him, contempt chasing disbelief.

'Thirty-plus people from this "piddling town" work up there. Not zero-hours, so called "self-employed", minimum-wage jobs, but proper well-paid ones with decent salaries and pensions and conditions. Plus, we get the Park and the Nature Reserve and the walled garden. And what do they ask in return? Nothing! Abso-bloody-lutely nothing, except that we respect their privacy and leave them alone. What did you think you were going to find up there – the frickin Mafia?'

By now, he was shouting, and the newsroom had fallen silent, the better to catch every word.

'I got an interview out of him!' Rivers shouted back, defiant.

'Oh yeah? And where's the write-up then?'

'They are going to make an appointment for me to go back.'

The editor shook his head.

'There are a couple of weddings and a flower show on today. That's about your level. Get your arse out of here.'

'Laura, bring your camera,' Rivers snarled as he passed through.

'I'm with you today, mate,' replied a mean-faced old hack from the next desk. 'Love a good wedding, me.' Humming

'Here comes the bride' and grinning at his colleagues, he followed Rivers out.

Chapter 20

Richard went directly to Eileen's office where she sat thoughtfully in front of a screen showing the now empty Training Room.

'Jasmine and Chris both did well, didn't they? You were right to select them. But Jennie?' Richard shook his head.

'I think you might be being a little harsh,' Eileen replied mildly. 'She has a good grasp of the economics and operational issues.'

Richard stared at her. 'Her whole philosophy is completely wrong! As was her understanding of how The Gilbert works.'

'Well, she was only given half the story…'

'And who's idea was that?' Richard laughed. 'She only had to ask, though – the others did.'

'She is a product of the modern world, Richard. Perhaps she just needs re-educating.'

*

Jennie did what Jennie always did. She pulled herself together; re-did her make-up; changed into a fresh, formal outfit. Then she sat herself down, went back over her reports; deleted the rubbish; identified the gaps; filled them with what she should have said; changed the emphasis. She tried to anticipate the questions and how she could bring this new emphasis into her answers; re-present herself; convince them that she was what they were looking for.

Jasmine was called first. The questions were fairly standard stuff. What did she feel she had to offer? Why did she want the job? How had she encouraged teamwork in previous posts? Then a few knotty problems. What would she do if a worker experienced discrimination? What would she do if a worker stole from colleagues?

Richard had been an excellent barrister. His body language invited confidence. His concise open questioning was effortlessly leading her into revealing her personality, work ethics and history, and even her philosophy of life.

Chris followed. Expecting a gruelling session, he was pleasantly surprised by Richard's non-confrontational manner – his attentive listening, his skilled questioning. 30 minutes later, he emerged feeling that he had done well.

Jasmine and Chris gravitated to Jasmine's balcony, looking out at the view, drinking tea. After a while they began to talk, exchanging their life experiences and their hopes for the future.

'We are very different,' Chris said. 'We would complement one another. It's a pity we can't both get the job. Combined, we would make the perfect manager!'

*

Jennie was surprised to see that it was just Richard interviewing – she had expected a panel.

The questions were as open-ended as she had hoped. Her words flowed. She expanded on points that she had not actually made in her report. She re-invented herself. Richard listened, nodded.

'Examine her work record. Why so many moves?' Eileen's voice came through his earpiece. He nearly jumped. She had not intervened in either of the other interviews.

'I would like to look at your work record,' he said smoothly, studying her CV, then up at her face. ' You have had, let me see… eleven jobs in eighteen years.'

Jennie was used to this question, prepared.

'I have been something of a trouble-shooter,' she said. 'I go into organisations that are struggling and turning them round. The social care and training areas have changed so much in recent years and many organisations have found it difficult to adapt and change to new ways of thinking. I have the ability to see the bigger picture – to see through the layers of outdated practices to the essential structures beneath. Under my guidance, organisations become lean and fit. These roles are often temporary, so my contracts come to an end. I am also ambitious, of course. I have enjoyed ever-increasing levels of responsibility as my skills have increased, so have moved for promotion, or to widen my skill set. However, I now feel ready for a permanent post where I can settle.'

'Probe!' In his ear.

He studied her CV.

'The maximum time you have stayed in any permanent job has been two years. That was your first job…after that…14 months…18 months…7 months.'

He lifted his gaze back to her face and waited.

'I generally achieve my aims quite quickly.'

'Aims?'

'When I go into a post, I can soon assess where action is needed. It is important to move ahead, to accomplish the modernisation and rationalisation as quickly as possible so that the organisation can move forward.'

'I would be interested to hear about some of the modernisations and rationalisation…Standby Rehabilitation and Care, for example. A small charity set up by a group of parents, to provide care for their adult children, using compensation payouts… Several small group homes…staff support…physio…occupational therapy… You were there for, let me see…six months.'

'It was a fixed-term contract. They were barely breaking even,' Jennie replied. 'Spending half their time fundraising. Endlessly trying to persuade care managers to pay extra for the rehab work. Social Services don't want to pay for that, they just want people kept safe. I was employed to rationalise, get them straightened out. I recalculated their cost base, enabled them to make realistic funding bids.'

'How did you recalculate their cost base?'

'By reducing staffing, mostly. I also reduced the rehabilitation element to the minimum, trimmed social budgets – outings and suchlike for residents. The usual economies.'

'How did the parents and residents feel about that?'

'They weren't happy about it at first. I think that they expected me to work some kind of miracle, so they could carry on as before. They accepted it in the end, of course. The residents continued to get good physical care, which is what counts, isn't it?'

'How have Standby Rehabilitation and Care fared since you left?' Richard asked, prompted by yet another whisper in his ear.

'They were taken over by one of the big private care providers,' Jennie said.

'And the benefactors?' Richard asked.

'Benefactors?' Jennie was puzzled.

'The compensation payouts…the fundraised money…'

Jennie looked blank. There was a trap here somewhere, she could sense it.

'How do you feel such modernisation and rationalisation would fit here, at The Gilbert?' Richard added.

'Well, it is different here…you don't have to deal with the same financial constraints…your money comes from private donors…'

And there it was.

Richard stood up. 'Shall we have refreshments? I am ready for a break. There are toilets just outside on the corridor if you need them.'

He could have phoned through, but instead went himself.

'Eileen Gilbert's vision is to support those that help others,' he thought. 'Is she also planning to punish those who hinder them? Is this what this is about? If so, she is taking a very tortuous route. There are countless Jennie Greens out there. Does she plan to pick them off one at a time?'

Jennie stared into the mirror in the toilets. After a while she straightened up, smoothed her hair, checked her make-up and returned to the office.

'As you know,' Richard said, when they resumed, 'teamwork is key at The Gilbert. What methods could you use to build and nurture teams?'

Jennie was relieved. This was a standard question – she was on safe ground here.

She spoke at length on various team-building theories. Richard listened attentively.

'Perhaps we could relate that to your experience with teams in previous posts,' he said.

'The Fanshawe Trust!' the voice in his ear instructed.

Richard scanned down her CV.

'Let's say…um…The Fanshawe Trust…social care provider… temporary training manager. You took over an existing team?'

'Yes, fourteen in the training section, though I had responsibility for training right across the organisation, which employed over eleven hundred people nationally. The training was fragmented, people doing their own thing all over, no consistency. It was a mess, frankly. My brief was to reorganise and standardise it across the organisation.'

'Why temporary?' Richard asked.

'I was given to understand that if I did a good job of restructuring the training section, I would be made permanent, which I was. But then I got an offer from a bigger organisation and moved on anyway.'

'Tell me about the restructuring.'

'I decided to look at what training should be offered in-house; what could be commissioned from outside training providers and what could be discontinued. I decided that only mandatory training – such as health and safety; fire safety and manual handling should be offered. The other courses would be discontinued as workers completed them.'

'So there would be redundancies.'

'Well, yes, but most of the trainers were on hourly rates with no guaranteed minimum.'

'That must have been really difficult news for them. How did they react?'

'Oh, I didn't tell them. I didn't want them leaving while courses were still running. I told them that we wouldn't be taking on new learners until the review was complete.'

Jennie stopped, suddenly aware how that sounded, and thought for a long, long moment, staring at the floor.

She looked up at Richard's face. He returned her gaze, his face expressionless, but his eyes, surprisingly, kind.

Richard smiled at her. 'I think we are done, now. Thank you, Jennie.'

They stood up and Richard extended his hand.

'I could settle here,' Jennie said sadly, as she shook it.

*

'You are really very good!' Eileen said to him later. 'Do you miss the law? Are you ever tempted to go back to it?'

'Never in life!' Richard replied.

'I am glad. I don't think I could manage without you.'

'Well, are we going to have her?' Richard asked, touched by her remark but choosing not to acknowledge it.

'I think not. It's just too risky. Think of the damage she could do. Maybe already has done. I do think we should look into her dealings with Standby, don't you?'

Richard nodded, 'I'll get onto it.'

'Besides,' she continued, 'we have two good candidates in Jasmine and Chris. They are so very different though. Combined, they would make the perfect manager. Do you think they would consider a job-share?'

'Neither would have sufficient income though, surely,' Richard replied.

'I have been thinking about that. Do you think it might help if we threw in accommodation?'

Richard raised his eyebrows. 'Where?'

'It's time the old gate house was renovated. It would make two cottages, don't you think?'

'I agree they complement each other... Cap'n Chris could do operations... Mother Jasmine could do people. There is nothing to be lost by asking them, I suppose. Right now, I am going to take Tilda out for a trot. Poor lass has been shut in all day.'

Jennie, too, felt that she had been shut in long enough. After a quick drink, and some of the snacks that appeared daily in her kitchen, she changed into comfortable shoes and slipped out. Taking the steps which dropped down at the end of the mews, she found herself on the gravel road that ran behind Gilbert House and headed for the Nature Reserve.

Deep in a reverie, she did not hear the pony and trap behind her until Harry gave a warning shout. He pulled up.

'Can I give you a ride, Miss? I'm going to The Reserve.'

'Why not? Thank you'.

Harry jumped down and handed her up onto the front board next to him.

It was a relief to make small talk, to stop going over and over the interview in her head.

Eileen watched her go from her office window and rang Richard to go and talk to Jasmine and Chris while Jennie was away.

'How do we approach it?' he asked. 'Do we let them know that we mean with each other, not Jennie?'

'Oh, I think so. No more games, eh?'

He knocked on Chris's door. Receiving no response, he tried Jasmine's. As she let him in, he saw that they were together, on Jasmine's balcony.

'We want to ask you two about the idea of a job-share. Being offered the post is absolutely not dependent upon you being willing to consider this. You understood when you came that this is a full-time role and we will honour that and appoint accordingly if either of you say no, ' he said to them. 'We are aware that this could lead to issues around income. However, we could offer you each a rent-free tied cottage with the post which could make it more viable. We would just like you to consider it and let us know.' He gave each of them a card with his mobile number on.

After Richard had gone, Jasmine and Chris agreed that they needed to think, and Chris went back to his apartment.

Jasmine was the first to ring Richard to say that she felt that she could work with Chris in a job-share. Chris soon followed.

'So, we are decided, then,' Richard said to Eileen. 'No second interviews required?'

'I feel that they are right for us. Do you?' Eileen replied.

'Two gooduns for the price of one, absolutely. But what about innovation, boldness, pioneering? Do they offer that?'

Eileen smiled. 'Do we value those qualities above all others?'

'I don't,' Richard replied mischievously. 'It was you who valued them so highly in Jennie, as I recall. Shall I tell her she was unsuccessful and let her go?'

'Yes, that seems best. No more games…I am going to slip down and have a quiet word with Jasmine on her own before we bring Chris in. She might want to stay up here until her cottage is ready.'

Having seen Jennie go out earlier, Eileen knew she wouldn't be seen by her as she made her way along the conservatory veranda and tapped on Jasmine's door. Had Jennie seen her on the patio yesterday? She really did hope not.

Eileen had to laugh at Jasmine's surprised expression.

'You're one of the Friends of the Refuge.'

'I am. I also own this Foundation. I am Eileen Gilbert and your new employer.'

'You managed to get my whole life story out of me last time you visited.'

'It's why you were chosen, Jasmine. I hoped you would do well in your interview, and I was not disappointed. You deserve this job and The Gilbert is lucky to get you. Now then, don't cry. Tell you what, I'll put the kettle on. That's my answer to everything. Nothing like a brew to settle the mind.'

She busied herself as Jasmine sniffled into a crumpled tissue.

'It will take a few weeks to convert the old gatehouse, and I presume Chris will be working his notice, but I wondered if you would rather stay up here till it's ready.'

'I did try to go on working, but he turned up at the Home, causing a scene and frightening the old people. I tried to explain to the owners that there was an injunction against him bothering me, and it wouldn't happen again, but they told me to go off sick while they decide what action to take. You can't blame them, I suppose. Oh, to be free of him!' she began to sob and Eileen gathered her into her arms.

'Come on, sit down now, drink your tea. You'll be free of him up here, I promise. It will be good to have a woman on my team. I miss having a woman around. We are going to do great things together, I just know it.'

Chapter 21

Quentin Rivers sat in the window of The Beckside Hotel bar, staring morosely up at Gilbert House, idly running his finger round the rim of his glass.

'You can shatter a glass that way, you know,' a voice said behind him.

'What?'

'I said you can shatter a glass running your finger round the rim like that. It's a scientific fact.'

Quentin stared blankly up at the man. He looked him up and down, noticed the logo on his T-shirt and changed his expression from disdain to welcome.

'Is that a fact? Well, I never. Will you join me? Simon! Get this man a pint, will you? Stick it on my tab.'

Dean flushed with pleasure and sat himself down.

'Quentin Rivers, Cheppingham Argos.'

'Dean Magson, Ranger, The Gilbert Nature Reserve, and Chairman of Cheppingham Wildlife Group.'

Quentin shook his hand firmly.

'Impressive,' he said. 'You could be just the man I'm looking for. We're doing a big spread for The Gilbert anniversary edition. That Nature Reserve is quite something.'

'It certainly is. And they couldn't have done it without us, you know,' Dean replied. 'We know this area inside out – what thrives and what doesn't. Oh, John Hardy knows his stuff well enough but he's not *local,* is he? I keep him straight though, with my local knowledge. I have devoted my life to the study of nature and conservation in this area.'

'And you do it all for free!' Quentin said, pointing at the 'Volunteer' embroidered on his chest.

'I do! And I don't begrudge it, I will say. The environment is what matters and they certainly haven't been mean with the money they have spent on it. Whatever we have needed has been there, I'll give them that.'

Dean was getting into his stride now. Quentin made a few notes on his pad, encouraged him to talk. He resisted the urge to move Dean on to the House and what went on up there. Another pint appeared at Dean's elbow.

'Mind you,' Dean said, 'I did have to go up to the House and have a word with Richard about the lax security down there. People without passes in and out at all hours.'

'Do you have much to do with him?' Quentin asked quickly.

'He's more up at the House, really. John runs the outside operations. Richard is the one with the real power, though. Smart bloke.'

'Did you get any joy out of him about the security?'

Dean hesitated.

'He didn't seem to think it was an issue. Said the Rangers keep an eye. We'll see.'

'It won't be his money behind it all though, will it?' Quentin said confidentially, leaning towards Dean and glancing round the bar.

'That's what I have said all along!' Dean replied in a conspiratorial whisper.

'What do they actually *do* up there?'

'Half the damn town works up there and not a one of them'll tell you!' Dean said, triumphantly, leaning back.

'Sounds a bit fishy to me,' Quentin said.

'I don't think there's anything, you know, criminal, goes on,' Dean said uncertainly. 'I mean, I know most of the people who work up there and they wouldn't get involved in anything like that. It's a charity. They help people from what I can gather. Nothing underhand.'

'No, no, of course not, I wasn't suggesting there was,' Quentin said, aware he had spooked Dean. 'I just meant that the money has to be coming from somewhere. Maybe it's some sort of tax avoidance scheme or something. All perfectly legit. Goes on all the time.'

'There's all sorts of theories like that in the town,' Dean said. 'No-one actually knows though.'

'What's it like inside?' Quentin asked.

Dean was relieved to be off the subject of the money. He didn't want to be responsible for the wrong sort of stuff going in the paper. He loved the feeling of status that the Reserve had given him, didn't want to appear disloyal.

'Oh, it's grand,' he said. 'No expense spared. The cafe is something else. Proper fancy food, on the go all the time. And it's all free!'

'Free? You mean, no charge?'

'Yup, hot and cold food, fancy cakes, proper coffee, day and night and all free to workers.'

That had to include him, didn't it? Dean stopped and thought this through. Why shouldn't he go up there? He as good as worked for them, didn't he? He would ask John Hardy, on the quiet, like.

'What's the rest of the House like inside?'

'Oh, I don't know. I don't have anything to do with that side of things.'

Quentin sat back, disappointed.

'Tell me about Aubrey,' he said.

'I haven't had that much to do with him, really. I see him about with that little dog of his and he is always civil enough.'

Quentin sighed. This was going nowhere.

'You've been very helpful, Dean,' he said. 'Thank you.'

'It's a good place,' Dean said anxiously. 'I wouldn't want you putting anything against them in the paper.'

'Don't you worry about that. It would be more than my job's worth! Everybody loves The Gilbert.'

The men laughed together.

'Well, this won't do,' Dean said, standing up. 'Back to work!'

Quentin went back to staring out of the window, running his finger idly round the rim of his empty glass.

Dean went in search of John Hardy.

'Can I use the cafe up at the House like the workers?' he asked when he found him.

'I don't see why not,' John replied. 'Just you, mind. Don't you go taking your friends up there. It's strictly for the workers.'

Dean watched him ride away. Why had he never realised? Why hadn't they told him?

Perhaps they had mentioned it, way back in the beginning and he'd missed it. Never mind, he knew now. He would walk up there right now, for his supper.

He didn't quite have the courage to use the front entrance, instead slipping in through the French doors.

'Good evening, Dean,' James said cheerfully, as if he came in every day.

Dean collected himself, strolled over to read the specials board, wandered around the carousel, nonchalantly selected a seat near the garden.

'Hot or cold meal?' James asked.

'Hot, I think. And lemonade please.'

He surveyed the room just as Jennie came in. He realised he was staring…again.

'Hi,' she said, smiling. 'Dean, isn't it?'

He hastily got to his feet. 'Will you join me?'

She hesitated, and her smile became a little fixed.

'Why not?' she said and sat down. 'Just tea, please, James.'

Dean could think of absolutely nothing to say.

'I have just been down to the Reserve,' she said. 'It is beautiful down there. You're very lucky to spend your days in such a peaceful place.'

'I work at the agricultural store during the day, but I spend most evenings and weekends there.'

She nodded, pouring her tea.

'I would be happy to give you a proper tour,' he added. 'I can show you things that most people miss. You have to know where to look, see.'

'That would be great, thank you.'

He was about to try to make firm date when Richard came in.

'Good evening, Dean. May I have a word please, Jennie?'

They left together, Dean gazing longingly after her.

*

Jennie was not surprised to be told she had been unsuccessful, and she did not ask for feedback – she already knew why. Richard politely declined to tell her who the successful candidate had been.

'You are welcome to stay until tomorrow as arranged, of course.'

'No, I don't think so. I only live an hour or so away. I'll go home. It'll be a pleasant surprise for my husband.'

'I will have your car brought round into the courtyard for you.'

Jennie fled back to her cottage, managing to stave off the tears until she had closed the door behind her.

'Why am I so upset? It was just a job!'

But she knew why, really. This place was different.

'Well, of course it is!' she told herself. 'They think they are so special, but they don't have to worry about money. It's not the real world here. They will have to come down off their high horse when their "Private Donors" find a better use for their spare cash!'

She flung her things into her case. She swept all the toiletries in as well. The boxes of pastries and snacks went in next and the packets of teas and coffees joined them for good measure. That childish gesture made her laugh. Feeling better, she lugged it all outside, threw it into her car and drove away.

She saw Jasmine and Chris outside the old gate house with the 'ghost woman' as she went by and this time, she got a good look at her.

'Both still here? They must be still deciding who to offer to. And there's that damned woman again. She must work here. Where do I know her from?'

As she was about to turn left out of The Gilbert House drive, Jennie remembered where she had seen the woman before.

'Eileen Croft! That was Eileen Croft!'

She stopped and tried to think it through. Changing her mind, she headed right instead, down the hill to the Beckside Hotel.

Ordering a drink, she sat at a table outside and studied Gilbert House, her mind working, fitting the pieces together.

'Still here then? I'll be up there myself, tomorrow. I'm interviewing Richard Aubrey,' Quentin Rivers said as he came up behind her.

'Are you, now…' Jennie replied. 'I might be able to help you with a bit of inside information if you are interested.'

'Let me get you another drink…something to eat.'

'No, thanks. What do you know about the place?' Jennie asked.

'Only what is already public knowledge.'

'I've been up there after a job. I didn't get it. That doesn't bother me – what does is that I went in good faith, but I think it was some sort of set-up. I'm still trying to work it out.' Jennie was thinking aloud.

Quentin held his breath, his small mind working.

'Everyone round here thinks they are perfection itself,' he said tentatively.

Jennie looked at him hard.

'Don't you?' she asked.

'Well, I'm new around here. What do I know? I did have some dealings with Richard Aubrey in London, though, and he's not my favourite person.'

'I can tell you what the Foundation does and how it does it,' Jennie said, making up her mind. And did so.

Quentin was disappointed. It was interesting enough and would make good copy, but it was hardly the stuff of National scoops.

'Take my card,' he said. 'If you think of anything else, you get in touch, yes?'

'I will,' Jennie said absently. 'I'm still trying to work out what happened up there. I have a feeling there is a piece missing.'

*

Richard, walking Tilda across the meadow, noticed a little red sports car down in the valley bottom. Raising his binoculars, he studied the people sitting outside the Beckside Hotel.

*

Jasmine carried a tray loaded with goodies through to her balcony. Chris followed with the bottle of champagne and two glasses that had appeared in his kitchen.

'This balcony surfing is becoming a habit!' Jasmine said. 'I'm shattered, I don't know about you.'

'I certainly am! But this'll help perk us up!' Chris replied as he expertly drew the cork. They toasted each other and settled on the loungers.

'I saw Jennie leave when we were at the gatehouse…'

'Yes, so did I. I was sure she would get it, at the beginning.'

'I did too! She seemed the obvious choice.'

They fell silent for a while.

'You were OK about job sharing, then?' Jasmine asked.

'Of course. Didn't we say we would make the perfect manager if we joined forces?'

'We did!' Jasmine laughed. 'Who would have thought it would actually happen?'

'I have a little house that I already let out. I live in at the hotel complex, but my pay is reduced accordingly, so even at half the salary, I will hardly be worse off than my current job,' Chris said.

'My marriage recently broke up and our house is being sold anyway. I shall have to think about what to do with my half…'

'I'm sorry to hear it,' Chris replied. 'I have never been married, myself. I am not the marrying kind. No doubt they will have experts here who could advise you.'

Jasmine said, 'You mean *we* will have experts!'

'Yes!'

They stared at one another for a moment and then laughed with delight.

'To the future!'

'The Gilbert!'

*

Dean, uncomfortably full, saw Jennie leave as he emerged into the gardens. He watched her go with regret.

'I'd better go and check all's well down at the Reserve,' he said to himself, turning away.

Chapter 22

'Please come through to my office, Mr. Rivers,' Richard said, guiding him across the foyer.

'Call me Quentin.'

Richard regarded the man opposite him with some distaste.

Quentin was looking forward to this. He had rehearsed the interview over and over in his head, imagining the knots he would tie this man into as Aubrey wondered how he knew so much.

'I imagine you have a list of questions to ask, Mr. Rivers. Do fire away.'

'Well, as you know, we are planning a piece for the Argos to mark the anniversary of the opening of the Park. A spread of before, during and after photos; write-ups about the Reserve, that sort of thing. What would be of real interest, of course, would be an in depth look of the work of the Foundation: what goes on *inside* Gilbert House.'

Richard didn't respond, merely sat back and waited.

'So, what does the Foundation actually do then, Richard?'

'Very much as it has done in Cheppingham, Mr. Rivers.'

'You establish Nature Reserves and children's playgrounds?'

Richard smiled faintly. 'We support people and communities.'

'You support the people who help others,' Quentin said, slyly.

'Precisely.'

In his fantasies, Richard had been stunned that Quentin knew the Mission Statement, had blustered and lost his composure. Trying to keep his own, Quentin decided to change tack.

'This is a fine building. It must be a sizeable foundation to have afforded the conversion…'

Again, Richard did not respond, merely nodded.

Quentin was becoming frustrated. In his imagination, Aubrey had taken his hints. He needed to make it more direct or he would get nowhere.

'How many people work here?'

'About forty altogether.'

'You will have the usual cleaners and cooks and suchlike, of course. Tell me about the Project Workers. How many of those are there?'

'Twenty-one at present.'

At last, a direct answer! Now he was getting somewhere!

'And what do they do, exactly?'

'They pursue the work of the Foundation. They support people who help others.'

Quentin consulted his pad, buying himself some time. This was not exactly as he envisaged.

'I might as well go straight for it,' he thought.

'Where does the Foundation get its money from?'

Richard paused, as if considering the question.

'That is, of course, confidential. However, I will say that the funding comes entirely from private donors who wish to remain anonymous. The Foundation expects the town to respect that. I am sure The Argos would not want the donors to reconsider their support of Cheppingham.'

'That was a threat! A bloody threat!' Quentin thought. This was a waste of time. He had the information from Jennie, he had really only come here to wind Aubrey up.

'It would be interesting to have a look round,' he said.

'Of course,' Richard said, rising. Quentin scrambled to his feet. He hadn't meant right now, he had more questions to bait him with, but Aubrey was holding the door open, waiting.

Richard took Rivers into the foyer, pointed towards the reception hatch and housekeeper offices, shepherded him into the Refectory.

Rivers whistled under his breath. She had said it was plush….

'Perhaps you would like some refreshments, Mr. Rivers. James here will look after you and see you out. Thank you for coming. Please remember that we do not allow photographs.'

Richard gave James a meaningful nod and disappeared. James was looking hostile – he remembered this man from the incident in the foyer. He sat Rivers where he could keep an eye on him, then followed him out to his car. Rivers noticed John Hardy sitting outside his cottage.

'It's like the bloody mafia, heavies on every corner,' Quentin thought sourly as he drove away.

Chapter 23

Gemma sat in Richard's Office, clutching a folder.

'That charity, Standby Rehabilitation and Care, that you asked me to look into, Richard, funny carry on. It's got a nasty smell to it. I think it was what could be called a "hostile takeover." I can't make any sense of how Alkenby Care got their hands on it. The original arrangements look competent enough to me.'

Richard scanned the report.

'It's not really my field either,' Richard said, 'but the set-up looks fairly watertight. Do we know who owns the houses now?'

'That's what I can't work out. This legal stuff is a bit beyond me.'

'I know an excellent man, Rex Wiltshire, in London who can work with you. I'll email you his details. Keep me informed, will you? Alkenby... that name rings a bell,' Richard said, reaching for the dossiers on the manager candidates. Selecting Jennie's, he turned to the biography section.

Name: Jennie Green... spouse/partner Gerald Alkenby.... of Alkenby Care.

Richard made a copy of Jennie's work history and handed it to Gemma.

'Gemma, I need you to do some more digging for me, strictly confidential and off the record. Can you see if there are any other links between this and Alkenby Care?'

Gemma glanced down the list and raised her eyebrows.

'Anybody we know?' she asked.

Richard gave her a long look, weighing up how much to tell her.

'Just keep it out of the database, will you? Our eyes only for now. I'll be able to tell you more when I've spoken to Mrs. Gilbert. It's complicated.'

Gemma tapped the side of her nose. 'Say no more.'

Richard went straight to Eileen.

'I asked Gemma to see what we could do for Standby Care. Based on what she has uncovered so far, I'm calling in a specialist lawyer I know in London.'

'Of course, whatever is needed.'

'It was taken over by a company called Alkenby Care. The name rang a bell, so I had a quick look in the manager dossiers. Jennie Green's husband is Gerald Alkenby. It's his company,' Richard added.

'Well, I'm damned,' Eileen said.

'I've asked Gemma to follow up her job history, see if there are any other links. I'll keep you posted.'

'Please do, Richard. It looks like that woman needs more than just re-educating.'

Chapter 24

'Richard! So this is where you have been hiding out! How are you?'

'I'm well, Rex. You?'

'Fighting fit...fighting fit.'

'This is Mrs. Gilbert, the owner of the Foundation. She will be sitting in. Let's get straight to business, shall we, Rex? What's the situation with Standby?'

'Well, first of all I have to say what excellent people you have here. Gemma – if ever you fancy a move to the big city, you come and see me at my chambers, d'you hear? The brief she wrote for me was first class, Richard, first class.'

'Once the families understood that we genuinely wanted to help them, they gave us access to all the documents and information we needed. They were suspicious at first, of course. They'd trusted people who had taken their money, then let them down,' Gemma put in.

'Well, thanks to Gemma's work, I was able to dive straight in. There were six families involved, as you know. Between them they bought three bungalows on a small new-build estate. Two residents to each. Some families had compensation money, others used their own resources, even mortgaging their own homes and suchlike. Because not everyone put in the same amount, there had to be a lot of trust involved, but they had worked it out, to their credit, though the resulting agreement was pretty complex, as you can imagine. All the residents had various benefit entitlements, and these went into the running costs. It was a bit nip and tuck, but just doable with Social Services input and a bit of fundraising. But cuts to benefits, Government squeezes on social care budgets and all the rest meant that they were struggling. They decided to get someone in to see if they could maximise their income, ensure all the residents were getting everything they were entitled to, look at economies. They scraped together the money to pay this Jennie Green woman for a six months temporary contract, goodness knows how. She took the axe to their expenditure – reduced staffing to one on at a time, got rid of the residents' vehicles. Some of the residents have challenging behaviour or are in wheelchairs so it effectively meant no-one could go out. No new furniture or fittings, no new clothes, all that sort of thing. She then persuaded them that they should hand the running over to Alkenby Care.

There had to be provision in the agreements for any resident who died to be replaced – no house was viable with only one resident's income. Alkenby somehow used this to shoe-horn a third resident into each ...shared bedrooms.' He shook his head. 'The families tried to challenge it all but Alkenby stonewalled them. They would have had to go to law and they had no resources left.'

'We had a big meeting with all the families,' Gemma put in. 'Parents, brothers, sisters, aunts, uncles, friends. Half of them were in tears. All the years of working together for their loved ones gone, counting for nothing.'

'Do they still own the properties, though?' Richard asked.

Gemma beamed, 'They do, thank goodness! Alkenby tried to persuade them to sign them over, but they held firm on that at least!'

Richard and Eileen sighed with relief.

'I looked at the contract they had signed with Alkenby. Whoever drew it up was no legal eagle, that's for sure! Did it on the cheap, like everything else. Didn't take me five minutes to pick it to bits,' Rex said, chortling. 'We paid our friend Alkenby a little visit and informed him that Standby would be terminating their arrangement with them with immediate effect and transferring it to a reputable national not-for-profit care trust, who had already done a cost-analysis, and benefits and entitlement checks and determined that the properties had always been viable with sensible housekeeping. The extra residents would be transferred to more suitable accommodation within their existing housing stock.

He blustered and fussed, of course, threatened to sue. When I gave him a run-down of the Government inspectors and pressure groups and advocacy organisations and possibly even the police, and all the rest, who would be keeping an eye on his future activities he declared that he was getting out of the care business anyway, "cos there's no money in it." Let us hope he doesn't go into the used car trade!'

'Oh, well done all of you!' Richard said. 'Will we need to put any money in the longer term?'

'Probably not, the families are happy to continue their fundraising and there are enough benefits going in to cover all the basics. We worked with the local garage to reinstate their Motability vehicles and put some funds into their account to front-load the reintroduction of the rehab regime etc.,' Gemma said.

'We'll keep an eye on it, Gemma.'

'Of course we will. Don't we always?' Gemma replied.

'We do,' Richard sighed. 'This place keeps money like a sieve keeps water.'

'Except…well…that list you asked me to look into,' Gemma said.

'Go on,' Richard replied.

'There were three other cases linked to Green and Alkenby. All asset stripped. We thought we might as well sort those at the same time.'

'Busy little bitch, your Jennie Green,' Rex put in.

'And are they sorted?' Richard asked.

'Oh yes! The same care trust has taken them all off Alkenby!' Gemma exclaimed.

After the others had gone, Rex said, 'Quite a set up you have here, Richard. You want to show me around?'

Strolling across the gardens, Rex said, 'I saw Sophie in town last week. We had dinner.'

'How is she?'

'She seems well enough, a bit thinner maybe. She came back from New York after a couple of months, you know, but you had disappeared. She tried to find you, but she was told that you had left the law, dropped out of sight. Even your old phone and email weren't working, so she went back to New York. She said she still doesn't know where you are. I didn't tell her, of course, that's up to you.'

'I haven't dropped out of sight, just changed jobs.'

'Have you not? I wouldn't have known where you were if not for this Standby business. How long were you planning to hide away up here? It's been two years!'

Richard avoided the question. 'What else did Sophie have to say for herself?'

'I got the impression that she would like to be in touch with you again. I told her the same thing that I told you when she went, that it would have to wait till the time was right.'

'I don't know, Rex. Sometimes I think there is nothing I want more. But I'm at peace here. Life is simple. She does have my current email address now – I let her know I will be selling the London flat – so she can contact me if she wants to. There are very few people that I have truly missed. Perhaps it is time I got in touch with them. '

'Well, she never was the easiest person to live with, I imagine. But then neither are you! Is there anyone else in your life?'

Richard thought for a while. 'Only The Gilbert,' he replied.

'Changing the subject, Richard, you know I do the occasional bit of pro-bono work with domestic abuse cases? Well, I need to lose someone. A young woman, and her little girl. We've got her out, but the bastard has sworn to kill them both and we believe him. He's turned up at several women's refuges looking for her, but the police seem incapable of catching him. We need to get her out of London. You've got those nice little apartments doing nothing very much. What do you reckon – would Eileen take her in? Not permanently, of course, just until they get him banged up.'

'I think I can safely say that Eileen will have no problem with it, Rex. Where is she now?'

'In an emergency B&B.'

'How will you get her up here? Do you want us to come and fetch her?'

'One of the volunteers from the Refuge will drive her up. The sooner the better, Richard.'

'Well you had better get on with it then. We will be waiting for them.'

'Good man. Tomorrow, then. Her name is Shari, by the way, and the little girl is Tanya. And thanks, Richard.'

'You're welcome, any time.'

*

Eileen quietly told everyone at The Gilbert who they were and why they were there. She knew the Gilbert's people had never let slip about her own existence and that they would not betray the wretched pair that slipped into the mews under cover of darkness, where Eileen was waiting to tuck the sleeping child into the big double bed. After a hot drink, her exhausted mother was glad to join her.

The mother and child hid in the apartment, Eileen flitting to and fro with hot meals for them. Jasmine was dispatched with a shopping list with instructions not to shop in the town, but to go away to York to avoid arousing curiosity. It was two days before the young woman trusted Eileen enough to let the volunteer return to London.

A steady stream of packets and parcels were thrust into Eileen's hands whenever she appeared: little toys and treats for the child, mostly.

Eileen knew that their presence could not be kept secret for long – they needed a story.

'It is called a Legend in the espionage community,' Chris informed her. 'A new identity,' he explained when she stared at him. 'It's called a Legend. And we will be her babysitters – that is what they call the bodyguards, or people who look after Assets. Assets are the people they take care of, usually undercover agents....' he tailed off, looking a little self-conscious. Eileen smiled fondly at him – she was getting used to his flights of fancy.

Eileen generally employed local people, so Shari had to be a visiting relative or friend.

'She can be my cousin,' Jasmine said.

'Good idea,' Eileen said. 'We will worry about the details another day.'

*

As the days passed, Tanya grew a little bolder, watching the comings and goings in the courtyard from the safety of the conservatory, but disappearing back into the apartment if anyone came too close.

It was Jo's little boy that managed to prise her away from her mother. Catching sight of her in the conservatory, he ran across the courtyard and poked his tongue out at her through the glass. She shrieked and ran away to hide behind her mother, who flung aside the door to see who had frightened her girl. Jo, hurrying after him, came face to face with the young mother on the doorstep.

'Hi, I'm Jo. Sorry about my boy. Paul, say sorry for scaring the little girl.'

Paul scowled at the girl, who scowled right back and poked her tongue out at him.

Jo roared with laughter. 'She can give as good as she gets, I see!'

The young woman's face softened. 'I'm Shari, this is Tanya.'

'You are very welcome,' Jo replied.

Very soon, it was as if Shari and Tanya had always been there in the little mews cottage. Paul and Tanya could be heard shrieking around the gardens, hurling balls for Floss and Milly. Even Tilda occasionally abandoned Richard to join in the fun. Jasmine persuaded her 'cousin' to visit her in her cottage and, eventually, to join them all in the Refectory.

'There's not a pickin' on either of 'em, poor lambs,' Susan said to George. 'That poor lass is far too young to have a four-year-old. And have you seen the scars and burns on her arms? God knows what he did to her. There are some wicked people out there. They need looking after, both of them.'

'Now don't you go crashing in there taking over, you will frighten the life out of 'em.'

Susan turned on him. 'How can you say such a thing? When did I ever crash in anywhere, George Sanders?'

George had to concede that Susan was not known for crashing in.

Chapter 25

Gerry Alkenby stormed in through his front door, slamming it behind him.

'Jennie! Jennie! Are you home? Where the hell are you?'

'Whatever's wrong? Has someone died?'

'Not someone, something!' Gerry raged. 'Some bastard London lawyer just trashed our business, with the help of your Gilbert Foundation! What the hell did you tell them?'

'What? For god's sake, Gerry, calm down. I'll get you a whisky. Sit down and tell me exactly what's happened.'

Gerry took some deep breaths, swigged his whisky, threw himself in an armchair and explained exactly what her interview with the Gilbert Foundation had led to.

'Well?' he demanded.

'Let me think...' she said. 'Right, let's look at this rationally. I get invited to interview for a job. They give me a hard time. I don't get the job. All fairly standard stuff except that I see someone there – Eileen Croft – who I know has a grudge against me. So maybe I was set up, played. OK. I got over it. But it doesn't stop there. They come after me. The big question is, what is her connection to the Gilbert Foundation? How come she has the power to launch the whole damned outfit against me? It has to be money – it always is. But, as far as I know she has none. She certainly showed no sign of any when I knew her. Perhaps she has influence with one of the Foundation's backers... Help me out here, Gerry. Don't just sit there.'

'Where does the name Gilbert come from?' he asked.

'Good question. From the research I did before the interview, the house was Cheppingham Manor before they took it over. Which means that "Gilbert" must be significant. We need to find out if she has any connection with anyone called Gilbert. Who do we know who does family history type stuff? They seem to be able to trace extended families, no trouble. What about your sister – isn't she into all that sort of thing?'

'She is,' he replied, reaching for his phone.

It didn't take his sister very long.

'You have to search on the family history websites – I have a subscription, you know. I put in the names you gave me – Eileen and Croft and Gilbert – from what you told me of her age, I was able to put in some rough dates. I had to try all the combinations. It was a nightmare.

'Never mind all that, Lou. What have you found out?'

'There's no need to be rude, Gerry. It took some doing, I'll tell you. They're not exactly rare names, you know, Croft and Gilbert. Not so many Eileen's, though – that's an old-fashioned name. Anyway, after a lot of false leads and elimination, I found a Daniel Croft who married an Eileen Gilbert in the right time period. If your Eileen Croft has reverted to her maiden name, she will be Eileen Gilbert now. There's your connection.'

'You are a star, Lou! I owe you!'

'So she is using her maiden name. Nothing unusual in that, of course,' Jennie said. 'There was a husband, now I come to think of it, a son too. But that doesn't explain the money. If it is her outfit, where's the money come from?'

'Perhaps she inherited it,' Gerry suggested.

'Lou, see if you can find out if this Eileen Gilbert had any rich relations. Can you search wills and things?'

The results were disappointing.

'I can't find any money in the family at all. They seem to have been a very ordinary lot.'

'So, is she the financial backer? If not, who is? And why does she hide away? Nobody mentioned her existence. I wouldn't have known if I hadn't happened to see her.'

Jennie stopped. 'Or *did* I just happen to see her? Was I *meant* to see her?'

Gerry laughed. 'Now you are being paranoid!'

'Maybe you're right. She must be Queen Bee, though – the Foundation carries her name. So, wherever she got the money, I think we can safely assume it does come from her.'

'True. But now that we know, how does that help us?'

'I can understand her not wanting me to see her, but she seems to go to extraordinary lengths to remain anonymous. I read up as much as I could about the place before I went for the interview and there was no mention of her in any of the local newspaper coverage, which is odd. Or the husband and son either. What has she got to hide? We need to find out,' Jennie said. 'Where did I put that creepy reporter's card? He has history with Aubrey. I think he could be an ally.'

'Don't you go telling him about me losing the homes! If our associates get wind that she is trying to break us, they'll run a mile and then we would be sunk!' Gerry responded.

*

Quentin Rivers spent the next weeks preparing his anniversary spread. He chatted with people in the Park and the Reserve and met with Jennie again. He checked and double-checked his story. He was frustrated at being unable to definitively establish whether Eileen Gilbert was the financial backer of the Foundation or find out more about her. Jennie was unable to help him there – she told him that Eileen had just been an incompetent employee that she had had to get rid of and there had been no hint of any personal wealth. He sensed that the ex and the son could be key, but they seemed to have disappeared into thin air. He just wished he had someone on the inside.

Quentin was not downhearted, though. He planned to keep digging and would save what he found out for the piece he planned to sell to the Nationals. There was a story for them here, he felt it in his bones. His article for the Argos would just be a teaser, designed to bring them out into the open, desperate to find out what else he knew.

River's editor was surprised that the interview with Richard Aubrey had apparently yielded such rich fruit. He could only begrudgingly congratulate Quentin and concede that he obviously had investigative skills hitherto unsuspected. Unfortunately, it didn't occur to him that Rivers had a second source.

'And is this all absolutely factual?' he asked, suspiciously. 'No bending of the truth, no spin? I trust you are not up to your old tricks.'

'Absolutely one hundred percent fact,' Quentin said, proudly.

'I bloody hope so,' Eddie said. 'I've rewritten a few of your more sensational paragraphs. The town won't thank us for cheap shots at The Gilbert.'

'Absolutely, boss, no problem.'

'This bit about the Gilbert woman – are you sure she exists? And this, about the staff not being allowed to talk about her.'

'Oh yes, quite sure, she exists alright. And I have asked some of the workers myself!'

'So, is she the financer of the operation?'

'Ah, now that's still a bit of a mystery, but it's her name on the organisation, so it seems likely. I haven't put that in, of course, I don't want to be accused of making things up!' he added meaningfully.

'Nobody is accusing you of making things up, Quentin, but the practice was not exactly alien to you in the past, you have to admit.'

'And I learnt my lesson, boss. All facts checked and verified for me, nowadays, you can rest easy on that. Of course, young Laura must take the credit for the picture spreads,' Quentin added, magnanimously.

'They are excellent,' his editor agreed. 'I particularly like the before, during and after photos of the Reserve and Park.'

'Great girl. Hard worker, too. She will go far.'

Distracted from his feelings of unease, Eddie Mason approved the copy for publication in the Argos and its sister publication, the County Press.

'It is two years since *The Gilbert Foundation* came to Cheppingham and opened its doors to our men and women, who are helping it to realise its philanthropic vision. Gilbert House, formerly Cheppingham Manor, has given meaningful employment to many of our citizens but, without their unstinting loyalty and hard work, it would not be the place it is today.

With a staff of over forty, and a legion of volunteers, mostly drawn from the locality, The Gilbert has brought relief and enjoyment to many, not only locally, but throughout the land. If you need support for your charity or cause, The Gilbert Foundation will be there for you; offering money, advice and assistance.

Its small army of domestic and admin staff work with the team of Project Workers, whose sole aim is to find and support those dedicated to relieving poverty and injustice wherever they find it.

The stunning house and grounds provide the perfect setting for the endeavours of its dedicated workforce.

The Refectory, offering free sustenance to the staff, is a haven of comfort – and some of the best food in the district – thanks to James and the Catering Team, and Jo and Amy lead the domestic staff in maintaining the facilities to the highest standard.

Cosy, well-furnished cottages provide homes for the Estate Staff, and the mews apartments, overlooking the valley below, are available for visitors and staff alike.

The Estate Manager, John Hardy can be seen with his trusty pony and dogs, patrolling and maintaining the Reserve and Park. The Director, Richard Aubrey is a familiar sight with his little dog, Tilda, always at his heel.

Add to this the pioneering work of the Project Workers in their busy workroom, and out in the field, giving away money to deserving causes, and we are looking at a multi-million-pound enterprise funded entirely by private donors.

Who are these donors? Who is the mysterious "Gilbert" of its name?

We can reveal one Gilbert: a reclusive and retiring woman who most of you do not even know exists. Ask any one of your friends who work there, and they will tell you that they are not allowed to speak of her outside their workplace. Why the need for such secrecy, you may ask? Why isn't this fine woman as familiar to us as Richard and John? What does she have to hide? Step out of those shadows, Eileen Gilbert – and let us meet you and your family and shake you by the hand!'

*

Richard came into Eileen's office, clutching a copy of the Cheppingham Argos, to find her standing with one in her hands, staring sightlessly out of the window.

'How did he know about me?' She looked at Richard in bewilderment. 'He interviewed you. Did he get it from you, Richard?'

He stared at her in disbelief. 'Do you really think that?'

'I don't know what to think!'

'Well, I can tell you exactly where he got it from. He got it from Jennie Green. Did she go home when she left here? She did not! I saw her sitting outside The Beckside Hotel with that snake, Rivers. Why did you bring her here, what was it for?'

'I knew her already. I worked at the Fanshawe Trust. I was one of the team she got rid of. I wanted to punish her; see her squirm; dangle a prize in front of her then snatch it away. Not just for me – my sister was in that team, too. She had a breakdown because of that woman and now she is dead. I don't know what you are making such a fuss about – messing with Green's head with a job interview can hardly compare to that!'

Suddenly her defiance crumpled and she began to weep, silently.

'Is that what it was all about – the interviews – revenge? You risked your precious anonymity for *revenge*? If you wanted to bring her down, why didn't you just say so? When

124

I asked Gemma to look into her activities, did she hesitate? No, she did not, because she trusts me. The Gilbert. You. And she wants to see justice done. Did you trust me to help you give that woman what she deserved? No, you brought her here, right into the heart of The Gilbert. You let her gather ammunition to hurt what you say you care about. What I *do* care about. We honour and respect your wish for anonymity and privacy and what do you do? You give it all away, to that poisoned woman! What did you think she would do? Go off home and forget everything she had seen and learnt? Did you think she wouldn't work out what had happened, who was behind it? Because if so, you were a fool. She gave –probably sold – those bullets to that weasel Rivers, and we will take the consequences. The Gilbert is built on trust. I thought our relationship was built on trust. Where was that trust when you used me to play your little games? And what is all the damned secrecy for anyway, Eileen? Don't tell me it is about some vague fear of the media and some long-gone ex-husband, because I really don't think I believe you anymore. What is it I am not trustworthy enough to know?' Richard waited. When there was no reply, he made for the door. 'I am going to London. I need time to think.'

When he had gone, Eileen sat on, hunched over, her arms wrapped around herself, tears dripping from her nose.

Dearest Jack
Oh, what have I done?

Eileen paused and sat back in her chair.

'What have I done, exactly? What was so terrible?' she said to herself. 'She must have seen me, dammit. I'll write to him – apologise – tell him to take some leave. I certainly owe him some. Then he will forgive me and come back and we can forget all about it.'

Suddenly she threw her pen across the room, screwed up the piece of paper and flung it at the bin.

'I am sick of it all. Sick to death of lying and hiding and writing letters Jack will never read. I should have killed that bitch, never mind interviewing her! If she comes within a mile of this place again I bloody well will!'

*

Jasmine found Chris sitting on the patio.

'Have you seen this?'

He scanned the article and looked at her, puzzled.

'Where have they got this from, the stuff about Eileen?' he asked

'They must have got it from someone in the House. Who would do that?'

They were distracted by Richard coming out of the French doors.

He sat himself down with them.

'I see you have read the piece in the Argos,' he said. 'Don't worry, it wasn't anyone here. It was Jennie Green getting her own back. Look, I have to go to London. You are going to be dumped right in the deep end, I'm afraid.'

'Will you be gone long?'

Richard stared across the garden, his eyes inexpressibly sad.

'I don't know,' he said after a while. 'It's complicated…I don't know if I will be back at all. You have a good team here: trust them. You will report directly to Eileen. This is her Foundation, after all. I am just an employee. Good luck.'

They all rose. He hugged Jasmine, shook Chris's hand.

'You'll be fine, I know you will.'

They watched as he drove away.

'Oh, whatever has happened?' Jasmine said, close to tears.

'That bloody Jennie Green!' Chris said fiercely. 'I will kill her if she's the reason for him going.'

'And I will hold her down while you do it! What do we do now? The thought of stepping into Richard's shoes terrifies me.'

'We have to talk to Eileen. Richard is right, though. The team probably don't really need us in the short term – they are an incredibly dedicated lot. They will help us get established.'

They were interrupted by John Hardy's dogs bounding across the grass.

'You two, lie down. Now, I tell you, lie down! And stay there.'

John stood looking down at them.

"You've seen it then,' he stated. 'Do we know who it was?'

'It was Jennie Green, the other candidate for our job, John. We got it from Richard.'

John sat himself down. 'I've seen her around a few times these last weeks. At The Beckside Hotel, but also some odd places like down in the Reserve. I did wonder what she was doing here. Speaking of Richard, I've just seen him loading his stuff into his car. He didn't tell me he was going away. It's not like him.'

'He's gone back to London. From the way he was talking, he might not be coming back. We think it might be something to do with the article, but we don't know.'

John was silent for a while. 'Hells bells…' he muttered. 'The staff will need to know. We need to talk to Eileen,' he added. 'Drink up, you two. Now is good.'

They made their way to the discreet door towards the end of the patio. None of them had ever been through it, let alone up the staircase to Eileen's private apartments.

'Floss, Milly, lie down. Stay,' John ordered. 'Right then you two, up we go.'

He opened the door and they followed him through and up to the apartment door. Jasmine tapped tentatively. There was no response. She looked desperately at Chris and John. John knocked firmly.

The door opened. 'You'd better come in,' Eileen said and stepped back.

The apartment was large and airy. Vertigo inducing, floor to ceiling dormer windows, set into the sloping roof, looked out over the garden from the living room. It was decorated in the same calm, soft pale green as the Refectory below. The carpet and furnishings, however, were splashes of vivid jewel colours which shocked and excited the eye.

'What a beautiful room!' Jasmine exclaimed.

'Thank you. May I offer you some refreshment? I was about to make some tea.'

Eileen Gilbert looked exhausted.

'Please let me,' Jasmine said.

Eileen smiled faintly and sank into a chair. 'The kitchen is through there, Jasmine. Thank you.'

'We have just spoken to Richard.' Chris said. 'He has left for London, with little intention of returning in the near future, we gather. We've seen the Argos article, by the way. We thought we should come and see you about the way forward…the running of The Gilbert…' he tailed off.

'Have you thought about the implications of that article?' Eileen asked.

Jasmine returned and laid out the tea things. There was a pause as they dealt with them.

'What did you mean about implications?' John asked.

'Every con artist, scammer and free-loader will descend on The Gilbert. In amongst that rabble will be genuine people who need our help. We will have to find those people and weed out the riffraff.'

'It's only a local paper, though. The circulation can't be that big, surely? There won't be too much extra work,' Jasmine said.

'Let us hope you are right, Jasmine. I will try to fill Richard's place while you find your feet, though there is much that I don't know of the day-to-day detail. I think we'll have a full staff meeting tomorrow morning. Perhaps you would work with the admin team to call everyone in. They will all pull together, I'm sure. I also think it would be a good idea if we had a weekly meeting of section heads. Would Wednesday mornings, in my office at ten suit you?'

They nodded their agreement.

She paused for a long moment. 'I have to tell you that this situation is entirely my fault. I knew what Jennie Green was before she ever came here. She bullied my sister into a breakdown and an early death. I wanted to punish her. Richard left because I didn't trust him with that information. I shouldn't have brought her into The Gilbert. He was right to tell me a that I was a foolish, vengeful woman.'

She stood up.

'Shall we say ten o'clock tomorrow morning?'

The others rose and followed her to the door.

Floss and Milly greeted them enthusiastically. Jasmine dropped to her knees, hugging and kissing them, wetting their heads with tears. She had not quite had the courage to do it to Eileen Gilbert.

Chapter 26

The circulation of the Cheppingham Argos and the County Press might have been small, but the circulation of social media is limitless.

The same groups that spread the word about the opportunities for local interest groups during the establishment of The Gilbert, did the same with the article. Here was an organisation that offered 'money, advice and assistance' to the thousands of people who were trying to help their communities. People tagged friends who were involved in charity work who, in their turn, shared and tagged and shared and tagged. There was just enough information in the article to identify the address of The Gilbert and an ever-increasing tide of rogues and heroes used that address to appeal for support.

'Morning, Magda. You lot are popular all of a sudden,' the postman said, coming into the foyer. 'Three sacks for you, would you believe, half of them with no postcode. You would think people would look it up online. It's easy enough.'

Magda looked at the sacks with dismay and rang through to the workroom for help.

The Right Hons didn't do social media, but they did take the Cheppingham Argos and were as surprised as anyone by the article. The town's people knew that they had a special relationship with The Gilbert and reasoned that if anyone knew the truth of it, it would be them. They were accosted by the gossips everywhere they went. The article itself was soon supplanted as the topic of concern, however, when visitors found the sign on the Park gate, that told them it was '*CLOSED UNTIL FURTHER NOTICE*'

Having received a tight-lipped 'no comment' from The Gilbert staff who lived in the town, the people made their way to The Old Rectory. The Right Hons were persuaded to go up to the House, but all they got was a statement which Magda told them was soon to be released to The Argos. Mrs. Gilbert was not receiving any visitors, even them.

*

'I would like to speak to the proprietor. My name is Eileen Gilbert.'

The receptionist scrambled for the phone.

'There's an Eileen Gilbert here to see you Eddie… Yes…OK…. Eddie will be out in a moment.'

He appeared almost before she had finished speaking.

'Mrs. Gilbert! What a pleasure!' He held out his hand. Eileen ignored it. He ushered her through the newsroom to his office. As the door closed behind them, the receptionist put her head into the newsroom and mouthed 'Eileen Gilbert!'

The word quickly went around, and all activity stopped.

Jim, whose desk was nearest the editor's door, rolled his chair over and put his ear to it.

Inside, his smile fading, Eddie slid behind his desk, as if to protect himself from her icy glare.

'Do sit down' he said, as he did so. Mrs. Gilbert remained standing.

'Mr. Mason,' she began. 'What requirements does The Gilbert place on Cheppingham for access to the Reserve and the Park?'

'Well…none. And we appreciate it, of course...'

There was a silence.

'Mr. Mason,' she repeated patiently. 'Do we ask anything of Cheppingham?'

Eddie met her gaze as the answer came to him.

'No, Mrs. Gilbert, except that we respect your privacy?'

Eileen nodded.

'Does The Gilbert advertise its services in your paper, have social media accounts?'

'No...'

'Have you ever wondered why?'

He had to admit that he had not.

'Then let me explain. The Gilbert Foundation, like any other charitable organisation, has limited resources. To remain within a finite budget and to provide employment and make bequests long-term, it has to husband its resources. An overwhelming flood of applications, I am sure you would agree, would naturally threaten this long-term viability. As a result of your article, this flood has become a reality. Hundreds of letters have been received at Gilbert House and continue to arrive daily. We could burn the lot, of course, but I'm sure you would not advocate that course of action. No, we must read every letter; evaluate the claim to establish if it is credible or merely a scam or con-man or free-loader; respond in a timely manner; offer support according to our mission statement. Consequently, the normal daily activity of Gilbert House has had to be suspended. Every member of staff has had to be diverted to deal with this. Our workroom has become a mailroom. At present, we are unable to do anything except acknowledge receipt of these applications. That diversion of personnel has had to include those who run and maintain the Reserve and Park. Therefore, we have had to take the decision to close them to public access until further notice. I have prepared a statement to this effect which I would be grateful if you would publish in your papers. Thank you. Good morning.'

Placing it carefully on his desk, she turned and left.

Eddie stared at the door for an age before picking up the statement and staring at that instead. Yanking open a drawer, he scrabbled at the back and pulled out a battered packet of cigarettes. The lighter took longer to find. He lit up and sat back in his chair, clouds of smoke filling the room. He watched it absently for a few moments, before jumping up and opening the outside door. He took his cigarette out into the delivery yard just as it came on to rain.

'What did she want, Mr. Mason? Did she come to congratulate you on Quentin's insightful piece on the inside workings of The Gilbert?'

He turned to see Laura standing in the doorway.

'Not exactly...' he said ruefully, forgetting that this apprentice had no business talking to him like this, even if he had known her since childhood.

She stood aside as he went back into his office. He handed her the statement and she read it through slowly.

'Quentin interviewed Richard Aubrey.... why would Aubrey give a reporter the information if he didn't want it published?' he said in bewilderment.

'That information didn't come from Richard Aubrey! You didn't really believe that, did you?' Laura shook her head. 'Unlike you, I've only been in journalism for a few months but even I know you can't trust someone like Quentin Rivers!'

'Photocopy the statement will you and hand it round the office.'

He opened the door. 'I presume you toe-rags got most of that. As they say in the movies, "hold the front page". Read her statement. I want a damage limitation piece for the next edition. And I want it on the social media pages and the websites tonight. Nobody is going home till I have approved it.'

'Mr. Mason,' Laura said. 'Do you think we should run it past The Gilbert before we publish?'

He considered for a while. 'You might be right.'

'I'll take it up there, if you like,' Laura said. 'Magda is on duty today. I could ask her what she thinks.'

'I'll come with you, lass. Hold your hand.'

'Thank you, Jim. I might need it.

Quentin breezed into the newsroom addressing his cheerful 'Afternoon!' to no-one in particular. No-one responded.

'What's up with you lot, then?' he asked.

'Ah, Mr. Rivers. Could I have a word? In my office,' Eddie said.

He closed his door behind them. Jim rolled his chair back to it.

'Morning, Eddie!'

'Mrs. Gilbert paid me a visit earlier.'

'Great!'

He handed the statement to Rivers who read it, then read it again.

'Clear your desk, Rivers. You're out,' Eddie stated simply.

'You can't do that!'

'So sue me,' Eddie replied. 'You let me believe that piece was sanctioned by Richard Aubrey. You are a lying piece of shit. Get out. And leave that statement behind.'

'He's out!' Jim announced in a moderately roared whisper.

'Good riddance!' he muttered as Rivers stormed through the newsroom.

Chapter 27

Eileen stood in Richard's office for the first time since he left and saw his work laptop and phone lying on his desk. She flipped the lid of the laptop to find his passwords neatly written on a Post-it Note and absorbed what that implied. She wandered around the room. Tilda's blanket and toys had gone. His desk was tidy and bare. A solitary, rather magnificent cactus on the windowsill was all that remained of Richard here. She began to weep quietly.

Giving herself a shake, she booted up the laptop and accessed the personnel records. Having found Richard's, she wrote down his home and personal email addresses and mobile number.

'He had a life before The Gilbert. What did I know of it? I was too taken up with myself to take the trouble to find out.'

She tried to imagine him now, in his London flat, in a busy restaurant, being welcomed back by his old friends, walking Tilda in a park, greeting the other familiar dog walkers. What had that occasional far-away sadness meant? A woman, maybe. A lost love? She shook her head at herself for thinking like a bad romantic novelist.

Snapping the laptop shut she folded the piece of paper into her pocket. She picked up the cactus and left, closing the door gently behind her.

'You can come and stay with me,' she said, taking it through to her office.

'Ah, there you are, Eileen. I've been looking all over for you,' John Hardy said as she emerged into the Refectory.

'Still treating me with the respect due to your employer, I see,' Eileen said drily.

'Don't be silly,' John replied. 'I've been apprehended by a delegation of local worthies, led by the Right Hons, no less.'

'Oh yes? And what did they want?'

'They brought a letter.' He handed it over.

It was long and very, very wordy and Eileen found she really could not be bothered to read it.

'Summarise for me, please, John.'

'Well, in essence, the school summer holidays are about to start. No park means no school sports day, no cricket nets competition, no five-a-side football contest, no fundraiser summer fair, no out-of-school activities. Defenceless children will be wandering the streets. You get the general idea. Anyway, they are suggesting that they try to run the park over the summer. Put together a team of volunteers. And they want to form a "Save The Gilbert" fundraising committee – give us the takings from the summer fair, have coffee mornings, that sort of thing. Your statement has frightened the life out of them. They want a meeting.'

'Good heavens!' Eileen sat down. 'You had better bring us some tea, James.'

'What are your first thoughts, John, about opening the Park?'

'Well, I will still have to mow the grass and maintain the facilities whether it is open or not, else it'll go to ruin. I can't be there all the time, though. A few volunteers to litter pick and keep an eye on the kids wouldn't come amiss. It works in the Reserve. But I won't be able to keep up with maintaining the rest of the grounds and buildings single-handed. I really don't think I can do without my team for long, Eileen. We need to think how we are going to manage if you are planning to divert all the staff long-term. You can't just pull twenty-odd people away and expect things so go on as usual.'

'So, what you are really saying is that I have to give up trying to sort the letter mountain.'

'Not give up, no. But The Gilbert has always had a dual remit. "Charity begins at home," you said that first day. Nurture the workers so they can nurture others. Doesn't that still apply?'

Eileen had to admit to herself that he had a point.

John said, 'I don't think it is necessary to close the Reserve either. There is a danger that we'll lose our volunteers if we do.'

'They can still work in there even though it is closed, surely?'

'It's a delicate situation. If they are expected to continue to maintain it, but prevented from bringing their friends and family in, they won't be happy.'

'Fair enough. You are right, of course. If in doubt, compromise…' Eileen said. 'Have your Rangers back, by all means. They aren't much use to us, anyway – it is taking longer to train them to use the systems than it is worth. And someone for the entry booth, to keep an eye on the volunteers. But it wouldn't hurt the town to help us maintain the park and run the refreshment booth. Could volunteers be relied on, do you think?'

'They would be better than nothing.'

'OK, let's give it a try. But what about this fund-raising committee? Do they really have any idea how much it costs to run this place? Their efforts might keep us in tea and biscuits, I suppose, but it would just take the money away from all the other local causes. We would only end up giving the money back when they were struggling.'

'And you would be daft enough to do just that!" John said, and Eileen had to laugh with him.

'Besides, I don't want their money!'

'Why ever not?'

'Because it would compromise our independence! So, what have you spent our donations on, Mrs. Gilbert? A luxury headquarters? A free Refectory? *A Nature Reserve?* We are not paying for that! We want representation, a committee, to ensure our money goes to causes we approve of.'

'You do like things your own way, don't you?'

'I do, and I intend to continue doing so.'

'Fair enough,' John said. 'It's your money.'

That had been a shrewd guess. Eileen could deny it. She chose not to.

'That's that little question cleared up,' he stated, and moved on. 'I suppose we had better have this meeting that they want. Do you think we should make it a public meeting?'

Eileen considered. 'Why?'

'Well, all they have to go on is what they read in the paper. If we're going to let them on board, it might be an idea to lay out some boundaries.'

Eileen thought back to that other public meeting, when Richard had taken the stage and she had lurked at the back.

'Who would lead this meeting?' she asked.

'Well, you, of course. Who else?' John replied. 'Don't worry, me and Jasmine and Chris will be there with you. They're fine people, by the way. I thought they were a job share. They both appear to be working full-time.'

Eileen laughed. 'I have tried reminding them, believe me, but they seem to have a selective hearing problem. And if Richard doesn't come back…and before you ask, no I have not heard from him. I'm going to write to him tonight.'

'Good,' John said. 'I'll have a word with Chris and Jasmine, get this meeting organised. The sooner the better. I'll put a notice in this week's Argos. Meanwhile, shall I get someone in the booth and take the closed notices down from the park gate?'

'No, the town needs to know how things are going to be. They can wait a few more days. And I am not going to lead your public meeting, either. You three can do it.'

'Mrs. Gilbert, Laura and Jim are here from the Argos,' Magda said from the door.

'What the devil do they want?' John muttered.

'Show them in here please, Magda,' Eileen told her.

'Mrs. Gilbert… sorry to disturb you.' Laura's flushed face was all terror. 'We thought we should show you the piece we plan to put in tomorrow's edition, and on social media and the website…'

'Run it past you…see what you think…' Jim echoed.

'Pity you didn't do that with the last one!' John snorted.

'Oh, we are so sorry about that…it was that Quentin Rivers and Mr. Mason has sacked him!' Laura said.

'Has he, now? Good man!' Eileen said. 'Come on then, let's have a look at it. Just the one copy? Well, perhaps you could read it out, so we can all share in the enjoyment.'

The words would not keep still on the page and Laura began to panic.

'Oh, you do it Jim!' she said desperately.

Jim cleared his throat and squared his shoulders

'For goodness sake, sit down,' Eileen said. 'You're not addressing Parliament.'

Jim did so and took a deep breath.

'*Local Charity Overwhelmed By Desperate Pleas For Help*' - that's the headline,' he said

'*Following intrusive revelations, which appeared on our pages last week and for which we take full responsibility, Cheppingham's Gilbert Foundation has been flooded with thousands of begging letters. Local postie Bill Johnson said: 'They are arriving in sack loads. I am having to make special trips up there with the van several times a day.'*

So overwhelmed are they, that they have had to call in all their staff to work around the clock in an attempt to deal with the situation.

In a statement, The Gilbert said: 'The diversion of personnel has had to include those who run and maintain the Reserve and Park. Therefore, we have had to take the regrettable decision to close them to the public until further notice.'

Locals are understandably upset and angry that the leaking of private information about The Gilbert has led to the withdrawal of the amenities that the Foundation so generously gifted to our town. The Argos shares that anger and can reveal that the reporter concerned has been dismissed.

Sadly, this flood threatens more than just our amenities.

The statement also describes the threat to the Foundation itself as it attempts to meet the huge increase in demand on its limited resources. The Gilbert is the largest

single employer in our town and these developments could jeopardise the livelihoods of our hard-working men and women.

The statement concludes: 'We ask those who have written to The Gilbert to be patient. We will try to respond to every genuine request for help but, if The Foundation is to survive long term, it must be prudent and responsible with the funds entrusted to it.

We regretfully request that no further applications be made for the present.'

Jim took a deep breath and looked up from his document.

Eileen shook her head. 'Well, I suppose it was too much to ask that it shouldn't be sensational. You may remove the reference to the Nature Reserve. John has convinced me that, with the help of his valued volunteers, he can keep it open.'

'I will write that in, just as you have said it. *Valued volunteers…*' he muttered, scribbling.

'We will also be holding a public meeting in response to a request from some of the townsfolk. Next Tuesday evening, 7.30, the Memorial Hall. Get that publicised too, please.'

Chapter 28

Eileen addressed the second, full staff meeting within a week.

'Thank you all for coming,' she began. 'Our worst fears have been realised and we will not cope unless we formulate a plan. The Foundation will not survive long-term if we do not. I have had a letter from a group of local people led by the Right Hon Champleys, who want to form a volunteer group to open the Park over the summer. John feels this is viable if I give him back his Rangers and someone for the entry booth. And he feels they can keep The Reserve open with the help of the volunteers. So, John and the Rangers will remain on normal duty. They can call on the rest of their people if they need them. The letter asks for a meeting, which we are going to make public – Jasmine and Chris are organising that. It will be next Tuesday evening, the 12th July at 7.30 in the Memorial Hall. The Argos are aware and will be publicising it. You may put it on your personal social media pages, and posters will be going up straight after this meeting. I would like James and his team to remain in the Refectory and keep you all fed and watered, if that is OK.'

The catering team nodded their agreement.

'One or two people will remain in the reception office – there will be plenty of photocopying and mailing to keep them busy down there and someone has to take delivery of the sack loads. In the workroom, I propose that we set up sorting stations. The first will open all mail and reply with a standard letter explaining that we are inundated but will be back in touch as soon as possible, making it clear that it may be weeks or even months before we are able to do so. I want this letter to be informal and explain in detail the predicament we find ourselves in. However, do feel free to bin those that are obviously from fraudsters. You may also

141

discard, without reference to me, any more offers of marriage that Eileen Gilbert might receive.'

When the laughter had died away, she continued;

'They will pass the appeal letters on to the second station who will sort the applications into two categories. One will be applications from individuals seeking help for themselves. The second will be those from the champions who are helping others. Our first priority will be to help the second category. This will serve two purposes. Firstly, it will prioritise our mission statement. Secondly, it will enable them to cope when we refer the applications from individuals to them. As soon as possible, we will set up a third station, which will evaluate and respond to the claims. It is important to remember that we must not be overwhelmed or lose track. Work steadily, keep detailed records, don't panic. People will have to wait longer than we are happy about, but it cannot be helped. If not for this crisis, we may never have found them at all. We will work through this and try to keep The Gilbert on track.'

Chris stuck his hand up

'You said that the long-term survival of the Foundation is threatened by this. What did you mean?'

Murmurs of concerned agreement were heard all around.

Eileen thought for a moment before replying. She looked around the room at their anxious faces. She could trust them, or not. Richard's words came back to her "*The Gilbert is built on trust*".

'The Gilbert has its capital and it has the income from the investment of that capital. It has no other funding. By limiting the number of Project Workers and monitoring expenditure, Richard and I have ensured that we spend only the income. So far it has worked well. By this means, The Gilbert would survive my lifetime and beyond. If we spend the capital, the Gilbert will run out of money. It is that simple. This huge increase in demand threatens that balance.'

'Then we will just have to be very responsible in how we make the bequests,' Chris said stoutly. 'That might sound hard, but we can't solve all of the world's problems single-handed. The champions that we support know that. They just try to help as many people as they can for as long as they can, and we must do the same. Once the capital was gone, we would be able to help nobody at all.'

'Hear, hear!' someone called out and it echoed around the room.

Eileen found herself both tearful and smiling.

'In that case, I am going to hand oversight of the Project Worker budget to Chris and Jasmine, and the Estate budget to John, if they are agreeable.'

They nodded their agreement.

'We could keep everyone up-to-date with what percentage of the year's budget has been spent, if that's OK with you, Mrs. Gilbert,' Jasmine said.

'We could have one of those thermometer thingies that fund raisers have,' someone called out and everyone laughed.

'Of course, the financial affairs of The Gilbert are our business and no-one else's,' John said. 'We will all remember that, won't we?'

There were nods and 'Of course' and 'Understood' from around the room.

'Shall we have lunch, then?' Eileen said. 'It will be cold food only today as James and his team have been in here. And then we can get started.'

After the rush was over, Eileen, Chris, John and Jasmine sat on in the Refectory.

'Thank you for trusting us with the information about the funding,' Jasmine said. 'Like everyone, I imagined there were a number of backers and funding sources. To have the whole Foundation in your hands alone is a huge responsibility. You were brave to start it at all.'

'When Richard went, I felt the full force of that responsibility, believe me. I do feel better for sharing it with you. Perhaps between us we can stop The Gilbert from imploding,' Eileen replied.

'Will Richard come back, do you think?'

'I haven't heard from him since he left. I have written to him, though, so let's see, shall we?'

There was a long, sad silence.

Chapter 29

Richard sank into as dark a place as he had ever visited when Sophie went. He read and re-read Eileen's letter – there was an apology of course, but where was the explanation for what she had done? Where was the true understanding of how shoddy and used she had made him feel? The whole tone, ending with the suggestion that he took some leave, just fueled his anger and pride, stopping him from responding. He had none to spare to turn Sophie away when she appeared at his door, as if nothing had happened. She did not move in this time. Neither quite had the courage for that. Occasionally she would stay the night. Sometimes they made love, more often not. They did not talk about his life in Yorkshire.

The Gilbert had put a decent amount of money into his account every month, and continued to do so, of which he had spent very little. Thankful that he had no need to find work, he devoted the summer to bringing his garden back from three years of neglect. Digging and clearing and burning occupied his mind and body, giving him sinews of steel and rich brown skin, melting every ounce of fat from his already lean frame, despite his voracious appetite. Tilda helped by furiously digging random holes, yelping with excitement, often flinging the dirt in his face. Sophie teased him about his increasingly wild hair, declaring that she wouldn't be seen out with him until he got it cut. He had no wish to be seen out, so let it grow.

'Will you tell me about The Gilbert?' Sophie asked one quiet evening, fully two weeks after she had reappeared.

'I would rather not,' he replied

'You dream about it, though; you talk about it in your sleep. Such sad and angry dreams, as if you have lost your homeland…'

She looked embarrassed to admit she had been watching him in his sleep.

'It's just a workplace…a house,' he said hesitantly,

'Not to you, though,' she replied. 'What makes it so special that you dream about being there when you are here with me?'

So, he told her. It took him fully an hour to describe the exhilarating, exhausting months of the renovations; he and John and Eileen working and laughing together; the anticipation as the teams came to life; the excitement of the project moving into action; the intense reward of seeing its streams of benevolence flowing out into the town and the communities beyond. Then he went back over it again, filling in the gaps. Once he started, he found himself reluctant to leave out any detail, as if committing it to memory. When he finally slowed to a halt, the wounds of loss raw from the telling, she asked:

'This Eileen Gilbert. Do you love her?'

He stared at her, dazed that this, of all things, was her first reaction.

He took a deep breath and brought himself back to her world.

'Yes,' he said, 'but not in the way that you mean.'

'Good, because, as you know, I'm of a jealous disposition,' she said mischievously, getting up to make coffee.

He watched her go with something like despair, and a bleak wave of loneliness. She had said she was lonely when she had left him, back before The Gilbert had claimed him. He could not wish her back in that place.

'Sophie,' he said, when she returned. 'I have to think about my future. I can't spend the rest of my life in the garden, I need to work.'

'There are plenty of charities in London. With your experience, they would snap you up.'

'The small ones can't afford me, Sophie, and I couldn't work for some big outfit, stuck in an office block all day, juggling figures… not after The Gilbert.'

Sophie looked away. 'You could go back to the law, I suppose.'

He stared at her averted head.

'You left me because I wouldn't give up the law. Now you suggest I go back to it?'

'I had a lot of time to think in New York,' she said. 'If it's the law that you need then I will just have to get used to it.'

He thought for a while then, pulling his chair up to face her and taking her hands in his, he said:

'What I need is The Gilbert, Sophie. Come with me.'

'Oh, Richard, please don't! I'm a city girl. Theatres, galleries, shops, black cabs and the underground…. The countryside is all very well for a weekend break. However grand the house might be it's still in the middle of nowhere! I can just imagine it. A lot of small town busy-bodies watching my every move. And what would I do? Join the Women's Institute? Don't be silly, Richard. I would fade away and die.'

She pulled her hands away.

'Please let's not mention it again. I can live with you practicing law if I must. I'll get a little job. Crispin and Anna are looking for someone for their new gallery. You do what you think best, Richard,' she said, closing the subject.

And so they went on, sharing some of themselves, keeping some of themselves back, as so many couples do. As long as Sophie stayed, he must stay too.

Tilda, at least, was content, though she would never leave Richard, resisting all Sophie's efforts to claim her for herself.

Hearing that their valued companion was back in town, his old friends gradually re-appeared. Refusing to be deterred by his preoccupied manner, they were content to sit and watch him work and drink his wine. Gradually, as they determinedly drew him into their easy company, he slipped gratefully back into the warmth of their regard.

Chapter 30

The Gilbert's people, weary from toiling through the hottest summer that anyone could remember, were grateful when awesome thunderstorms swept away the heatwave. Somehow, they had survived the crisis, though it had been many weeks before the tide of letters had receded to a manageable stream.

Eileen had increased both Chris and Jasmine to full-time, but stubbornly refused to terminate Richard's salary. Until she received that letter of resignation, they all hoped that he would one day return to them. They might be able to manage without him and Tilda, but they didn't want to. The Gilbert was poorer for his absence.

The Right Hons had formed a committee and mustered the retirees of the town, bullying them away from their leisurely lunches to take their turn in the park. At first reluctant, they had found, to their surprise, enjoyment in tending to scraped knees and organising games of rounders. The children had never heard of rounders and it quickly became that year's craze. Teams rapidly became unmanageably enormous and a knock-out league had to be organised. A grand final was held in the last days of the school holiday and grateful parents clubbed together to buy medals for all the participants and a Gilbert Trophy for the victorious team. James sent down daily picnic baskets to sustain these volunteers, though the goodies were soon appropriated by the children. Hearing of this, James increased the quantities to such an extent that a pony and trap were needed to transport them all. The volunteers, pleased to be appreciated, refused to allow afternoon games until the children had dutifully sat at the picnic tables to make thank-you letters and cards. These went up to the house in the empty picnic baskets, bringing pleasure and amusement to the busy staff.

The volunteers anticipated that their duties would probably come to an end when the schools went back. However, the children clamoured for after-school rounders and the volunteers found themselves still wanted. Some fell away, exhausted and glad to get their lives back. Others settled into a pattern of evening park duties, secretly hoping that The Gilbert's own staff would never return.

Some, reluctant to return to idle days, transferred their efforts to the walled garden. Eileen had offered a decent amount of money but had quietly decided that the spadework must come from the town. If they wanted it, they must do it for themselves.

She noted with interest that its committee's ambitious aims had never been realised, though a small group of die-hards had soldiered on. She was not surprised: Cheppingham was a small town and people are busy. They had livings to earn, children to raise, grandchildren to mind.

The glorious colours of autumn usually suited The Gilbert. The house merged against the hill as the leaves fell away from its woodland. Eileen's favourite Michaelmas Daisies massed blue and purple in the gardens and early frosts silvered the lawns.

This year, however, the thunderstorms were followed by weeks of wind and rain which stripped the trees and battered the daisies, sending the children scurrying home from the Park to their video games.

Chapter 31

John was concerned that he had, early in the morning, twice found the Nature Reserve workshop unlocked, with signs of occupation. It was understandable that the bat and owl watchers should run for cover in such weather. Several groups held keys for just such an eventuality, but it was unheard of that they should forget to lock up after themselves or tidy away their coffee cups. He took to making a visit down there his first job of the day.

On a bleak and gusty morning when daylight struggled to come, John pulled on his waterproofs and went to fetch his pony from the barn.

He didn't bother to saddle up. Wet leather was the very devil and he rode as well without as with it.

The pony dropped its head, flattening its ears and squinting against the driving rain as they trotted along the back road. Floss and Milly cared little about the weather – it was good to be out and they raced ahead. John had fired up the range and they could steam luxuriously on the rugs when they returned.

John heard them bark and whine as he came into the carpark, saw the workshop door banging in the wind and the figure on the ground. He called them sharply to him, halting the pony. He slid from its back and ran through the flying rain and leaves but stopped when he saw the spreading crimson rivers around the body. He approached cautiously. She lay on her front, her head turned sideways, her arms flung wide, her eyes open and staring. The dogs hung back, their eyes anxious.

'Lie down,' he said automatically. 'Stay.'

He wrestled, cursing at his waterproofs, until he found his phone and dialled 999.

'There is a body in our carpark. I am pretty sure she's dead. The back of her head is stove in,' he said grimly.

'Then please don't touch anything. Stay well away. Don't let anybody near. The police and ambulance are on their way.'

Eileen, peering out of her bedroom window at yet another dreadful day, saw the flashing lights on the bottom road and heard the sirens, just as her phone shrilled.

'John?' she said as she glimpsed the lights appearing in the Reserve car park. 'What on earth has happened?'

'We have a bit of a problem down here on The Reserve, Eileen. A bloody body in the car park. I hope you are sitting down because it's that woman Jennie Green. And it looks to me like she's been murdered.'

'Please move away, well back, that's it. Thank you.'

This was the extent of Cheppingham Community Policeman's personal experience of murder scenes. Keep everyone away and wait for the big boys. They were not long in coming.

John was taken aside. Details were taken.

Did he recognise her? Was she local? Did he know what she was doing here? Had he seen anyone else down here?

Once they knew he was from The Gilbert, they told him to go home and wait for them there. They would be up to take a statement shortly.

As he led the pony away, they were battling to erect a tent over the body. Figures poured from cars and vans, some trying to don white suits, which were instantly soaked by the driving rain. Crime scene tape was going up around the nightmarish scene behind him.

He met Eileen, wet and breathless, as he went. He helped her up onto the pony and they trudged back, the dogs hugging his heels.

'Go up and get changed – you're wet through,' he said when they arrived in the yard. 'I'll come up when I've finished with the police.'

She didn't argue. Chilled to the bone, she climbed to her apartment.

John sorted the pony and took his dogs into his cottage. He saw lights in Harry and George's windows but didn't knock. He needed time to think. It was still only just after seven-thirty and Gilbert House slept quietly in the watery grey light.

'Let it sleep,' he thought.

As John waited for the police to come and take his statement, he busied himself making tea, feeding Milly and Floss and shutting them in the back room, changing out of his wet clothes and dumping them in a heap by the door. Would the police want them? They would want to compare his shoes to footprints around the body, test his clothes for bloodstains, wouldn't they? Not that there would be much in the way of footprints in this weather. They did in books and on the TV. His knowledge of such things was entirely gleaned from such sources. He was surprised that they had let him go, really.

His mind moved on. What was that damned Jennie Green doing there, anyway? He thought about The Gilbert and its people. There was no shortage of candidates for the police to suspect. Everyone now knew she and Rivers had been in cahoots over the Argos piece that had led to a summer of upheaval and the loss of Richard. The more he thought, the more uneasy he became.

He booted up his laptop and accessed the personnel database,

'There are some advantages to being on the Management Team,' he muttered.

He copied a number into his phone and pressed "call."

A disgruntled voice muttered, 'Do you know what bloody time it is?'

'Never mind your London hours, Richard, I need some professional advice. We have a nasty situation up here. I think we might need a lawyer. I hoped you could put us on to someone if you prefer to stay out of it.'

'What sort of nasty situation?'

'I found a body down the Reserve this morning. Not just any old body, either. Remember that little bundle of joy, Jennie Green? Well, someone stove her pretty head in.'

There was a long silence.

'Richard? You still there?'

There was a snort from the other end.

'Well, you don't mince your words, John! "Nasty situation" doesn't half cover it, though.

I'll give it some thought. How have things been up there?' he added, his voice hesitant. Did he really want to know?

'It's been bedlam, Richard, I won't lie. That Argos article went viral on the Internet and half the world wrote begging letters. Thousands of them. We had to pull all the staff in to tackle it. We only managed to keep the park open by using volunteers. Eileen went to the Argos and had a right go at the editor, by all accounts. They sacked Rivers. Hahahaha!'

Richard felt The Gilbert pull at his heart. His people, struggling while he dug his garden…

'Eileen went in person?' he asked.

'Yup. Stormed in there, shot the place up, no prisoners taken. I wish I'd been there! I'd better go, the cops will be up to interview me soon. Get yourself up here, Richard. We miss you, you old fool. Fatted calf and all that.'

'John, tread carefully. You don't have to answer their questions without a solicitor present. Do our people know about Jennie Green and Rivers?'

'Of course they do.'

'There is more to the story than you know. The Gilbert has enemies.'

'Enemies? The Gilbert?'

'Stick to what you know with the police and guard your tongue. And brace yourselves for a storm.'

'Hells bells, Richard, you are really spooking me now.'

'Keep an eye on Eileen, make sure she holds that temper. I'll make some calls, get you a good defence lawyer.'

'Richard! You're the best defence lawyer we know!'

Richard laughed grimly.

'And I'm in New York!'

'Who are you talking to, Richard? You woke me up!'

'Ah, I see!' John said, laughing. 'Awkward! Sorry about that. I think the plod are here, so I'll let you go. Happy holiday!'

Richard stared at the dead phone in his hand, then turned on Sophie,

'That was important, Sophie! What is the matter with you?'

She pouted. 'I wasn't to know that, was I? Who was it, anyway?'

'John Hardy, the Estate Manager at The Gilbert. A body has been found in the grounds.'

'Oh, Richard! How horrible! But why did he ring you? It isn't really anything to do with you anymore.'

'He wanted the name of a decent lawyer.'

'Oh, I see, fair enough. Are you coming back to bed now?'

'Yes, in a minute,' he replied, absently.

*

'Thank you for seeing us, Mr. Hardy. I am Inspector Letwynd. This is Detective Constable Hallam. We are here to take a statement from you.'

John took them into his warm kitchen and studied the pair. The Inspector was a shrewd, intelligent looking man of middle age. The DC was a bright, cheerful woman, about his own age.

'Sit yourselves down. Tea? Coffee?'

'Tea would be very welcome. Filthy morning out there, we are chilled through, lovely and warm in here, though. Are you often out early in the morning in such foul weather?'

'Of course,' John replied. 'The Estate needs managing whatever the weather.'

'There was no particular reason for this morning's visit to the Reserve, then?'

John weighed up the question, remembering Richard's warning.

'I had found the workshop unlocked a couple of times, first thing, so I've been making it my first visit of the day.'

'Is that unusual?'

'Oh yes. Local groups use the workshop and have keys, but they always lock up after themselves.'

'At night?'

'Occasionally the owl and bat watchers go in at night, yes, though not normally in this sort of weather.'

'We will need details of all the key holders.'

'No problem. I'll get you a list.'

'Tell us exactly what happened this morning, will you, please, Mr. Hardy.'

John described the blinding rain and half-light, the dogs whining and hanging back, calling them away, seeing the blood and going no nearer.

'It sounds like you did everything right. Well done, sir. And you didn't touch anything?'

'No. I could see she was most likely dead, so I rang you lot. Do you know how she got there?'

'We found her car behind the workshop. So, you are the Estate Manager here, sir. How many other people work here?'

'There are about forty or so. You'll have to ask the Boss for the details. Not my area.'

'The Boss?'

John paused. Did they really not know the set-up? It seemed unlikely, so what was this about?

'Mrs. Gilbert. She owns the Estate.'

The DC carefully wrote this down. John waited for the next question.

'Can you tell me more about how you came to know the deceased?'

'She came here for a job interview back in the Spring, with a couple of others. I gave them a guided tour of the Reserve and Park. She didn't get the job.'

'And have you seen her since then?'

'I saw her a couple of times outside The Beckside Hotel, once down in the Reserve.'

'You said she wasn't local. Did that strike you as odd?'

'This is a popular tourist area. I assumed she liked what she had seen and came back to explore.'

'For the record, where were you last night?'

'Here, tucked up in my bed, alone.'

'Thank you, Mr. Hardy. I think that will do for now. We will need to talk to you again. Are those the clothes you were wearing when you found the deceased? Bag them up will you, DC Hallam.'

John watched as the DC pulled on gloves and carefully loaded the wet heap into bags. 'Can you tell us where we can find Mrs. Gilbert?'

'She has an apartment on the top floor. I'll ring through and see if she's there, if you like.'

'No need, Mr. Hardy. If you could just direct us, that would be appreciated.'

John sat, pondering over his tea when they had gone. His phone shrilled.

'John. Richard here....my work phone. It has some contacts on it that I need. I left it in my office. Courier it to my London address, will you? In a packet small enough to go through the letter box. Don't bother with the charger; I've got another. I'll pick it up when I get back to London. And keep this under your hat.'

John chortled as he wrote down the address.

*

Eileen let the police in and led them through to her living room.

They introduced themselves. She introduced Chris and Jasmine.

'Thank you for seeing us, Mrs. Gilbert. We won't keep you long. Just a few preliminary enquiries, to get a feel for the set up here. You own the Gilbert Estate?'

Eileen nodded.

'You are the sole owner?'

Eileen nodded again.

'You live here, I presume. How many people live here altogether, on the Estate?'

'Including myself, eleven plus one child.'

'Could you give me their names, please, and their role?'

Eileen listed them all. Jasmine was about to tell her that she had left Richard out, but thought better of it.

'How many people work here altogether?'

'Thirty-eight at present, plus a number of volunteers, mostly in the Reserve.'

'This is a charitable foundation, I believe. What is its purpose?'

'The Foundation supports people who help others. Individuals, groups, small charities. We give them money, information, advice.'

'And you also own the town's Park and Nature Reserve, I gather.'

'I do.'

'Tell me about Jennie Green.'

'Ms. Green came here in the spring for three days for a job interview along with Chris and Jasmine. She was unsuccessful. I have not seen her since then.'

'We'll need to talk to all of the staff, Mrs. Gilbert, and will no doubt need to talk to you again. Is there a room we could use or would you rather people came to the station?'

'Cheppingham doesn't have a police station, Inspector. It went in the last round of cuts. The nearest is over twenty miles away, unless you want to cram into our Community Policeman's front room. We will find you a room here. You can use one of the offices. There's also a Refectory here that your team are welcome to use. There is no charge. This is a terrible business. I cannot imagine how she came to be in The Reserve. We want to help in any way we can.'

'That's good of you. Thank you. We will be setting up a Mobile Incident Room, probably in that car park near the hotel.'

'By all means, you may put it in my car park,' Eileen said. 'I will take you down to reception. They'll be on duty by now and will give you a list of the staff.'

She took them down the staircase and into the Refectory. The great French doors were closed against the weather, though she noticed that it was clearing, and a weak sunlight was breaking through.

'Perhaps you would like a hot drink, or breakfast, while I get the list and arrange an office for you.'

Seduced by the aroma of cooking bacon, they willingly allowed James to lead them to a table.

'The police are in The Refectory, Magda. Could you take them a list of all the staff and volunteers, please? They will want to talk to everyone. I am giving them Richard's office to use.'

Eileen did not need to tell her why the police were here. Bad news has wings in a small town.

She went down the back corridor and into Richard's office. She was about to clear his desk when she realised his phone was not there, though its charger was. Puzzled, she searched the floor under the desk, and the drawers. Taking his laptop, she tucked it into a drawer in her office and returned to the foyer.

'Jo,' she said, putting her head around the Housekeeper's office door. 'Richard's phone was on his desk. It seems to have gone.'

'I'm sure it was there last night when I dusted, Mrs. Gilbert. No-one's been in there this morning, that I know of. Nobody has started work yet. Everyone is at sixes and sevens over this dreadful business. Leave it with me. I'll ask around, it must be somewhere. We don't get theft here. Poor John, fancy finding a body like that! It's that woman who came for an interview, I have heard.'

'Yes…Jennie Green…' Eileen replied. 'The police want to talk to everyone. They will be using Richard's office. I had better get back to them. Tell everyone to take it easy. People will be upset.'

*

158

Letwynd assembled his team in Richard's office. It was an impossible squeeze, but it would have to do until The Powers That Be got their finger out and brought the Mobile Incident Unit.

The Refectory had given his people a good breakfast, at least, though he was not sure if it didn't amount to fraternising with the enemy.

'Right then,' Letwynd said, 'the pathologist says that death was likely due to the heavy blow across the back of the head, some time late on Monday night. It was a swinging blow from a long heavy wooden object, something like a pickaxe handle.'

'Is it likely to have been a man?'

'Either – a long heavy object like that could be swung with enough force by either a man or a woman. Death was not instantaneous. She died some time between about ten pm and three am, so she had been dead some time when Hardy found her around seven. No sign of sexual assault. The rain and wind have played havoc with the scene, of course, so forensic evidence is going to be limited. There is no trace of car keys, handbag or phone, unfortunately. The forensic boys are checking the car against her partner and other known associates for prints and so on. It's a bit of a nightmare. It seems to be more about what they have *not* found than what they have. We should know more when they have been over the scene properly and done the post mortem. We will be doing a proper search of the area for the weapon, handbag and phone, of course. There are pools and undergrowth and all sorts in The Reserve, so it is going to be a long job. We will know more when the full post-mortem report comes through. Meanwhile, what did you find out from the partner, Gerry Alkenby?'

Hallam recounted how they had told Gerry Alkenby that Jennie Green was dead.

He had stared at them in disbelief but when he heard that she had been found in Yorkshire, he had laughed with relief and declared it couldn't be her. They had made a mistake. Jennie was at a conference in Manchester. When told exactly where she had been found, he had erupted into a terrifying, incoherent rage. Leaping to his feet, he had ranted about The Gilbert Foundation, accused them of deliberately ruining his business, of stealing it off him and giving it to their mates. It was some considerable time before they were able to calm him sufficiently to get any sense out of him. The tale he told was an interesting one. Jennie had been invited to apply for a job, but it was all a front for that bitch Eileen Gilbert to get her own back for Jennie firing her. Not content with that, they had paid some big-wig London lawyer to trash their business. He had described in great detail how the care home business they had so lovingly built up, providing a refuge for so many vulnerable people, had been asset stripped by The Foundation, who had shared the spoils amongst their mates. He said Jennie had been kept away from Mrs. Gilbert but had caught a glimpse and recognised her. That was when she realised that the whole interview business had been a set-up, so she started working with a reporter to expose their filthy operation. This reporter had had some sort of run-in with them before. Eventually Alkenby had thought to ask how she had died. They had told him that it was likely she had been murdered and that brought on another bout of accusations and bile. They had done it…. they must have found out she had been working with the reporter. Somehow, they had lured her to the place and done her in to shut her up. But it wouldn't work. He had all the details – he could give them all the evidence they needed. He would not be silenced. He would make sure the bastards paid.

Hallam handed the statement to Letwynd.

'Well, well,' Letwynd said. 'Do we know who this reporter is?'

'His name is Quentin Rivers. He was with the Cheppingham Argos, but they sacked him when he wrote a bit of an exposé about The Gilbert. We don't know where he is now.'

'Get down to the Argos, talk to the editor, look in the paper's archives, get their side of the story. And check out the obvious stuff – have a look at The Gilbert's website and social media pages, etc. See if there have been any other unhappy customers'

'They don't have any social media accounts.'

'What?'

'Nope. They are a secretive bunch, it would appear.'

Letwynd pondered.

'So, this place may not be quite what it seems, and we may have a possible motive. I think we need to have another word with Mrs. Gilbert, but I want a clearer picture of the set-up first. Hallam and Atkins will interview the live-in staff. Get someone down to that little hotel and the park, see if anyone saw anything. Find anyone who has seen this woman in the area,' he said, handing out copies of a photo that Alkenby had supplied.

As his team fanned off to make a start, Letwynd sat and read the papers supplied by Alkenby. There was nothing immediately revealing. Various contracts, emails and letters about a charity called Standby and three other homes that the Foundation had taken off Alkenby. He made notes of people to talk to and further details that he needed. He briefed a couple of officers and sent them off to investigate.

When he had finished with them, Letwynd sat back in Richard's chair, twirling a pen between his fingers and staring down the valley. At least the rain had stopped.

He was getting two completely opposite impressions of The Gilbert. Was it a benevolent charity or a 'bunch of crooks'?

*

Eileen sat in the window of her apartment, a laptop tilted on her lap, watching Letwynd on the screen as he twirled his pen. So he knew it all, then. Would he believe Alkenby's version – that The Gilbert had asset-stripped his business to give it to their mates? Hopefully not, when they saw the evidence, but it was going to get sticky for a while.

She accessed the database and searched for Standby. There was nothing there. She sat back, baffled.

She rang through to the workroom and asked to speak to Gemma but was told she was abroad, on leave. Should she warn Chris and Jasmine? No, the less they knew the better for them. They had not been here when the Standby business was going on anyway.

There was nothing she could do, and she suddenly felt vulnerable.

Richard would know why it wasn't on the database. Richard knew everything.

'Oh, Richard,' she thought sadly. 'I told you I could not manage without you, and it looks like I was right.'

But at least she knew what Letwynd knew.

'Keep your friends close but keep your enemy closer,' she muttered. The first hint that Letwynd was poking about in her past, she would know. Quite what she would do, she had no idea.

Chapter 32

Hearing a car pull up in the yard, John glanced out of his window.

'Well, well, my lovelies,' he said conversationally, 'we have a rat in the yard.'

John hated rats, so his dogs did too. Flushing them out of the barn was almost their favourite game. They wagged their tails and whined to be let out.

'Wait now. You shall have it soon enough.'

He went into the back, fetched his shotgun and propped it behind the front door. The dogs bounced excitedly round his legs.

'Heel, now. You stay with me,' he said as he opened his door and stepped into the yard.

Rivers had been surveying the scene, taking photographs, and turned as John spoke.

'You can sling your hook,' John said, matter-of-factly. 'You're trespassing.'

Rivers sneered and raised his camera, snapping shots. John walked up to him and smacked the camera out of his hand. It arced through the air, smashed on the cobbles and slithered away. Rivers stared after it in disbelief.

'I said, sling your hook,' John said calmly.

Rivers took a step backwards but then squared up and stuck his chest out.

'What you going to do? Call the cops? That'll do you no good. Trespass is a civil offence, not criminal, you know.'

John laughed. 'I'm sure the police have better things to do than clean up shit. No, I'll set the dogs on you.'

Rivers looked at the cheerful looking dogs and grinned.

John called them to heel.

'Bad rat,' he said. The dogs growled and whined. Rivers took several steps back.

'Speak, Milly. Speak, Floss,' John muttered, and they barked at Rivers.

Suddenly uncertain, Rivers said, 'You wouldn't dare. I'll have the law on you.'

'You are trespassing. I'm entitled to use reasonable force to protect the property.'

He ambled back to his door. Reaching round, he picked up the shotgun, broke it over his arm and turned to face Rivers.

'Bugger off,' he said, 'and don't come back.'

Affecting unconcern, but watching the dogs and the gun, Rivers retrieved his camera.

As he opened his car door he snarled, 'I'll have you and this whole damned outfit, you mark my words. You cross me, and I never forget it. I told Aubrey five years ago that I would have him and I will, however long it takes. You can tell him that from me. Got that? Good.'

He climbed into his car, then swung it as if to turn it round, but drove it at John. John didn't flinch, and Rivers was forced to stop. He reversed, then drove away.

'Sorry, girls,' John said absently. 'Maybe next time.'

He stood watching Rivers go, wondering what he had meant about Richard.

Letwynd came from the front door.

'Trouble?' he asked.

'A reporter. We have had bother from him in the past. Just seeing him off the premises.'

'Was that Quentin Rivers?'

John nodded.

'Damn, I wanted to talk to him.'

'He used to stay down at The Beckside Hotel when he first came here, till he got himself sacked and slunk away. You could try there.'

'Thanks. You really can't go smashing cameras and waving a shotgun about, even if it isn't loaded, you know.'

John looked at him, appraisingly.

'Can I not?' he said.

Letwynd shook his head. 'Look, just watch yourself. You don't want to get yourself arrested. My people will be interviewing the staff and volunteers, starting with the live-in people. Perhaps you could make yourself available for another chat later today.'

He turned and went back inside.

John took himself off upstairs to Eileen.

'I've just had a run-in with that Quentin Rivers in the yard.'

'Yes, I saw you,' Eileen replied. 'I was outside my door.'

'I saw him off, but he swore he would be back. What did he mean when he said he had been looking for revenge on Richard for five years?'

Eileen told him.

'And to think I have brought all this on myself,' she added, sorrowfully. 'Why on earth was she here, John?'

'Search me. We do get courting couples down there in the carpark at night sometimes...'

'I don't think anyone says "courting" any more, John,' she said, laughing.

'Well, what do you want me to call it?'

'Fair enough. Are you saying she could have been meeting someone down there?'

'It's just a thought. But she wouldn't come back unless it was someone she met around here. Rivers?'

Eileen pondered. 'Nobody is that hard up!'

'Oh, I don't know. Birds of a feather and all that, and we know they had been cooking up that Argos story together,' John said. 'We must make sure Letwynd considers the possibility – that would get Rivers off our back. Two birds of a feather with one stone, eh?'

He chortled at his own wit and Eileen found herself joining in.

'The only thing I can't work out is how they could have got hold of a key to the workshop. The door was open when I found her,' John said.

'That does rather scupper your theory, John. We will let the police find the answer to that one. It is what they are paid for, after all. Let's go and get some breakfast. It will be lunchtime if we don't go soon!'

Arriving in the Refectory, she found it full of policemen and women, enthusiastically tucking in to full English breakfasts.

'I'll be back in a minute,' she told John and, after stopping at the Admin Office, headed for Richard's office.

'Inspector Letwynd,' she said as she entered, without knocking, 'the Refectory is full of police officers. You not going to try to cram them all in this office, are you? That won't do at all. We will put them in our Training Room. Come with me and I will show you.'

Letwynd allowed himself to be led into the foyer and up the stairs. Eileen unlocked the door and handed the key to him.

'This is a murder inquiry, Mrs. Gilbert, centered on this Estate. It is entirely inappropriate that we are here at all.'

Eileen smiled. 'Of course, of course, I quite understand. You must do as you think best. You will need the office as well, for your interviews, I expect, and now you have the keys to both rooms. I will get a keypad put on this door. I will get onto it this morning. You can set the code so nobody except your officers can get in. There are three empty cottages in the courtyard that would sleep at least two each if you need accommodation. Just let me know if you want them. I am going for a late breakfast. I will leave you get yourself organised.'

Letwynd was about to tell her that modern policing doesn't work like an Agatha Christie novel. Pad or no pad, the room was simply not secure; that only preliminary enquiries would take place here; that the ongoing investigation would happen back at HQ; that they would not have access to their secure databases, contacts, files, books, documents, templates, recording equipment, evidence bags…. when he realised that she had gone.

Letwynd surveyed the room. Well, it wouldn't hurt to have a bolt-hole for the men with the weather the way it was; and it would do for briefings especially as there was still no sign of the Mobile Incident Room. He let himself out, pocketing the key, and followed Mrs. Gilbert down the stairs to the Refectory.

He was wished 'Good morning' from all sides by The Gilbert staff.

Amongst them, little groups of his officers were tucking into plates of food, while trying to maintain a professional distance by studiously avoiding eye contact.

'Food's amazing,' Hallam said. 'We've landed on our feet here.'

'You do realise we shouldn't be here at all,' Letwynd snapped. 'This is a murder inquiry, Hallam. Everyone in this place is a potential suspect!'

'Well, you can tell that to the men, because I'm not!' she said and went back to her food.

'Mrs. Gilbert has offered us a big room upstairs to use as a base. She is even going to have a keypad put on the door. Totally inappropriate, of course, but what is it with this place?' Letwynd muttered. 'Why is everyone so damned nice all the time? It's not natural.'

'Has it occurred to you that maybe this place is just what it seems? A lot of decent people helping other decent people to do good things?'

'Ask me again when we have caught our killer,' Letwynd replied. 'The Mobile Unit will be here any minute,' he added lamely. She ignored him.

James appeared at his elbow.

'There is a hot meal available or you can help yourself to cold food or a sandwich from the carousel to take away.'

Tempted though he was, Letwynd decided to set an example. He selected a sandwich and headed back to his office.

John Hardy, quietly listening at the next table, smiled to himself.

'I like her,' he thought. 'She's a canny lass.'

Hallam caught him watching her and smiled.

'Are those your dogs?' she asked, nodding towards the French windows. Floss and Milly sat with their noses pressed against the glass, following John's every move.

John laughed. 'Daft buggers!'

'I was tempted by the Dog Unit,' she said, 'but I do like the detective work. Is it OK to pet them?'

'Unless I tell 'em otherwise,' he replied.

John opened the door and they stepped outside. Floss and Milly wriggled around their legs. Hallam stroked them, and Milly rolled on her back, her whole body wagged by her tail. Hallam bent to rub her wet and muddy belly as John watched. Before he could stop himself, he blurted out. 'Are you spoken for?' and immediately blushed a fiery red. 'Hells bells, that was unforgivable…unprofessional…forget I said it….'

She laughed out loud. 'Ask me again when we have caught our killer.'

*

John didn't bother with the niceties when more reporters started to turn up in the yard. He set the dogs on them with instructions to 'Kill the rats!'

He phoned down to Chris and told him to close and padlock the great gates at the end of the drive. When they tried to get to the house across country, he, George and Harry fired their shotguns into the air and sent their dogs after them. Thankfully, the police stopped them from coming in along the back road past the Reserve.

Eileen was heartily glad that The Gilbert had no landline phones for them to track down. There was something to be said for secrecy.

It didn't stop the reporters from plaguing the staff as they came and went, however. Eileen arranged for the minibus to transport them as The Gilbert took on siege status.

The interest wouldn't last long, though. Murders have to have an angle for the National Press to take a sustained interest. Rivers was determined to find that angle: this was too good an opportunity for him to let it go.

Chapter 33

Letwynd started Hallam and Atkins on the interviews with the live-in staff and then headed back to HQ.

The first few told them frustratingly little that they didn't already know.

James had seen her only during the interview days, in the Refectory. Jo had spoken briefly to her when she had settled her into one of the cottages and when she was being shown round. George had fetched her car for her when she was leaving. George's wife had never seen her at all.

Only Harry had a little more to contribute. He had driven the three candidates down to the Reserve and Park on their tour and helped to show her around and had given her a lift down to the Reserve on the day she left. If they wanted to talk to Annie, his partner, they would have to go down to the town. She was staying with her sister, who had just had a baby. He seemed ill-at-ease. Hallam picked up on this and probed. In the end, Harry admitted that he and Annie hadn't been getting on for a while. The baby was an excuse for her to get away for a bit. No, he hadn't spoken to her since she went – they were giving each other some space.

Hallam was disappointed. She had thought he smelt of guilt for a moment, but the man was just embarrassed that his girlfriend had walked out on him. They would be interviewing her, though, and could check that there wasn't more to it. She let Harry go.

Chris and Jasmine's interviews were a little more enlightening.

They had spent the three interview days in her company and that had been quite enough. They each described a rather pushy, brash, confident young woman who had made life difficult for The Gilbert by feeding confidential information to a local reporter out of spite for not getting the manager's job, despite having signed a confidentiality agreement. They described the chaos that had ensued: the sacksful of letters; the complete disruption of the normal working of The Gilbert; the diverting of all the staff to help deal with it; the near closure of the Park and Reserve. The Gilbert was a wonderful place and she was a spiteful woman who had been determined to have a go at it for rejecting her.

Their anger and distain for the woman was obvious and they made no effort to hide it and no apology. They had only been in post for two months. Neither had seen her since those three days.

Neither had ever heard of Standby.

'Apart from Mrs. Gilbert and a four-year-old boy, Hardy is the last of the live-in staff. I am saving Mrs. Gilbert for later. Let's have him back in,' Hallam said.

'Mr. Hardy. You gave Jennie Green a tour of the Reserve and Park. What were your impressions of her?'

John thought for a few moments.

'That was the only time I met her to talk to. First impressions? I wondered why she was here – she didn't seem our type.'

'Our type?' Letwyn echoed.

'The people who work here are genuine, open, honest. She was one of those modern hard-faced business women. Designer clothes; cold eyes; sharp tongue. You know the sort.

I did a bit of a talk about the work of the Reserve in the workshop first. She didn't pay a lot of attention. She seemed more interested in admiring young Harry, our Ranger.

She was better when we went out and about, asked lots of questions, mostly about the money side of things, which didn't surprise me. She flashed her eyes at one of our volunteers, Dean. Poor devil didn't know what had hit him. One of life's innocents, our Dean.'

'You said earlier that you had seen her around since.'

'Yes. I can understand her being at The Beckside Hotel. She was in cahoots with that snake, Rivers. But I saw her leaving the Reserve once.'

'Was she alone?'

'When I saw her, yes.'

'Have you any ideas about how she came to be at the Reserve on the day she died?'

'I have been thinking about that. Perhaps she and Rivers came up there for a bit of nookie. We do get courting couples in the carpark. It is very secluded,' John said thoughtfully.

'How would they have got into the workshop, though? They wouldn't have had a key.'

'Now, that I don't know the answer to. Perhaps they were just lucky and found it unlocked, like I have done.'

Letwynd thought it through. It didn't quite hang together. Hardy was possibly right about the nookie, as he called it, but the whole key thing was not credible. Why would they go up there if they thought they couldn't get in? Unless they had been using Rivers car…there certainly wasn't room in hers. And it was not a night for lying under the trees.

Letwyn changed tack.

'Do you know if Mrs. Gilbert knew Ms. Green before she came for interview?'

'I have no idea.'

'What do you know about Standby Care?

'Never heard of it.'

'Can you think of anyone who would want to kill Jennie Green, Mr. Hardy?'

John laughed out loud. 'They would have to form an orderly queue!'

Letwyn decided to leave it there.

*

Hallam and Atkins returned from their visit to the Cheppingham Argos and reported back to Letwynd at morning briefing.

'We spoke to Eddie Mason, editor and proprietor, guv. Rivers is a nasty piece of work by all accounts. He got himself sacked from a national paper, The World, about five years ago after they got sued in a big libel case. Mason only took him on as a favour to a friend. Rivers didn't last long.

He was asked to do a birthday spread about The Gilbert for the Argos and told to respect their privacy. They keep themselves very much to themselves, apparently, but they are well thought of for giving the town the Park and Reserve and employing a lot of local people. Instead, he stomped up there making a nuisance of himself. The Director, Richard Aubrey, gave him an interview sometime later and Mason assumed Aubrey had OK'd the piece he wrote. This is the piece.' She handed it over and Letwynd read it through.

'All hell broke loose. The Gilbert was inundated with begging letters. Mrs. Gilbert was not best pleased and threatened to close the Reserve and Park. She gave Mason this statement.

'The town was up in arms –they love their Gilbert. Volunteers rallied round and kept the Reserve and Park open. Mason sacked Rivers.'

'This Richard Aubrey, I haven't heard him mentioned before,' Letwynd said.

He pulled out the staff list. Richard's name was listed as Director, his address as Gilbert House.

'Odd. His name isn't on the list of live-in staff.'

'Nobody has seen him around since the business with the article, guv.'

Letwynd mentally filed that away as another question for Mrs. Gilbert, along with her dealings with Jennie Green before she came for interview – and the Standby business. She was an enigma, and his unease about using Gilbert House as a base resurfaced. Something told him to hold fire till he had a thorough grasp of the whole picture though – he wanted to be sure of his facts before he tackled her. He had a feeling she was more savvy than she appeared. Then he changed his mind. He had had enough.

'Get Mrs. Gilbert in here'

Eileen, sitting in her office next door, watched on her screen as Hallam headed out. She closed her laptop and tucked it in a drawer.

'I was a fool to leave Richard out of it. I have no rational explanation for it,' she said to the cactus. 'Why am I talking to a cactus?' she said and shook her head. She knew why, really. It was the nearest she could get to talking to Richard himself.

'Mrs. Gilbert,' Letwynd said rather belligerently, when Hallam eventually found her and brought her in. 'Why is Richard Aubrey's name not on the list of live-in staff?'

'I am sorry, Inspector, I assumed you meant staff living in *at present.'*

'Where is he now?'

'He is taking a well-earned break.'

'Two months? That's a hell of a holiday!'

'Richard Aubrey has worked for me for three years, Inspector, without taking any leave. I felt it only right that he had a proper break.'

Letwynd gave up for now – the woman had an answer for everything.

'Thank you, Mrs. Gilbert. That will be all for now'.

Eileen smiled sweetly at him as she left.

She sank into her office chair, her heart pounding.

'Where the devil are the Standby records? It doesn't make sense. And why the hell did I ever bring that woman here?' she muttered.

She could feel things slipping out of her control and she didn't like it one bit.

Eileen went in search of Jasmine and Chris. Whatever chaos had ensued from her rash decision to interview for a manager, it had at least given her these two gems. Having been given a shared office when they job-shared, they had elected to continue the arrangement when they went full-time. The Gilbert would have really struggled if it had not been for their complete loyalty and commitment and she had told them so many times.

She had wondered if they might become a couple. She had spent so many years on her own that she could not imagine a life where she was not; but it did not stop her match-making everyone else.

She found Chris and Jasmine in their office, poring over spreadsheets.

'I have given the police team the Training Room as a base. Inspector Letwynd is still using Richard's office when he is here. I am not sure he felt they should be here amongst all us potential murderers, but I don't think they have anywhere else to go and at least here we can keep an eye on them. He asked me why Richard is not here. I told them he was taking three years accumulated holiday.'

'Why did you leave him off the list?' Jasmine asked

'I don't really know... I suppose I didn't want them to think there was any discord here...' Eileen said, struggling to pin down exactly what had been in her mind.

'Do either of you know where Richard's phone is? It was in his office and now it isn't.'

'Jo was asking earlier. I haven't seen it.'

'Nor I,' Chris added.

'I'm sure it will turn up,' Jasmine said. 'Perhaps it got knocked off and kicked under a cupboard or something.'

'Maybe you're right.'

'Do we know how the investigation is progressing?' Chris asked

'They have a team down in the Reserve searching every inch. They won't let John in there and he is beside himself in case they do any damage. They seem to be coming and going all the time; closeted in with Letwynd and flying around the country, but who knows how far they have got with solving it. They still have most of the staff and volunteers to interview but I saw DC Hallam go off out just now.'

'It's a dreadful business,' Jasmine said. 'I can't say I took to Jennie Green, but I wouldn't wish her dead, whatever havoc she caused us.'

'Mmmm,' Eileen said, noncommittally.

Chapter 34

The police interviews with the staff were tedious and frustrating. Many had seen her during the three days that she had been here, but they had been asked not to engage with the candidates: to give them space and to ensure confidentiality was maintained. That in itself struck Letwynd as suspicious. Why were they so obsessed with secrecy?

Apart from Harry Watson, only Dean Magson had had any personal contact with Jennie Green – he had sat with her briefly in the Refectory. Mindful of John Hardy's information that Jennie had flashed her eyes at him, Hallam had probed. Dean had been reduced to a blubbering ruin within minutes. She had been kind to him, she was looking forward to him showing her the Reserve, she was lovely, why had she had to die?

Hallam let him ramble on. Was this just the reaction of a lonely man who had mistaken a bit of attention for real regard, or something more sinister?

Dean admitted that he often went to The Reserve in the evenings – he was at work during the day. Yes, he had been up there on the evening in question. He and Harry had been repairing the fence in the car park, but they had seen no-one else and he had left at dusk. He'd spent the rest of the evening, and the night, at home alone.

Hallam picked up on the mention of the fence.

'You said you were repairing the fence, Dean. What exactly were you doing to it?'

'Somebody had backed their car into it and several of the palings were bent and broken. I said to Harry, "I'll help you fix that." We replaced the palings and one of the thicker uprights.'

'What happened to the old ones?'

'Harry said he would take them home. They would make good firewood. There was one new one left over and Harry said he would put it away in the workshop for next time. It was always happening. People don't take enough care with their cars.'

Dean denied ever seeing Jennie Green after she left The Gilbert, not in The Reserve or anywhere else.

Hallam gently convinced him to give a DNA sample before he fled.

Some of the other people were reluctant to give samples. The officers knew that this didn't mean a lot – many people are suspicious of Big Brother.

Rivers was the only one who had tried to refuse outright – he had blustered and prevaricated. However, he thought he knew enough about such things to believe it could be seen as suspicious if he refused, so, in the end, reluctantly submitted to a swab being taken.

They had Harry back in. Why had he not mentioned that he had been down at The Reserve on the night in question?

Harry looked startled then realised they must have been talking to Dean.

'I can see it was a stupid thing to do. I panicked,' he admitted. 'You didn't actually ask me…we didn't see anyone else down there and I came home just after Dean went. Another storm was coming in.'

'Did you take the old fence posts home?'

'Yes, they've gone on the fire. The nights are getting a bit nippy now.'

'What about the new one that was left over?'

'I left it leaning against the workshop. I meant to put it away before I went, but the rain came down and was so busy hurrying to get back home that I forgot. I forgot to lock the workshop, too.'

'You have obstructed our investigation by omitting to tell us these things, Mr. Watson. That is a serious offence.'

Harry hung his head. 'Everyone knows she was giving me the eye when she was here. I thought you would think I had something to do with it.'

'And did you, Harry?'

'No! I didn't! I haven't seen her since she was here for the interview.'

'She has been seen in The Reserve since then, Harry.'

'Well, I didn't see her.'

'Thank you, Harry. That will be all for now.'

*

Letwynd had just collected his team in the Training Room for the morning briefing when there was a tap at the door.

'Yes?' he barked to Jo as he opened it.

'I am sorry to disturb you, sir. I wondered if I could collect some crockery. We're running a bit short downstairs. I've brought a trolley. If you leave it outside the door, I'll collect it later.'

Letwynd scowled and turned to look around the room. Dirty mugs and glasses and empty sandwich boxes huddled in clutches in amongst the steaming wet clothes draped over tables. Plates hung precariously from desk edges, interleaved with papers. Random pieces of cutlery were dotted about the floor and there were several dried coffee puddles around the tables.

Suddenly ashamed, the officers surveyed their horrible litter.

'Hrmph...' Letwynd said awkwardly. '... we'll get onto it...'

Jo thanked him and left.

'God, you are an 'orrible lot,' Letwynd said, wheeling the trolley in. 'What would your mothers say?'

They hastily piled the evidence of their guilt onto it and tried vainly to scrub the stains away with tissues.

Letwynd parked the trolley outside the lift and the briefing got under way.

'Right,' he said. 'We have a possible weapon, though it has no doubt long since gone on a fire somewhere.'

Hallam described her interview with Harry.

There may yet be more that Harry Watson hasn't told us. We spoke to his partner, Annie Lovidge. She works at The Beckside Hotel. She saw Jennie Green there with Quentin Rivers several times in the weeks following Green's job interview. On a couple of the occasions she stayed overnight. She and Rivers had separate rooms but that doesn't mean much.

Rivers left after he was sacked by The Argos, but he is back there now, as we know.'

'So, if she was passing information on to Rivers, Harry could have killed her to try to protect The Gilbert,' Atkins said.

'But why now?' Hallam asked. 'Rivers had gone, the article had already come out. Rivers only came back after the murder, presumably to cover it.'

'Perhaps Rivers was coming back to meet Green and Harry saw them.'

'Why would Rivers and Green meet round here? Neither of them is local. They could have met up anywhere,' Atkins said.

There was a long silence as they digested that they were at a dead end.

'So perhaps she was meeting someone else,' Hallam said.

'That does seem the most likely answer,' Letwynd said. 'But who? Harry? Dean Magson? Or someone else? Without forensic evidence we are looking for a needle in a haystack. Annie was up at the hospital, with her sister who was giving birth, on the night of the murder. She confirmed that she and Harry had split up several weeks ago. All he ever did was work or talk about it. She had had enough, so Harry was here on his own.'

'What else have we got?' he asked the assembled crew and was depressed that they appeared to have very little that was new.

'Green and Rivers had upset everyone at The Gilbert with that article,' Atkins said.

'So, in other words, we can't rule anybody out,' Letwynd growled.

'I think our best lead at the moment is this Standby business. How did you get on with the residents' families, Atkins?'

'They couldn't praise The Gilbert highly enough. They didn't know a lot about the Foundation, just that it had rescued them from that scoundrel Alkenby, as they called him. I got a lot of background about how Green and Alkenby got their hands on Standby and it was all rather unsavoury by their account. Quite different to Alkenby's version. They dealt with a woman called Gemma Maitliss from The Gilbert. A London barrister, Rex Wilkinson, was dealing with the legal side.'

'Have we interviewed Gemma Maitliss?' Letwynd asked.

'Away on holiday in Greece, guv. Not due back for ten days.'

'Damn!' Letwynd muttered. 'We need to see The Gilbert's records. I will get on to that. How is the search of the scene going?'

'Not well, to be honest, guv. No sign of a handbag, car keys, phone or weapon. We are still searching. It's a big area and we have ponds and all sorts still to do. The weather isn't helping. Everything is saturated and blown about. There are no footprints or tyre marks around the workshop – the carpark is a hard surface. There are plenty of footprints inside the Reserve but then hundreds of people tramp about in it, so it's not surprising. It's the same with the workshop. The floor is a muddy mess. There was no sign of recent activity: no coffee mugs or anything. Half the town use it, so not much chance of any meaningful fingerprints. Her prints were on the door and inside, but so were dozens of other people's. Sorry, guv,' she added as Letwynd glared at her.

'And the lab has come up with no bloody matching DNA or fingerprints on the body either,' Letwynd snarled. 'No sexual activity or assault; no other injuries; no sign of a struggle.'

'Wouldn't there be blood spatter on the killer's clothes?'

'Well, of course there would, but unless you want to confiscate the wardrobes of the whole of Cheppingham, we aren't going to find them. That is assuming they haven't burnt them, of course, which is most likely. Get fingerprints from Rivers. At least let's establish whether he's been in there. He won't like it, if the DNA sample business is anything to go by.'

Letwynd came out of the Training Room after the morning briefing. He paused outside the workroom door, then opened it and stepped inside. The room was full of busy people, but every face turned towards him and all activity ceased.

A woman approached.

'Emma, isn't it?' Letwynd said. 'I need to have a look at your records.'

'I'm sorry, sir, they are confidential.'

'This is a murder enquiry. I need to see records which directly relate to our investigation.'

'I think you'll need some sort of warrant, Officer. Our records contain sensitive information, which we have promised to keep confidential.'

Letwynd gave her a patronising look.

'You give money away to people. What sort of sensitive information does that involve?'

'The locations of women's refuges for one, sir. You need to speak to Mrs. Gilbert.'

Letwynd looked around the room.

'Are those the letters you got after the Argos article?' he asked waving towards the stacks of boxes. Emma nodded.

'Have you had any threatening ones?'

'Oh yes,' Emma said, indicating a box under a table. 'There are always people who feel the need to inform us that anyone in need of charity is a work-shy loser who needs to pull themselves together and get a job. Charities just encourage them apparently and should be shut down, or even burnt down with all the lefty liberals locked inside. They are mostly anonymous, of course.'

'I would like to see those. Maybe one of them decided that actions speak louder than words, eh?'

'You would need to speak to Mrs. Gilbert, but I can't see a problem with that. There might be fingerprints or DNA or something.'

Letwynd grinned to himself. Everybody who watched a few crime dramas thought they were an expert. 'There may be indeed, Emma.'

He turned and left.

Eileen could think of no valid reason why he should not have the 'poison box' but refused outright his demand to access The Gilbert's database or the rest of the letters. Informing her that he would be getting a warrant, he followed her to the workroom and took charge of the box of abusive letters. His officers groaned as he dumped it on a table in the Training Room.

'Get this lot off to HQ,' he said. 'It's a long shot, but there may be something in there somewhere.'

Having got his warrant, it didn't take Letwynd long to establish that there was no record of the Standby business in The Gilbert's database.

Chapter 35

Quentin looked at his phone screen as it rang. Not a number he knew.

'Hello?' he said.

'Is that Quentin Rivers?'

'Who's asking?' Quentin replied.

'Gerry Alkenby, Jennie's husband. They've killed her. Those bloody bastards have killed my Jennie.' Gerry could be heard sobbing on the other end.

'Steady on, old mate,' Quentin said, his mind working. 'Slow down, now. Where are you?'

'In Cheppingham. I went up to that Reserve where they found her, but the police wouldn't let me in. That Gilbert woman is not getting away with it. You know what they're really like. I've got enough evidence of their shady dealings to hang them, you don't know the half of it. You have connections – we could use them to expose the bastards.'

Quentin couldn't believe his luck.

'I'm staying at The Beckside Hotel. You will have passed it. Come and find me. Let me buy you a drink and something to eat.'

Gerry arrived, sweating and blotchy faced, clutching a folder. Quentin settled him in the window, bought him a drink, ordered food, made sympathetic noises while Gerry got a grip. He studied Gerry with interest, remembering what a go-er Jennie had been in the sack that night back in the summer and wondering if Gerry had been up to it. She had seemed to quite like it a bit rough, giving as good as she got. It was a pity she had declined to repeat it, but that was women for you.

As they ate, Gerry launched into a detailed account of the Standby affair and Quentin listened with mounting excitement.

'So, they bankrupted you?' Rivers asked.

'They tried to, believe me, but I'm too canny for them. They took four homes off me, but I still have a decent portfolio – I shan't tell them that, of course. I wouldn't let Jennie tell you in case it spooked my backers, but now I don't care if it bloody does, if it means I can bring that bitch down.'

Rivers slid the folder over and opened it up, greedily scanning the papers.

He got Gerry to explain in detail what they all meant, asked if he could keep them.

'Sure, 'Gerry replied. 'They are copies, I have more. I was going to go up to the House, shove them under their noses, see what she and that Richard Aubrey had to say for themselves. But the gates were locked.'

'So, have you actually met this Eileen Gilbert?' Rivers asked.

'No, but I know what she looks like. Jennie told me enough that I would have recognised her if I had just managed to get in the place.'

'Describe her to me. I need to know her if I see her.'

There was not a great deal of detail, but Quentin was left with a good overall impression.

'Leave it with me,' he said. 'I'm going to go over this lot properly and do a bit of digging. Don't you worry, mate, you and me are going to hammer them!'

Back in his room, Quentin picked the memory card out of his smashed camera, blew the dust off it and held it up to the light. It looked fine. He pushed his camera carelessly out of the way sending it crashing to the floor. He ignored it. With a grunt of satisfaction, he slotted the memory card into his laptop and, a few clicks later, was studying the photos on the screen.

There were some good clear shots of the building. He scrolled on till he came to the half dozen or so nearly identical shots of the woman on the patio. He scrolled back and forth till he found the best two, cropped them, adjusted the light on them, then sat back, well pleased.

He scrolled on to the ones of John Hardy. He was gratified that one had caught a particularly unpleasant sneering scowl. He cropped and adjusted it before carefully labelling and saving the chosen ones. He saved them again on a memory stick and set off downstairs.

'Simon, old mate,' he said, 'can I use your printer? Just a couple of sheets, it won't take a minute.'

Simon sighed and let him in behind the reception desk, peering over Rivers shoulder as he put the memory stick into the computer.

'Sorry, mate. Private and confidential.'

'Suit yourself,' Simon said and left him to it.

Rivers watched the photos emerge from the printer, shielding them from any possible prying eyes. He gently tucked them inside his jacket and retrieved his memory stick. On his way out, he nicked a handful of pins from Simons desk and returned to his room.

He stood for a long time staring at the photo pinned to the back of the door, a look of intense satisfaction on his face.

He glanced at his watch before unpinning the picture and rolling it into his pocket, then he carefully hid the memory stick and card, laptop and photos under his clothes in the drawer and, with one last look round, headed out.

He parked opposite the door of the Argos building and settled down to wait. He knew he might have to do this for days before he struck lucky and was elated when, after only a couple of hours, Laura emerged alone. He hurried across the road.

'Hi, Laura, and how are you keeping, eh? I've been taking some photos. What do you think of this one of Eileen Gilbert?' He shoved the picture under her nose.

She reared away from him, her hand going to her mouth.

'How did you get that?' she cried, her voice full of anguish.

'So, it is her then!' he shouted. 'Thanks, Laura. I owe you!'

Laura watched him sprint back across the road and burst into tears.

'Eh, lass, whatever's the matter?' Jim said, emerging behind her.

'Oh Jim, he has a photo of Mrs. Gilbert.'

'Well, it can't be helped,' he said. 'I don't know what all the secrecy was about anyway.'

*

Quentin wrote and rewrote the copy: adjusting the headline, realigning the pictures. They would do it their way of course, but he wanted it to catch the eye.

Rivers was not a popular man in London, and it took him every last ounce of his persistence to get it in front of his old mates on the nationals. He wheedled, bought pints, spent ruinous amounts on dinners, called in every favour however old. He got increasingly desperate as the days slipped by. He was terrified the police would make an arrest before he got his piece out. At last, he got lucky. It was a quiet period news-wise and the The Quire had been running a sporadic campaign against corruption in charities. They bought the piece from him and he was rewarded with a front-page spread.

'Charity Boss Quizzed In Murder Probe'

The exposé described the secretive, cult-like nature of The Gilbert Foundation and its reclusive leader. It hinted at the dubious nature of the sources of its apparently immense wealth. It implied that Richard Aubrey had disappeared from London to avoid some unspecified disgrace, joining the equally shady Eileen Gilbert in seclusion. It suggested that they had somehow forced the previous owners to hand over their ancestral home. It insinuated that she had arranged, or at the very least condoned, Jennie's death to protect herself. It described the violent reaction of John Hardy and his vicious dogs when Quentin had got close to the truth. The police were systematically grilling the cult members, determined to uncover its guilty secrets. Eileen was being questioned long into the night to try to break down her implacable resistance.

Gerry's emotional quotes about The Gilbert's destruction of his caring enterprise for the benefit of its mates, and their vendetta against his beloved wife, peppered the piece. He described how Eileen Gilbert had lured Jennie to its luxury headquarters, hidden away in the Yorkshire countryside, to exact revenge for some petty and well-deserved slight from years before. John and Eileen's photos were prominently featured. Jennie's pretty face, subtly misted, gazed out, begging for justice.

It was a masterpiece of innuendo and implication; leading the reader to conclusions without actually stating them, and Quentin was enormously proud of it. He hadn't written such a piece since his days on The World, when Richard Aubrey and that bloody politician had picked his finest campaign to bits and convinced the court that it was all lies.

Chapter 36

Letwynd read the article with interest though there was nothing in it that they didn't already know.

'Do we have anything on the husband or son yet?'

'No sir, we haven't been able to trace either of them. We've tried the husband's known associates but they either don't know or aren't saying. He's certainly never been seen around here.'

'So, we have missing records, a missing husband, a missing son and a missing Director. Mrs. Gilbert seems to have a knack of losing things,' Letwyn remarked. 'Right, time to have that little chat with her. Fetch her in.'

Eileen was ready for him and followed Hallam willingly enough.

'Mrs. Gilbert,' Letwynd began, 'can you tell me why there is no mention of Standby in your records?'

'I can't, Inspector. I was not directly involved in the case…'

There was a brisk knock on the door, and it opened before Letwynd could respond.

'Good afternoon, Inspector. I am Richard Aubrey QC. I am the Director of The Gilbert Foundation. I am also Mrs. Gilbert's legal adviser and will be sitting in on any further interviews you may have with her or The Gilbert's staff.'

Tilda trotted to where Eileen sat. She put her front paws daintily on Eileen's knee and whined gently, her tail wagging furiously. Eileen dropped her face onto Tilda's head and caressed her ears as she waited for her self-control to return.

'My apologies for not being here sooner, Inspector,' Richard continued. 'I was holidaying in New York. The American papers don't generally report UK murder stories, so I was ignorant of the situation.' He turned to Eileen. 'You really should have recalled me, Mrs. Gilbert. I know that having worked for you for three years without a holiday, you considered that I deserved a good long break, but The Gilbert comes first, you know. I hope you are well. I trust you have been talking to my cactus in my absence. Plants flourish if they are talked to, you know.'

Eileen looked up and met Richard's smile.

'Every day, Richard. I am sure it has grown at least an inch while you have been away.'

Letwynd, bemused, looked from one to the other, suspicious of this pantomime, though he could not have said why.

Richard turned back to him.

'I expect you will want to see the records relating to Standby Rehabilitation and Care. As I had been advised by our legal adviser on the case, Rex Wilkinson QC, that Gerald Alkenby could be liable to prosecution, I felt that it was better that the information relating to the case should not be entered onto our general database. The basic records are on my laptop, but the paper files are held by Mr. Wilkinson. He has accompanied me today. Perhaps it would be better to continue your interview with Mrs. Gilbert after you have spoken to him. I will bring him in.'

'Thank you, Mrs. Gilbert, you may go for now,' Letwynd said.

Richard and Eileen left together. She reached up and hugged him as soon as they were in the corridor.

'Welcome back, Richard. I have missed you. Are you back for good?'

'I would like to…'

'Will you come to my apartment when you've finished with Letwynd? There are things I need to tell you – that I should have told you long ago.'

Richard's face softened and he leant to kiss her cheek.

'Thank you for looking after my cactus,' he said and winked. He disappeared into the Refectory before she could reply.

Almost overcome, Eileen slipped into her office and closed the door.

Word had spread quickly and most of the staff seemed to be waiting for him. His anxiety at leaving Sophie there evaporated as he saw her in a circle of Gilbert people, laughing and chatting, enjoying their attention. She barely noticed him enter. They surrounded him, patting him and greeting him. The bolder souls gave him a hug. John Hardy shook his hand firmly while Sophie watched, amused.

'They are waiting for us,' Richard said, and Rex stood up.

'Will you be alright here, Sophie?'

She beamed up at him. 'Of course, Richard. I'm sure these lovely people will look after me.'

*

Richard and Rex sat down opposite Letwynd and Hallam. Rex very deliberately extracted a pen and pad from his briefcase, squaring the pad neatly in front of him on the desk, and uncapped his pen.

'It might be helpful, Inspector, if I fill you in on some of the background to the Standby case,' Richard said.

Letwynd sat back in his chair and waited.

'As you are no doubt aware,' Richard began, 'Mrs. Gilbert knew Jennie Green before she invited her here for interview. Mrs. Gilbert had worked in the training section of an organisation called the Fanshawe Trust for many years and was highly regarded. Ms. Green was taken on to rationalise that training section. She deemed it necessary to rid the section of most of the existing staff and did this by the simple expedient of bullying them until they resigned. The impact of this on Mrs. Gilbert and her colleagues cannot be overestimated and it has remained with her. It was catastrophic for one colleague – her sister – who suffered a breakdown and later died. The purpose of her decision to bring Ms. Green here was an attempt to understand what drives a person like Jennie Green, to try to gain insight into the rationale behind her behaviour. A job interview is the perfect setting in which to explore a person's history and actions. As it was essential that Ms. Green did not feel constrained, the decision was taken that Mrs. Gilbert would not make herself known to Ms. Green, so I would conduct the interviews. Mrs. Gilbert was not previously aware of Ms. Green's involvement with Standby – it emerged during the course of the interview. Ms. Green did not consider that her actions were in any way reprehensible, either at The Fanshawe Trust or Standby. I was so concerned at what she disclosed about Standby, however, that I briefed one of our Team Leaders to look into it. That was when it emerged that Ms. Green's husband, Gerald Alkenby had gained control of Standby. Further investigations revealed that this was not the first time that this had happened. At this point I engaged the services of Rex Wilkinson QC, who is a specialist in such matters. Unfortunately, Ms. Green caught a glimpse of Mrs. Gilbert and recognised her. Not surprisingly, given her character, she looked for ways to get revenge. Quentin Rivers was the perfect ally for a person like Jennie Green and they set about causing as much trouble as they could for the Foundation. Mr. Rivers is equally as keen to cause trouble for us. I have had dealings with him in the past. He was a reporter on a national newspaper and set about destroying the reputation of a good, decent politician through its pages and she sued them. I was her barrister and we won easily, which led to his dismissal. He would not have forgotten that. Jennie Green and Quentin Rivers… A marriage made in hell.'

*

Eileen, sitting in her office, was so engrossed in Richard's narrative that she didn't hear the tap on her door until it was repeated. She closed her laptop and looked up as Jasmine bounced in.

'Oh, isn't it great to have Richard back?'
'Good news indeed, Jasmine.'
'And isn't his partner just lovely!'
'Partner?' Eileen echoed.

'She's in the Refectory! Haven't you met her? Her name is Sophie. They have been together for some years, apparently, though they split up before Richard came here. They got back together when Richard went back to London. Isn't that romantic?'

Eileen beamed at Jasmine. 'How exciting! No, I haven't met her. I haven't been out of my office since he arrived, and he went straight in to talk to the Inspector. I must go and make her welcome. You seem to know a lot about her!'

'She has been telling everyone all about it over lunch, though most people have gone back to work now. She'll be staying on here with Richard, I gather.'

They hurried through to the Refectory. Sophie sat alone at a table, looking a little lost.

The two women regarded one another with curiosity. Sophie was certainly lovely. She was as fair as Richard was dark. Glossy golden hair fell to the shoulders of her elegant figure.

Sophie was pleased to see that Mrs. Gilbert was just a rather homely sort of middle-aged woman, though she had to admit to herself that her clothes were unusual and rather beautiful. Eileen's fine silk top was an intricate, subtle confection of small, random tucks and pleats with the occasional patch of shirring, which accentuated its multi-coloured greens. Its asymmetric profile was created with floating points, some with tiny tassels, others with weeny beads. The crushed velvet trousers had picked out one of the greens and shimmered in the light. But no-one was ever born with that colour hair!

Sophie offered her cheek to be kissed and they sat down. James appeared from the kitchen.

'Tea?' he said. 'Coffee for you, Sophie, Jasmine?'

'Yes, please,' the three women chorused together and then laughed companionably.

'Welcome to The Gilbert, Sophie,' Eileen said. 'You've been in New York, I gather.'

'My sister lives there. I lived there myself for nearly three years. After London, I think it is the best city in the world.'

'We must seem very quiet after New York and London,' Jasmine said rather wistfully.

'Everyone has been so friendly, though they have had to go back to their work now. This is certainly a beautiful house. I can see that you used the top architects and designers for the restoration.' Sophie said. 'I'm so looking forward to exploring The Estate. I have heard so much about the Park and the Reserve from Richard. You have ponies, I hear. Perhaps I could borrow one to ride out. I do love to ride'

'Of course. They are just little working creatures, though. We will get you a proper riding horse to go out and about on,' Eileen said.

'Oh, there's really no need. We won't be staying that long. A pony will do me just fine.'

'You're not staying then?' Jasmine asked.

'Richard would come rushing straight here as soon as John Hardy rang him to get the name of a lawyer for you. I got to meet John earlier – a real countryman. I love his dogs, such characters. Anyway, Richard just had to come flying here himself as soon as he heard of your trouble; you know what he's like. I suppose it makes sense, he knows all the ins and outs of it all. But once this horrid business is cleared up, we'll be going home to London. Some friends of ours are opening a gallery and I have decided to go in with them. It will be such fun, I'm really looking forward to it. Perhaps we could make some suggestions for art works for here. We would be happy to advise you.'

She chattered on, responding to Jasmine's questions about New York.

Eileen sat apparently listening but reflecting that either Sophie or Richard was right about staying – they couldn't both be.

'Top architects and designers, indeed! Advise me on art works, would she?' Eileen thought. She examined her feelings. Was she jealous of Sophie? Yes, of course she was!

Sophie would take Richard away for good, if she could. Richard belonged at The Gilbert, not trailing around behind the lovely Sophie in some arty-farty gallery. But perhaps he wanted to go back to his London life. There were plenty of charities there who would snap him up if he didn't want to practice law again, or fawn over the idle rich in her fancy gallery. Maybe he was just being kind when he said he was coming back. waiting for the right moment to tell her that they would be losing him forever.

She was startled out of her reverie when Magda approached and said, quietly in her ear,

'Mrs. Gilbert, there is a man here who says he is your husband…'

Eileen leapt to her feet as a handsome, well-dressed man strolled into the room as if he owned it.

She swayed and gripped the back of the chair as he approached.

'Goodness me, Eileen, you look like you've seen a ghost.'

She stepped back as he pushed his face close to hers.

'Did you think I was dead?' he asked, spitefully. 'Where is that bastard of yours, by the way? Or haven't you found him yet?'

She uttered a strange, strangled cry which rose through a scream to a keening wail that went on and on and on.

He grabbed her shoulders and shook her.

'You can shut that racket,' he snarled. 'Get a bloody grip.'

She fought and screamed, all control gone,

'Get out of my house! Get out! Get out!'

'Shut the fuck up!' he snapped and slapped her across her face.

'Enough!' Letwynd roared from the door.

Daniel let go and stepped back and Eileen slid to the floor. Jasmine ran to her, sinking down beside her and wrapping her arms around her shaking body.

'Who's this then, wifey dear? Your new fancy man?'

Letwynd regarded him cooly. 'Inspector Letwynd' he stated and flashed his warrant card. 'Mrs. Gilbert asked you to leave, sir, but perhaps we could have a word before you do.'

Richard knelt by Eileen.

'Help me get her upstairs,' Jasmine said.

Richard nodded and between them they half dragged, half carried Eileen to the lift.

'Oh, my boy, my poor boy…all those wasted years…oh god!'

'Hush now,' Jasmine said soothingly as they helped her into her apartment and onto the settee.

'I'll put the kettle on, or would brandy be better?'

'No! Get me Chris! Please get Chris. He has to tell him. Oh god…my poor boy…my poor, lost boy…' she began to cry again, distraught.

'Chris?' Richard said, baffled.

'Yes, yes! Chris! Please just get him.'

Richard asked no more but pulled out his phone.

'He's on his way, Eileen. I'll make that tea. Stay with her, Jasmine.'

Eileen was shaking uncontrollably, though the tears had stopped. Jasmine sat with her arm around her, gently stroking her hair.

When the knock came and Richard opened the door, Eileen jumped to her feet.

'Chris, you have to tell him...you have to do it now.'

'Tell who? What?'

Eileen took a deep breath, calmed herself.

'You must tell Jack that Daniel is alive. He is not dead. I have seen him myself. He will understand. You must do it now, right now.'

Chris stared at her. 'Jack...?' he began and then stopped, realization dawning.

'You're Jack's mother...of course you are… and I thought the Gilbert name was just a coincidence.'

He nodded decisively, went away across the room and pulled out his phone.

'Jack, Chris here. I am with your mother, but I think you already knew that, didn't you? I am to tell you that Daniel is not dead, that she has seen him herself. Yes, I'm sure. That's fine, of course you do. We must speak again very soon, though, OK? Take care.' He came back and sat with Eileen. 'He needs time to think, Eileen. Maybe he will talk to you next time.'

Eileen nodded. 'Thank you, Chris,' she said, her voice limp. She looked into his eyes and took his hands in hers. 'Thank you for it all, Chris. For dragging my boy out of the gutter, for caring for him, for giving him a future, for doing what I should have been doing. I must tell you what it's all about. I owe you that.'

'I already know, Eileen.'

'You know?'

'Of course I do. In the dark reaches of the night, when your boy cried out in his nightmares, and needed someone to tell, what else could I do but listen?'

'And you didn't turn him in?'

'What for exactly, Eileen? For killing a man who might not even be dead? Oh, I made discreet enquiries, tried to find out, of course I did, but I drew a blank, as I guess you did too. Didn't your private eyes, with all their contacts, manage to find him?'

Eileen shook her head.

'They weren't looking for him – I was sure Daniel was dead. If he wasn't dead, why didn't he come back? Why wouldn't he come back if he was still alive?' she asked.

'Who knows?' Chris replied. 'Perhaps it was more satisfying to watch you tear yourselves apart. I did try to persuade Jack to let you know he was safe, at least, but his mind was so fragile, Eileen, I didn't dare push it. He hated you and Daniel and himself, and was convinced that you would never forgive him.'

'Me forgive him? What for?'

'For killing your husband of course.'

Eileen stared at him in wordless disbelief. 'Oh Jack,' she said sadly, 'It is me who needs forgiveness.' She looked around her, at Jasmine and Richard, quietly watching and listening. She went to sit down and they joined her, sitting close. She stared out of the window, her fingers twisting and picking at her nails.

'Here,' Jasmine said, passing her a mug.

'Nothing like a brew to settle the mind,' Eileen murmured and took a deep breath.

'It was Jack's idea – The Gilbert. We planned it together.' She looked up and smiled softly at them. 'It had always been just me and Jack, with our plans and dreams. I met Daniel when Jack was eleven. I was flattered – he was a good-looking man – and he showed such an interest in Jack. I thought a father's influence would be good for him. It was fine at first – they went to the football…for bike rides…they were genuinely attached to one another. But Daniel grew resentful when Jack got older… to want to be with other youngsters. Daniel took to disappearing for weeks on end, but he always came back. He was OK with me at first, too, but I soon saw the other side of him. He had…has…a cruel streak, took pleasure in putting me down. He didn't knock me about – he was more subtle than that. It was small, cruel things, like bending my fingers back or twisting my wrist until I cried. He never hurt Jack, or hurt me in front of him, though. And there were the other women. He soon got a reputation for making passes at my friends…colleagues… I realised that he married me not for commitment, but to avoid it. If any of the other women wanted more than just a fling, he could play the "married man with a son" card.'

Eileen stopped. They could see she was struggling. Jasmine squeezed her hand and Eileen smiled weakly at her and gulped at her tea.

'Anyway, it all came to a head at the Christmas. I was working for the Fanshawe Trust and really struggling with Jennie Green's bullying. We all were. Daniel always seemed to have money, though I rarely saw any of it. I couldn't really afford to, but I handed in my notice. We went to the work Christmas party, I wanted to say goodbye to people. Daniel knew what I had gone through, knew what Jennie Green had put us all through, but it didn't stop him –

I caught him with her, his trousers round his ankles, up against a wall. They just sneered at me and went right on shagging. I had no strength left. I just walked away, went home, left them to it, but by the time he came home I was angry. I said to him, "You're a real bastard, aren't you? Nothing is beneath you. Why do you hate me so much?"

"Because you're a spineless, pathetic little bitch. I can't think why I married you."

'For a comfy billet and someone to support you while you screwed around! But with Jennie Green, of all people…" I replied.

"Except you're not going to be supporting me, are you? You won't get a reference off Jennie, no chance. You're finished. You and that little bastard of yours will end up on the streets where you belong, but I won't be with you. Jennie now, ah she's got balls. She's going places and, if I play my cards right, I'll be right there with her."

I lashed out at him then, went for him, but he was ready. He had me by the hair in an instant, yanking my head backwards, twisting my neck. I heard Jack shout at him to leave me alone and saw him jab at him with the kitchen knife. It was a clumsy blow, of course. It only caught Daniel's shoulder, but it was enough to make him let go. I have never seen such rage…Jack saw it too and was gone, out of the door and away into the night, with Daniel after him. I followed but they were fast, too fast for me to keep up. I ran and ran, down the long road to the river and Jack was there, his eyes huge and terrified in the dark.

"I've killed him," he said. "He caught me, he had me, I was struggling, he went back against the wall and he was gone, over, down there."

I looked over the wall, down and down to the deep, fast river below. The moonlight was bouncing off the choppy ripples but there was nothing – no sight or sound of Daniel. He was gone, swept away.

"I killed him. I murdered Daniel."

"No, he will climb out, further down," I said, but I knew I was lying. We were on an estuary, and the tide was high, the river sweeping away to the sea.

"I've killed a man. Me…killed my step-father, your husband…"

"Jack, you didn't mean to, it will be alright…"

"But I did, I did. I saw him stagger back against the wall and I didn't stop to think – I pushed him over! It will never be alright! I'm a killer, do you hear? Nothing will ever change that! And it's all your fault. Why did you have to marry him? We were alright till you married him!"

I reached out for him, tried to cuddle him like when he was little, but he shoved me off and turned and ran, away into the night. I stood, stupidly staring after him, stunned. I called and called, all the way home. By the time I got there, he had been and gone. He had taken his backpack and his bike, the cash from my purse... He was fifteen years old, for god's sake, fifteen!

I searched and searched, tramping the streets, showing people his photo, waiting for Daniel's body to be found, for the police to come knocking. I dared not report Jack missing – the police might find him before I did. I volunteered at shelters, got a job at one, went out night after night with the street crews. The years went by. I never stopped searching. I was the biggest UK EuroMillions winner ever. If I became public property, the press would start poking into my background, my past, and it would all come out. They would hunt Jack down…crucify him. He would think I had betrayed him. I had to stay hidden. When I won the money, I was able to pay private detectives, as the press would no doubt have done. They traced Jack to your hotel in Leeds, Chris, goodness knows how. I wasn't even looking in the right places!'

There was a long silence.

'Eileen,' Richard said suddenly. 'Where's my laptop?'

'Your laptop? In my desk drawer, why?'

They watched, baffled, as he hurried from the room.

*

Richard sat in his office, intently watching his laptop screen.

'Yes, she was obsessed with Jennie Green, paranoid, convinced I was having an affair with her, that we were trying to get rid of her. She even managed to convince herself that Jennie was somehow responsible for her sister's death.' Daniel shook his head, sorrowfully. 'I had to leave in the end. She drove Jack away, too – he couldn't cope. She poisoned the boy's mind against me. We had been so close – he was like my own son.'

'So what brings you all this way here then, Daniel, if she was so toxic?' Letwynd asked.

'She's still my wife, when all's said and done. Her problems haven't stopped me loving her, or the lad.'

'Nothing to do with her winning the lottery then?' Daniel looked shocked. 'I didn't know she had, Inspector. How would I know that? I just saw that she was in trouble – that she was obviously still obsessed with Jennie. I lost track of Eileen when she moved away, only found out where she was when I saw the article in The Quire. That was a nasty bit of work. I came to help her set the record straight – that she is mad, not bad. She needs help. But you saw how she was out there – completely out of control. I probably shouldn't have come – I've just made things worse.'

'Well, I think that will do for now, Daniel. I appreciate you being so candid with us.'

'Any time, Inspector. You know where I am if you need me again. I won't be going back to Spain for a while yet. In fact I'm thinking of moving back here permanently.'

'What did you make of all that?' Letwynd asked Hallam when Daniel had gone. 'Whose version do we believe, eh? Aubrey's or Croft's?'

'I would far rather believe Aubrey.'

'Because he is a decent law-abiding citizen and Croft is a known rogue? Oh come on, Hallam, you know better than that. That was Eileen Gilbert's version we heard from Aubrey.'

'We don't have any evidence against her, guv, only Croft's word. We found nothing when we took The Gilbert's vehicles for forensic examination.'

'Perhaps we haven't been looking in the right places, Hallam. We need to go back – trace her associates at this Fanshawe Trust – get their version. And find that bloody son!

And we need to get ourselves out of this house. Sometimes I think the walls here have ears – they always seem to be one step ahead of us. We're about done with the preliminary stuff anyway. We'll move back to HQ today.'

Chapter 37

Eileen was supposed to be resting, but she couldn't settle. She wished she had something useful to do, to stop her mind squirrelling. Having a great team was all very well, but her staying in the background had just meant that they'd learned to manage without her. Jasmine and Chris stepped admirably into Richard's shoes. She couldn't believe that she had somehow managed to sideline herself in her own damned Foundation. This was not how she had seen it in her vision.

There was a tap at the door and she opened it to Richard's smiling face. She couldn't stop the tears as she hugged him. She held him at arm's length and studied him.

'You are thinner,' she said.

She did not say that he looked tired and strained and older, as did she.

She sat him down, poured him a glass of wine.

'Where is Sophie?' Eileen asked.

'I left her unpacking in my apartment. Rex will be staying over – I have put him in one of the mews cottages. I wanted to see you alone. As you have no doubt gathered, I have been watching the police online through my phone.'

'Who sent it to you? John Hardy?'

Richard nodded.

'He is a sly dog. He never dropped a word,' she said.

'I asked him not to.'

They talked quietly and at length as Eileen told Richard all that he did not already know about the weeks that he had been away. Eventually Richard dared to move on to more personal matters.

'I finally understand your need to be private, what has shaped you.'

'I should have told you long ago, Richard.'

'You were just trying to protect your son. You had learnt to trust nobody. That is a hard mind set to change. I would have defended him in court, Eileen. He was just a boy, trying to protect himself and his mother.'

'You told me the first day we met that you never defended a guilty person – you made it a rule.'

'Oh, Eileen…how was I to know it mattered to you?'

'Will you tell John for me? I can't go through it again.'

She felt her control slipping, the tears coming, and changed the subject.

'Tell me what has happened to you since you went,' she replied.

Richard looked thoughtful for a while.

'You have been brave; I must be too. I was angry – you had lied to me. It would no doubt have soon passed, and I would have come back, but then I got your letter – so cold… It was as if the ground beneath my feet tilted... I went to the darkest place. And then Sophie came back…' He fell silent.

'You never told me about Sophie – you had your secrets too,' Eileen said sadly.

'Ah, Sophie…' he said. 'What has she had to say?'

'That you will be going back to live in London when this horrid business is cleared up.'

Richard stood up and went to look out of the window.

'Did she, now? We have not agreed that. Sophie is a creature of the city. She doesn't want to live here. I hoped that if I brought her with me, she would learn to love The Gilbert and want to stay. She left me because I put my work before her. I couldn't do it to her again,' he said simply.

'What about you, Richard? Do you love her?'

He was silent for the longest time.

'I did. I loved her more than I can say. When she went, I don't know which was worse – that she had stopped loving me or that I had driven her to it. I owe her so much.'

Eileen said nothing.

Richard came and sat back down, facing her.

'I know you want me to come back, but do you really need me? Chris and Jasmine seem to have stepped up into my place. What does The Gilbert need me for, Eileen?'

Eileen looked startled. 'I have been thinking exactly the same about myself, Richard!'

He regarded her sadly,

'Then I feel for you, Eileen. We have both of us made ourselves dispensable to what we love.'

'We talked about research, development, specialising, branching out,' she said tentatively.

'Perhaps you could open a chain of Gilberts,' he said.

'I don't think even my fortune would run to that.'

'You never did tell me how much you won.'

'A hundred and fifty-eight million pounds.'

He looked staggered and whistled quietly.

'Good god!' he said. 'I know little about such things, never having been a millionaire, but my guess is that even if you had just put it in a building society, the interest would cover what we spend here.'

'That was the idea,' she said, 'I want The Gilbert to go on forever.'

He sat back in his chair.

'What sort of research and development?'

'I don't know,' she said smiling. 'Apart from making them weather-proof, we have never done anything with Home Farmhouse or the cottages... and the land is still rented out.... but whatever it was, I would need a consigliere.'

He shook his head, but his eyes brightened a little and a small smile flitted across his face. For that moment, he looked like the old Richard.

'There is no great rush,' he said. 'This business will take a while to sort out. Let's see what happens. Perhaps The Gilbert will cast its spell over Sophie, and she will change her mind.'

*

Richard went in search of Chris, who was in his office.

'Chris, Croft was in with the police while we were up with Eileen. Who knows what he might have said about Jack...have you spoken to him again?'

'I have. I was concerned. He isn't strong, Richard. I have been thinking I should go up there, spend some time with him.'

'Up there?'

'I'm not going to tell you where he is Richard. He knows now that he didn't kill that man, but that doesn't wipe away the six years he has spent in hell. It will take time. I wondered why he was so interested in hearing every last detail of my new job. Knowing his mother is realising their shared dream will help, but he has a long way to go yet.'

'The police will look for him, Chris. He needs to be prepared.'

'Why will they?' Chris asked. 'He hasn't committed any crime, we know that now.'

Richard was stuck. How could he convince him?

'Chris, think about it. They know that Eileen and Jennie have history. Croft and Jack were part of that history. Eileen brought Jennie here to punish her. Now Jennie is dead. Croft may have told the police that Jack tried to kill him, implied Eileen did more than just punish Jennie – that she killed her. They will go back, talk to the other people at Fanshawe. And they will want to talk to Jack. I was a lawyer – I know how it works. Their job is to identify the killer and they will keep digging till they do. Go and see him, Chris, persuade him to let me help him.'

*

The police were gone as suddenly as they had arrived. Eileen was informed that their preliminary enquiries were complete and that the investigations would continue back at HQ. Officers would come back as and when they needed more information or had lines of enquiry to pursue. The Reserve was still off-limits, for now. From that she gathered, correctly, that they still had not found Jennie's personal effects or a weapon. Her car had long since been taken away on a low-loader.

John raged at Hallam. His beloved Reserve would be going to rack and ruin if it was not maintained. Hallam was sympathetic, but she could give no indication of when John might be able to go back in, apart from reassuring him that it could not be long.

She disappeared along with her colleagues, leaving John aware of a gap in his life that he had never felt before.

Chapter 38

Eileen tapped on Shari's door.

'You want a cuppa?' Shari asked as she let her in.

'That would be lovely, thank you. I have good news, Shari,' she said quietly, seeing Tanya was absorbed in a cartoon on the television. 'Rex has been in touch. Your ex has been arrested.'

Shari turned frightened eyes towards Eileen.

'He has been charged with attempted murder and remanded in custody. He took a knife to someone outside a pub. With his record he will go down for a very long time even if you don't press charges. You can stay right out of it. You can go back to London. You can go home!'

'I don't want to go home!' Shari said desperately.

A hand plucked at Eileen's arm.

'I don't want to go to London, Auntie Eileen. Paul is going to school after Christmas. I want to go to school.'

Eileen looked down at Tanya's earnest face and smiled reassuringly.

'They have schools in London, pet.'

'But I want to go with Paul. Paul is my friend.'

'What about your friends in London?' Eileen asked. She turned back to Shari. 'Don't you have friends in London?'

'A few, I suppose,' Shari said and shrugged. 'But they're no better off than me. I grew up in care. Kids come and go all the time. You don't get much chance to keep any friends you make. There's nobody'd miss us. We could have a proper life up here, not like down there.'

Eileen was nonplussed. 'I need time to think about this, Shari.'

Shari nodded, resigned. Eileen saw her hopeless face and her drooping shoulders. Tanya went back to her cartoon. Neither argued with her. They were used to their fate being in other people's hands.

Eileen fled back to her office and stood staring down the valley. Richard followed her in.

'Eileen?' he queried. 'Trouble?'

'Shari and Tanya don't want to go back to London. Tanya wants to go to school with Paul. They have no family or friends down there.'

'They've got a council flat,' Richard said gently. 'Rex has made sure it will still be there for them when they get back. It's only one bedroom but it's more than many have got. There will be more Shari's and Tanya's if I know Rex. You can't keep them all.'

'We have so much, Richard. Chris once said that we can't change the world single-handed – and that our champions know that too. They just try to help people one at a time. But if everybody did that, the world would change, wouldn't it? That's how change happens – one person at a time. You will say that I want to keep Shari and Tanya because I've got to know them. Does it matter if it's someone I know or not, as long as I'm trying? People should have what they need, not what somebody else decides they need.'

To her surprise, Richard leant down and kissed her cheek.

'Well, when we are overflowing, don't come moaning to me!' he said, laughing.

Eileen took Jasmine with her when she went back to Shari.

'What would you do if you stayed up here?' Eileen asked Shari.

'What do you mean?' Shari asked.

'You would need somewhere to live and a way to earn a living,' Eileen said baldly.

Shari looked at her in bewilderment. 'Can't we stay here?' she asked desperately.

'Certainly you can for now, while you decide what you want to do long term. We will help you, of course, as any friend would. That's what friends are for.'

Jasmine smiled reassuringly, 'We'll support you, help you plan and get on your feet. Your future is yours to decide, Shari. You can build a good life for yourself and Tanya – you just need to decide what sort of life it's going to be.'

Shari looked from one to the other.

'We want to stay up here,' she said, her voice a little firmer.

'Well, that's one decision made,' Eileen said. 'Now you need to think about how you can achieve that. When you have some ideas, we will work with you. It's what The Gilbert does, Shari. You are your own person, it is your life. We're just here to give you a leg up when you decide what you want that life to look like.'

'I've never had a real job,' Shari replied. 'I've turned a few tricks when I've been really skint… I've never done drugs, though. Mug's game, that is! I've been helping James out in the café, he's been teaching me a bit of cooking. Could I do that?'

Eileen smiled. 'James has told me how hard you have been working in the Refectory and we really appreciate it. It is time we paid you for the hours you do in there. You can start to put a bit by for when you decide what you want for yourself. It looks like you are already coming up with some ideas. We will leave you to think about it.'

Shari watched them go, her expression thoughtful.

'Have we got to go back to London?' Tanya asked.

'Not if I can help it.' Shari replied.

Chapter 39

'We have a DNA match for Quentin Rivers, guv!' Hallam said, bursting into Letwynd's office.

Letwynd flinched. He appreciated Hallam's commitment, but her enthusiasm made him feel old.

'About time we had a breakthrough with the Green enquiry,' he replied.

'Not with the Green case, guv! He has come up as a match on some old unsolved Met cases. Two rather nasty date rapes.'

'Well, well,' Letwynd said 'No wonder he was so reluctant to give DNA. He doesn't have any form, does he?'

'No, nothing at all.'

'I suppose that means we'll have The Met stomping all over us. Is he still at the Beckside Hotel?'

'I have already checked that out. He booked out a week ago. No idea where he is now. The landlord seemed to think he had gone back to London. The Met are going to follow it up at their end.'

Letwynd sighed with relief.

'Anything new on Mrs. Gilbert?'

'No, guv. The Fanshawe Trust only have paper records for the period she was there. Not a single one of her old colleagues still works there, which is odd in itself, don't you think? Aubrey said Jennie Green drove them all out...They're in the middle of going digital and they seem to have just dumped the old records in the basement. It's taking time to find the people from her old team.

We are still searching for Jack Gilbert. I am waiting to hear from HMRC – if he is working anywhere, they'll know.'

Chapter 40

Harry sat hunched in his living room, with his hands between his knees, staring at the floor, remembering how it had started. Jennie had hopped down from the trap and said she would love another tour of the Reserve but why didn't they have a coffee first?

He had been plugging the kettle in when he heard her drop the latch on the door. Before he could turn round, she was close behind him, her hands brushing his belly. He reflected later that if he had done that to a woman, she would have slapped his face; probably had him arrested, but he had done neither. She had felt his body's involuntary response and laughed quietly, taking his hand, backing to the table, pulling him with her. She had hitched herself up onto it and unzipped him. He had smelt the tang of rubber as she slid a condom onto him. Where had that come from? She hadn't even bothered to take her skimpy little panties off, pulling them aside to let him in. She had made guttural animal noises, the like of which he had never heard before, all the while holding his gaze. He hadn't lasted long, but that didn't seem to bother her. She had slipped the condom off as he shrank, expertly tying a knot in it.

'We will have that coffee later,' she had said as she zipped up his trousers. He followed her, dazed, out of the workshop, watched as she dropped the condom into the litter bin.

They had wandered The Reserve, had seen no-one else, to his relief. Then she had gone straight back into the workshop and he had meekly followed her. This time had been much better. She had been entirely in control, teasing him to distraction, encouraging him to explore her, before slipping a condom on and riding him as he sat on a bench.

She had taken his phone number – how could he refuse?

It had been over a week before she had texted him. They had met at the workshop frequently, late in the evenings, over the summer. Annie was used to him going off out to patrol and to check The Estate and showed no curiosity. Jennie had shown no curiosity either – not in him nor his life and had shared nothing of her own with him. He hated himself, and her, but dreamed of her at night, tossing and turning in his sleep.

The guilt was with him all the time, yet he could not stay away from her.

Annie was not stupid – she sensed his distraction. In the end they were barely speaking; he could not look at her or touch her. He took to staying up late, until she was asleep before joining her in their bed. It could not go on.

Jennie had texted to summon him that day. Later, he had slipped away from home on the golf buggy, along the back road, down to the workshop. She was waiting, silhouetted in the doorway, the rising wind whipping her hair and skirt.

He had stood in the carpark and told her that he was not coming in, that he couldn't see her any more. She had laughed and told him not to be silly. He had insisted, and she had shrugged.

'Suit yourself,' she had said. 'There are plenty more where you came from.'

At that moment he had seen the headlights sweep across, as a car turned off the public road into the lane that led to the carpark and he had panicked. He had run away, got on his golf buggy and fled back up the track to The Gilbert, leaving her standing there in the dark, alone.

Chapter 41

Cheppingham was rocked to the core by River's article in The Quire. Copies passed from hand to hand. The newsagent had to order and re-order more. The website version was shared and shared. All over the country, the champions bought the paper and read the website. At first, The Quire was delighted at the surge in circulation and attention.

What collective consciousness decrees that one human interest story will pass unnoticed and another will capture the *zeitgeist*? Where is the tipping point from minority to majority? How many shares make trending? Unlikely as it may have seemed, the elements of this story united to catch the interest of the nation. An unsolved murder; a mysterious and anonymous woman philanthropist; open-handed, unconditional charity; a vindictive and intrusive reporter; a small town; the environment; real jobs….so many hashtags, so many resonances.

Reporters from the Nationals hastily returned to the town, having lost interest when more juicy stories caught their attention. Finding The Gilbert's gates locked, they turned their attention to the townsfolk and were amazed to find that everyone was more than happy to talk to them. The Right Hon Champleys led the charge and the town fell in behind them. The Gilbert staff shrugged off their confidentiality agreements and described their idyllic working conditions and the generous nature of Eileen and Richard and their vision. And everywhere it was the same story. – The Gilbert was the life-blood of the town – it had brought jobs and prosperity. The Park and Reserve were shown off. Quentin Rivers was a poison snake who had been sacked by their trusted local paper for his nasty vendettas.

The Quire became nervous as vitriol began to appear on their Twitter feed.

A hundred versions of the truth were circulating, rumour was rife, the papers were having a field day with Eileen – digging into her history, her life, her secrets, just as she had always feared.

'Eileen, I think we should call a press conference,' Richard said at the Wednesday staff meeting. 'Let them meet you. Face them down, answer their questions or they will make up the answers for themselves.'

He winced at her fearful face, but then she straightened up and lifted her chin.

'Here, I think, in the Refectory.'

The Daily World, remembering the grief that Rivers idea of the truth had brought to them, were the first to sense some good copy in seriously questioning his article. They searched out and interviewed the Standby families, who were happy to correct Alkenby's version of events. They decided to send their reporter to the press conference.

They were not the only ones. As word spread, champions announced their intention to attend. The Beckside Hotel filled up with reporters and every holiday cottage and B & B was suddenly in demand. Caravan and camping sites were soon booked up; the courtyard mews apartments were allocated; even the Right Hons bravely agreed to host half-a-dozen people. Eventually there was no more room to be had.

The Lads and Mrs. Marsh wanted to come *en masse* but had not a penny piece between them.

'What about the Farmhouse? One of the champions we support is a furniture restoration project. They take donations of second-hand furniture and homeless, disabled or unemployed people do them up,' Gemma told Eileen. 'Then they sell them to raise funds for their people. We could furnish Home Farmhouse from there.'

'Excellent! Get in touch with them,' Eileen replied. 'Hire a furniture van.'

Gemma contacted the Lads: 'We'll send a coach for you. There is an empty farmhouse on the Estate. It's in the middle of nowhere but you are welcome to stay there. We can put beds and other basics in for you. It won't be fancy but it's the best we can do in the time available.'

The reply was short and to the point. 'It can't be any worse than sleeping on the streets!'

The Gilbert realised that if everyone who promised to attend did so, it would need to be properly organised. They called in the wedding team from Chris's old workplace to work with the Refectory team and mobile kitchens went up in marquees on the lawns. Portable loos appeared in the courtyard.

Inspector Letwynd thought that DC Hallam's idea of a police presence was a good one. Mingling with the crowd, she and Atkins might pick up some gossip which could help to break the Green case. Maybe Quentin Rivers would be there – he seemed to have disappeared without trace.

*

Thankfully, the day of the press conference was one of those crisp, bright Indian summer days when the darkening green of old leaves is beginning to give way to the golds and ochres of the coming winter. The doors were flung open. Cars were parked end-to-end along the drive and the back lane. Groups of people tramped up the hill and crammed into the Refectory and the patio until every seat was filled and late arrivals had to stand. They eyed the bounty in the carousel but didn't quite dare to sample it.

There was a constant buzz of excitement from the local people. They were becoming one with The Gilbert at last. They told every stranger who would listen that this was *their* Gilbert. It was their town that had been chosen as its home and their people who had made it a reality. Neither could prosper without the other.

Sophie stood in a doorway to the back corridor, watching the crowd and listening to the buzz. She watched as Eileen, Richard, John, and Jasmine entered the Refectory to ragged applause and the clicking of cameras.

'So many people! Why did I refuse to sit with them?' she thought wistfully. 'What is it about this place and why can't I feel it?'

Someone turned round and, seeing her, beamed, and then unseen hands gently guided and propelled her along the room. A murmur ran along the seats, people rose and shifted sideways; she was passed along until she found herself sitting beside Richard. He turned to smile at her, and it was a smile she had not seen in so long that her heart hurt.

Dean lurked up at the back. He had, of course, recognised the woman in the paper as the person he had all but ejected from The Reserve. He could only hope that she had a short memory.

As Eileen and her team sat nervously taking in the faces before them, the Right Hons pushed through the crowd and stood behind them. They patted Eileen and smiled benevolently all around. The Standby families, emboldened, flooded in to flank them, defiantly facing the cameras. The Marsh Lads came next, shepherding their people behind and beside the Gilbert team so they were surrounded, Mrs. Marsh scarlet with embarrassment. Satisfied at last, one of them said loudly:

'I think we are about ready. Off we go!' which was greeted by another ragged cheer.

Shaking, Eileen stood up and the crowd fell silent.

'Good afternoon, everyone. Thank you for coming. I am Eileen Gilbert.'

Cameras flashed all around and a murmur arose as the local people recognised that here, in the flesh, was the mysterious Eileen Gilbert that the Argos article had revealed all those months ago. Eileen froze, overcome with nerves. The Right Hon William, seeing her confusion, rose to his feet and held up his hands for quiet.

'This house was built by my ancestors. I was born upstairs and generations of Champleys have raised their children here. Over those generations, the Estate provided work for the citizens of this area. They were not good jobs by modern standards, but they gave people some security. Now the Estate does so again, with working conditions your forefathers could only dream of. Far from being 'forced out', as some in the gutter press have suggested, I was proud to sell The Manor to Mrs. Gilbert for her Foundation and I am even more proud of what it has become. My greatest wish is that it provides continuity for many more generations to come.'

He sat down to cheers and applause.

A reporter stood up.

'Mrs. Gilbert, what about the murder of Jennie Green?'

Richard rose to his feet.

'The death of Jennie Green was a shocking event which violated everything we hold dear, and we send our condolences to her family and friends. We are not allowed to comment further except to ask anyone who has any information, however small, which might help bring the perpetrator to justice, to contact the police. We want to see this wicked killer caught as much as anyone. Cheppingham and The Gilbert will not rest easy until they are.'

'Where's the money coming from for all this, Eileen?' a reporter shouted.

Eileen stood up, her shoulders back, her expression defiant.

'What I choose to do with my money is nobody's business but my own!' she retorted and sat down.

'Why did you bankrupt Gerry Alkenby?' another shouted.

One of the Standby parents stood up, his hand on Eileen's shoulder to stop her rising.

'Gerry Alkenby is not bankrupt, though he should be. I am sure I speak for all of the six families when I say that we mortgaged our homes and laid everything we had on the line to give our children a meaningful, safe life. Gerry Alkenby damn near destroyed that by asset stripping their homes. The Gilbert Foundation rescued us, and others, from him. I only wish that the rest of his properties could go to organisations that care as much as The Gilbert, instead of to people who want to make a profit out of other's misfortune.'

That started an avalanche as the champions jostled with the locals for the chance to speak. The testimonies were seemingly endless and the press, punch drunk, gave up shouting questions and just listened.

Eventually Richard, seeing James waving from the back of the crowd, stood up and clapped his hands.

'The food is ready, folks!'

The crowd turned as one and headed for the marquees.

'Well, that wasn't so bad, was it?' Jasmine said to Eileen.

'I hardly needed to open my mouth,' she replied, laughing.

They wandered out onto the patio and Eileen was immediately surrounded by well-wishers. Richard and John stayed close by her, deflecting the more intrusive questions from reporters and brusquely rebuffing a hack who was determined to sign her up for an 'Exclusive'.

Eileen ignored the reporters, instead moving from group to group, greeting and speaking to the champions, hearing their stories, enjoying their affection and regard.

'You are the lady that comes to me to have her clothes made! I recognised your picture in the paper!' a young woman called out, laughing.

Eileen saw Dean lurking and deliberately approached him. His eyes widened with panic as he tried to decide whether to stay or run.

'Thank you so much for coming, Dean,' she said, her eyes dancing, 'and thank you for all that you do for The Gilbert. I don't know what we would do without you and the other volunteers. You are welcome here any time.' She held out her hand and shook his firmly.

Mouth open, he watched as she turned and moved on. A reporter made a beeline for him. Seeing him approach, Dean turned and fled indoors.

Having filled their stomachs, the journalists drifted away, their job done. They had heard quite enough good news for one day.

*

'I was hoping Quentin Rivers would be here,' Hallam said to John. 'He is wanted by the Met. I would have loved to be the one to nab him.'

'Is he now?' John said. 'What for?'

'I can't tell you the details,' she replied. 'Quite serious crimes, though, but he seems to have disappeared. Let us know if he turns up, won't you?'

They settled themselves on the patio with their plates of food.

Casting aside caution, John caught her eye and said quietly,

'Did you mean it, about asking you again when you'd caught the killer?'

Hallam held his gaze for a long moment and, seeing only sincerity, smiled.

'Yes, please,' she replied simply.

John beamed, 'Do we have to wait till then?'

'I don't know, John, I really don't. We have absolutely no real leads. It might never be solved – it happens, you know, probably more often than people realise. Unless they slip up or kill again, we may never catch them. I will talk to Inspector Letwynd…'

'Do you know,' John said, looking a little foolish. 'I actually have no idea what your first name is.'

'It's Marnie, but everyone calls me Hallam.'

'Marnie…' John said slowly, as if savouring the taste of it. 'Marnie…that's lovely.'

Richard, watching them chatting, smiled quietly to himself.

Hallam's phone buzzed.

'We have had a call from Annie Lovidge,' the voice at the other end said. 'She says she has some information for us. You interviewed her before, didn't you? Go down and see her while you are there.'

Chapter 42

If Hallam had known that Quentin Rivers was sitting by the window of The Beckside Hotel, with Gerry Alkenby, she could have had her wish.

They had planned to go to the press conference where Gerry would stand up and accuse Eileen Gilbert. Rivers would be there with Gerry's fancy camera to record their triumph and do deals for interviews with the Nationals. Huddled in Alkenby's living room they had plotted their finest hour. Rivers had invited himself to Gerry's classy detached house to show him the article and had somehow never left. Gerry didn't mind – he had no appetite for solitude.

Avidly following social media, they had, with dismay, watched the slow turning of the tide from hero to villain in a thousand tweets and tags. Yet they could not stay away. They dared not show their faces at Gilbert House, but somehow they had to see the spectacle for themselves. They had slipped into town just before the event was due to begin and taken up Quentin's usual Gilbert-spotting place in the Beckside window.

Simon greeted them with indifference – he cared not who he served as long as they paid.

For Annie Lovidge, however, it was too much. The minute Simon went off down into the cellar, she was in their faces.

'You've got a bloody nerve, coming here!' she spat.

'That's no way to talk to your customers, now is it, eh Annie?' Rivers sneered.

'My beloved wife was murdered in this town. I have every right to be here,' Gerry said bravely, his voice breaking.

'Beloved wife? That slag who shagged anything with a pulse? She got exactly what she deserved.'

'How dare you talk about my wife like that, you nasty little bitch!'

'Well, she shagged your mate here, did you know that?' she spat back. 'We could hear them all over the hotel!'

Gerry turned bewildered eyes to Rivers.

'She's lying,' Rivers stated confidently.

'Am I now?' Annie said, her face inches from Gerry's. 'And he wasn't the only one – believe me!'

'Annie! What the hell is going on?' Simon roared from the door.

'I'd get out if I were you,' Annie continued, her voice low and dripping with venom, 'before someone smashes *you* round the head with a big stick.'

She turned, took her coat and bag from behind the bar and, pushing past Simon, stalked out of the hotel.

*

Annie was still shaky when she opened the door to Hallam and Atkins.

'Are you OK?' Hallam asked.

'I've just seen that Quentin Rivers in The Beckside with Jennie's husband,' Annie said, waving Hallam into a chair. 'He was knocking Jennie Green off. Did you know that? I was on the nights when they were there. I thought he was bloody killing her, the racket they were making. I thought you ought to know.'

'Is he still there?' Hallam asked.

'No, they drove past me as I was walking home.'

'Why didn't you tell me this when I interviewed you?' Hallam asked.

'Well, I suppose I didn't want to speak ill of the dead and Rivers had never done me any harm so why drop him in it? And I suppose I didn't think it was important. But he was up there with her husband again, still stringing the poor bloke along, dragging him into telling lies about The Gilbert. He needs stopping before he hurts somebody else.'

Hallam regarded her thoughtfully as she rambled, near to tears.

'Shall I put the kettle on?' she asked gently.

Annie stared at her. 'If you like.'

220

'We'll have a nice cup of tea and you can tell me all about it,' Hallam said, getting up.

'What did you mean when you said that about Rivers hurting somebody else, Annie?' Hallam asked when they were sipping their tea.

'Well, I think he hurt Jennie that first night in The Beckside. I noticed that she didn't let him in her room again the second night. I asked her if she was alright at breakfast because she looked a bit shaken up. He looked really pleased with himself, of course, but the second night he looked really pissed off at breakfast. He was civil enough to her – I guess he had to be if he wanted her to help him dish the dirt about The Gilbert – but I could see he was angry with her.'

'Did they go out together, at all?' Hallam asked

'I heard her saying to him the first day that they should go up to the Reserve that evening, late –see if they could get in the workshop and have a poke about. They went off in his car just as it was getting dark.'

'Did you ever see Jennie or Rivers around after the article came out in the Argos, Annie?'

'They never stayed in the hotel again, but I saw her. I was walking the dog on the meadow one evening and I saw her car in the Reserve car park. I assumed she and Rivers were using the workshop for a bit of the other. Cheaper than a hotel! I thought it was odd, though, especially considering what I'd heard that night in the hotel, but it was none of my business. Maybe he threatened to tell her husband if she didn't give him what he wanted.'

'Annie, I still don't really understand why you didn't tell me all this before,' Hallam said gently.

'I didn't want to get involved, alright? If Simon found out I was talking about the guests outside the hotel he'd sack me. I couldn't afford to lose my job now I'm on my own. But I think I will now anyway – I just had a right go at that Rivers in the bar.' She laughed grimly.

'But Simon can't sack you for talking to us,' Hallam responded.

'You don't know Simon! He would find a way,' Annie retorted.

Hallam and Atkins went up to The Beckside as soon as they left Annie.

'We would like to ask you a few questions, please, Mr. Hance,' Hallam said to Simon.

'I remember you. I've told you everything I know already.'

'Maybe so, sir, but we would like to go over some of it again,' Hallam replied mildly.

Simon sighed heavily and took them through to his pokey office.

'Jennie Green and Quentin Rivers stayed here at the same time for two nights, is that right?' Hallam asked,

Simon nodded.

'Did you hear any unusual sounds coming from their rooms during either of those nights?'

Simon chortled suggestively. 'You mean did I hear them at it? It's far too noisy in the bar to hear anything from the rooms, so no, I didn't.'

'What about after the bar closed and the hotel was quiet?'

'I don't sleep in the hotel. I live in the annexe at the back, so I wouldn't hear anything anyway unless they were hanging out of the window!'

'Do you have a night manager?' Hallam asked patiently,

'A hotel this size can't afford a night manager!' Simon replied, his voice scathing. 'The phones come through to me when we're closed, and we don't do room service at night. I do generally leave the bar staff to clear up on their own, though, it's what I pay them for. So, I suppose they could have heard something. You would have to ask them.'

'So, who did the clearing up on the evenings that Quentin Rivers and Jennie Green were here, Simon?'

'You already know that. It was Annie Lovidge.'

'On her own?'

'Yes.'

'And was she on again the following mornings, for breakfasts?'

'Yes, she wanted as many hours as I could give her, she was saving to buy a house. Why are you asking about Annie? She hasn't done anything wrong, has she? She's got a sharp tongue on her, but she means no harm and she's a damned good worker.'

'Absolutely not, Simon. I'm just trying to get events clear in my mind.'

*

Back at HQ, Letwyn, Hallam and Atkins discussed what they had heard.

'It's beginning to look as if Rivers might be our man,' Atkins said.

Hallam shook her head. 'Much as I would like it to be Rivers, not Eileen Gilbert, it doesn't work. Why would they come all the way back here? That has always been the bit that didn't fit. Rivers had left Cheppingham long before Jennie was murdered. They could have met up anywhere. And why would Jennie meet up with him at all if he had roughed her up that first night? Rivers is obviously capable of it – date rape is what The Met want him for.'

'Perhaps she liked that sort of thing?' Atkins said.

'Then why didn't she spend the other night at the hotel with him? Unless Annie was right about blackmail…'

'I don't think we will ever know the answer to these questions, Hallam. What evidence have we actually got against him? Damn all! There is no way the CPS would let us charge him.'

'Did we double-check Annie's alibi?' Letwyn asked.

'Yes, she was up at the hospital all night – her sister's husband was away with the army and Annie was her birthing partner. The baby wasn't born until the morning.'

'Whether you like it or not, my money is still on Eileen Gilbert. The problem we have is that the evidence is all circumstantial. I don't think there's enough for a decent chance of a conviction,' Letwyn said.

'What about Daniel Croft, guv?' Hallam said. 'We know from talking to the old colleague that we found, that his version was a whitewash – she confirmed that Jennie Green *did* bully Eileen's sister into a breakdown and suicide, that Croft *was* having an affair with her. He went off to live permanently in Spain soon after. Perhaps Green dumped him and he never forgot it. She does seem to have picked up and dropped men without a second thought.'

'Croft didn't know about Eileen and The Gilbert until after Jennie was dead – when he read River's second article,' Letwynd said.' No, it just strengthens the case against Eileen Gilbert. She had the motive and the opportunity.'

'Unless he saw the earlier piece, in the Cheppingham Argos and decided to see if it was the same Eileen Gilbert,' Hallam said.

'That's a bit far-fetched, Hallam, even for you. How would someone living in Spain see an article in a Yorkshire local paper? At a push, I could see him keeping up with news from his old home town, but a Yorkshire paper?' He sighed heavily. 'I suppose there's no harm in checking out when he came back from Spain. We've got to the stage where I'll follow any hunch, however ridiculous.'

Chapter 43

The World published a four-page spread on the modern corporate nature of our social enterprises and set up the truly philanthropic nature of The Gilbert Foundation as the example that should be studied and followed by Governments of every colour. This was how it used to be, they maintained, in the good old days of social philanthropy, when those who were fortunate enough to be rich, shared that bounty with those less fortunate – not according to what they considered that its recipients should need, but what they actually did.

The Foundation's champions across the country cast aside their confidentiality promises and told their stories to anyone who would listen. They launched social media threads that started off by telling of their gratitude to The Gilbert and ran away into heated discussion of the evils of the money-grubbing modern world we live in and the seeming inability of any Government to address the problems of our time.

The Quire hung on for a few days, maintaining that such unanimity merely illustrated the hold that the cult had over the town, but even they had to admit in the end that such mass nationwide brain-washing was unlikely. They were reminded, by those with long memories in the business, of the eye-watering amount of the libel settlement that Rivers had cost The World and set about hastily publishing retractions, as their social media feeds were swamped with condemnation.

Everyone at The Gilbert feared that this marked the end of the cosy, autonomous Gilbert that they loved. The whole country knew about them now – no more would they be able to pick and choose their champions. The flood of applications for help had become the norm. Like any other modest charity, they would eventually be largely forgotten, known only by word of mouth. But that would be a long time coming and the frantic activity in the workroom would continue long into the winter. They were tempted to introduce a formal application process through the website but Eileen was adamant – that way lay ruin for all that she believed in. It was not about who could make the most convincing case, who had time to fill in endless forms and jump through hoops. No. The Gilbert's whole reason for being was to relieve them of such onerous tasks – to fight their battles for them, to take the support to them.

The Quire, horribly aware that they had been on the wrong side and, fearful of litigation, tried to mitigate the damage, but Richard was implacable in his determination for revenge on Rivers.

Eileen was startled by this side of Richard that she had never seen before.

'It won't cost us a lot, Eileen,' he said when she questioned the wisdom. 'You pay us anyway. It is a question of principle. Destructive people like him should be held to account – you of all people should understand that.'

'But look what it led to, Richard. I brought all this grief on to us with my wish for revenge. You told me that I was a foolish vengeful woman, now I am returning the sentiment. Let it go, Richard, please.'

'You may not need to sue anyway,' John later confided to Richard. 'Hallam told me he is wanted by The Met, I don't know what for, but it sounded serious. If we can find him, we can turn him in and save ourselves a load more grief!'

Quentin managed to convince Gerry that Annie had lied. It wasn't too difficult. Gerry had chosen to bestow on his wife the virtue of a saint, and who could blame him if it helped him through? Rivers was reassuring and solicitous and Gerry needed a friend. Two lonely, unloved souls, clinging together in a common cause, commiserating with one another through endless bottles of Gerry's wine.

Chapter 44

'Can we stay on for a few days?' one of the Lads asked Eileen. 'We could do a bit of sketching and that.'

'Of course you can,' Eileen said. 'I will send some more provisions down. You can come up to eat in The Refectory any time – George will come down in the minibus to fetch you. Do you need art materials? George will take you to York. Just text us when you need him.'

The Lads settled into Home Farmhouse for a week or two of art therapy and when they went, it was as if they had never been there, except that they had rather ineptly taken a scythe to the overgrown garden and cleaned the windows to let in the light. George brought back a portfolio of views of the estate that they had left behind as a thank-you to The Gilbert.

They varied from the impressionistic to the bizarre.

Eileen laid them out on the tables in the Refectory and everyone gathered around to study them.

Sophie had to admit that she was impressed.

'One or two of these are really rather good. Properly mounted and framed, they would not be out of place in a top gallery.'

Looking up, she met Richard's eye. He smiled questioningly at her.

'Well?' he said.

Sophie turned back to the pictures, studying them thoughtfully, buying herself time. Eventually she turned to Richard,

'To have any influence on what Crispin and Anna put in their gallery, I would have to have a financial stake in it. I do not have the resources for that,' she stated with some dignity.

Eileen froze, sensing that this was about more than just a few paintings and sketches.

'But we do,' Richard said gently. 'Between us, we have the resources.'

Sophie sat down, her hands reaching out to touch the pictures. Richard sat himself opposite her while Eileen and the others stood back.

'What are you suggesting, Richard?' Sophie asked.

'The Gilbert is supporting the Art Therapy Group financially and they already have a little shop, though it rarely sells anything as it is not in a good place to attract art buyers…I think I'm suggesting that we use your expertise and our money to somehow put these works in the public eye…I haven't thought it through….'

'But an Art Therapy Group is not about selling pictures, Richard, it's about therapy, surely? What about the members whose work is not commercial? Wouldn't that damage their self-esteem?'

Richard regarded her with some surprise. This was the wrong way round – Sophie was supposed to be the entrepreneur.

'However,' Sophie added, speaking her thoughts aloud, 'if the chosen pieces were just a small part of it – a few selected works – it would not seem so discriminatory maybe. Or, better still, if it was an exhibition rather than a sale…. I need to think this through, Richard. It is important not to lose sight of what a therapy group is about, you know,' she stated, firmly, as if Richard had suggested the wholesale exploitation of the Lads.

She collected up the pictures and carried them away to their apartment. Richard stared after her until Eileen's stifled snorts of laughter startled him. He smiled ruefully back at her, shrugged and made his way to his office.

'Good try,' John muttered to himself.

Chapter 45

Dean had taken to coming every night for his evening meal – staring morosely out through the windows at the garden as it lost its colour and slowly slipped into autumn gold and brown.

'We are a sad old pair, aren't we?' John said to Dean one evening as they sat brooding over their evening meal.

Dean looked surprised. 'You feel it too, then?' he asked tentatively. No-one ever confided in him, but he felt John was on the verge of doing just that.

John merely sighed.

Magda came hurrying in to the Refectory.

'I have just been notified that the police have finished with the Reserve!'

John and Dean leapt to their feet and hugged each other. Both immediately broke away, looking rather embarrassed, but unable to keep the grins off their faces as they headed off out.

*

Sophie had explored every inch of the Estate, riding out on every fine day. She was irritated that she was discouraged from entering the Workroom or the Reception Office.

She had described to James some dishes that were all the rage in New York, suggesting they would make a nice change in the Refectory. She had shown George the only right way to prune roses and told John all about an article she had read about the best way to manage the re-wilding of flower meadows. She had very much enjoyed George chauffeuring her around the district, poking about in the local shops as he sat waiting outside. Word soon spread that she was Richard's "lady friend" from London and she was welcomed and treated royally. Invitations came in for her to join everything from the Women's Institute to the

Walled Garden Committee. Her designer clothes were admired, and she was invited to tea at The Old Rectory.

For a while she had enjoyed the attention, but now she was bored.

She perked up, however, when the Police went: maybe now they could be gone too.

Far from being superfluous, Richard had found himself constantly in demand. Chris and Jasmine had a thousand questions about the workings of The Gilbert. They had been feeling their way in his absence and had never had the induction they had needed to get a grip of the detail. They were not afraid of the responsibility, merely relieved to share it with the man who truly understood The Gilbert so much better than they did.

The Project Workers wanted to update him on the progress of their cases and seek his advice. Everyone praised Chris and Jasmine, keen to stress that they could not have managed without them. But they had not wanted to burden them too much as they were new and had enough to do with managing the practicalities.

They decided to continue the Wednesday Team Leader's meeting, as it had proved so valuable in keeping everyone informed.

The morning after the police went, Richard rose as usual, showering and dressing for work.

'The police have gone, Richard. When are we going home?' Sophie asked.

'I have work to do, Sophie, can we talk about this later?'

'What do you mean, work to do? You don't work for her any more. You only came back to get her out of a mess.'

Richard stared at her in dismay. 'Of course, I still work for *Mrs. Gilbert*! What do you think we have been living on these last months? We will discuss it this evening,' he said and left, Tilda trotting after him.

*

Richard and John stood on the pasture overlooking the Reserve, leaning on the gate as the dogs chased each other madly around them.

'I am worried about Harry,' John said. 'He is not himself.'

'Not surprising, really. He and Annie are still apart,' Richard replied thoughtfully.

'I haven't told anyone else this, Richard...' John said, pondering for a while. 'There wasn't really anyone else I felt I could talk to about it...'

Richard gave him a questioning look.

John took a decisive breath. 'I told the police that I'd seen Jennie Green leaving the Reserve one night, back in the summer. She was alone when I saw her but there was a bit more to it that I didn't tell them. It was one of those balmy summer nights – a joy to be outside. I went out at dusk for a wander with the girls and thought I might as well go down the Reserve lane. I met Harry coming back upon the golf buggy. Fair enough, nothing odd in that. He said not to bother checking the Reserve – he had done it. I said I was just walking the dogs, no problem, but he wouldn't let it go. "It doesn't need you to check it again. Everything is fine down there. Leave it alone. Walk back up with me."

It was like he thought I was checking up on him. "No need to get shirty, Harry" I said, "If it's done, it's done, I am just taking the night air," and walked away. But he didn't drive off. I looked back and he was just sitting there in the gloom, watching me.

When I got near the car park, I saw that sports car of hers drive out the other way, onto the road. It set me thinking, I have to admit....'

'You think Harry had been down there with her?' Richard asked.

'He must've been. Why else would he be so anxious that I didn't go down? They were both leaving at the same time. But I felt bad, being suspicious of Harry. He's a good sort.'

'But she was not,' Richard said, grimly.

'I didn't tell the police – it might have just been a coincidence, meaningless. I wondered if I should have a word with Harry. I can't believe he would have had anything to do with her death, though, Richard. He might be stupid enough to shag her, but I can't see him killing anybody.'

'Nor me,' Richard replied. 'But people always say that, don't they? When the time is right, why don't you just mention it, see what his reaction is? He trusts you.'

'I will,' John said. 'Though heaven knows when the right time might be to ask someone if they whacked their 'bit on the side' across the head!'

Sophie was waiting for him when he returned. She took his coat, poured him a glass of wine, made a fuss of Tilda.

'You look tired, Richard. You work too hard. We will eat in, tonight. I'll ring down to the Refectory and have a meal sent up.'

Richard watched as she phoned down, ashamed at his guarded and suspicious response to her concern.

'We will eat first,' she said, 'and then we'll talk.'

As she leant over him to refill his glass, her perfume enveloped him, and her cool hair brushed his cheek. He reflected that once upon a time, this would have captivated him, but now he felt just a great sadness.

The food arrived, they ate, he brooded, she watched him.

'What are we to do, Richard?' she asked, at last.

'I belong here,' Richard replied.

'But I do not.'

'Yes, I can see that. Perhaps you could return to London and we could spend some weekends together,' he said tentatively.

'Some?' she asked, her eyes challenging him.

He held her gaze for a while before looking down at his plate.

'What are you saying, Richard? That I should just disappear off to London and be available when you have a few hours to spare for me, like some kept woman?'

'You need to make life for yourself, Sophie. Stop behaving like a kept woman.'

He regretted it immediately, of course, but it was too late. She was staring at him in angry disbelief.

'And what exactly does that mean?' she demanded.

'I don't know, Sophie. That's for you to decide. It's your life.'

Sophie slammed her napkin down onto the table.

'This life you have lined up for me…. where do you suggest I live it? Back with my parents? And what do you propose that I live on? I have been your partner for all these years, your helpmeet, your support. Now that you don't want me anymore, you'll just cast me off, will you?'

'You can live in the flat, of course. And you could go in with Crispin and Anna,' Richard said, a note of desperation in his voice.

'Well, that is generous of you, I must say. And where do you propose I get the money from to buy into their enterprise? I could've been working all these years, have bought a place of my own. But no, I devoted myself to you and your career and this is the thanks I get.'

Suddenly she stopped and stared down at her plate.

'Oh, Richard, whatever has happened to us? We used to be so good together, until you got drawn into this place.' She began to cry.

'Sophie, it was your choice not to work. It was you who left me, and it nearly destroyed me. I came here *because* you left me. I moved on because I had to, or lose my mind, you must see that?'

'I didn't think you would just disappear like that. I came back from New York and you were gone. I searched for you, did you know that?'

'Why didn't you tell me you were unhappy, Sophie? Why didn't we talk about it, like adults, instead of you flouncing off like a spoilt child? You made it absolutely plain to me that we were finished. What did you expect me to do, come running after you?'

She looked at him in anguish,

'Yes!'

'Then I'm sorry that I disappointed you, Sophie.'

He stood up. 'Come, Tilda. Time for your trot.'

He left, closing the door quietly behind him, leaving Sophie staring after him. She sat for a few moments before picking up her glass and hurling it at the wall.

Richard stood in the darkness of the courtyard as Tilda trotted about on the gardens.

His thoughts would not come clear. 'What am I doing out here? That is *my* home.'

'Is that you Richard? Fancy a brew?' John called as he came across the gardens, his dogs and Tilda romping around his legs.

'Why not?' Richard replied.

As they came into the light of his cottage, John frowned. 'A whisky, more like, going by the look of you.'

They settled in front of the range and Richard sighed and stretched out his legs.

'I was married once, it might surprise you to know,' John said.

'Why should it surprise me?'

'Well, you know, confirmed bachelor and all that. She ran off with my best man.'

'I trust she waited until after the wedding. And don't tell me, you still miss him!'

John snorted with laughter. 'It's not funny, you know, or at least it wasn't at the time.'

'I am sure it wasn't. Why are you telling me this now?'

'Oh, just a wild guess at the reason for your haggard look,' John replied. 'Sophie wants to go back to London, you don't. Am I right?'

Richard nodded and told him the history, John topping up the glasses as he listened. By the time he had finished, the whisky was working its magic and both men were mellowing nicely.

'So now what do I do?' Richard asked.

'Huh! Search me. I'm bloody useless with women. Hells bells, I let Hallam go without so much as a murmur!'

Richard looked at him curiously.

'Well, I did ask her if she was spoken for. She said to ask her again when they have found their killer.'

'The way things are going, it looks like you might have a long wait.'

'Look, Richard, you have your life. Sophie has her life. You can only be responsible for your own. You are The Gilbert. You can't just chuck it up – you would never be happy. Is that what Sophie wants? To see you unhappy?'

'But I don't want to see her unhappy either, John!'

'Well, you are stuck then, aren't you? Either you split up or you compromise with a long-distance relationship.'

'I suggested that. It didn't go down well.'

'Then she will have to come up with an alternative. The big question you have to ask yourself is: "Do I love this woman more than The Gilbert?"'

'If you had asked me five years ago, I wouldn't have hesitated, John. But I spent years learning to live without her after she left. It damned near killed me, but I made it, and I was content.'

'Well, there's your answer then.'.

Richard tried to be quiet as he made his way up to his apartment, but the whisky had somehow robbed him of his faculties. He need not have worried. Sophie lay stiffly in bed with her back to him, the covers almost covering her head. He wanted to care if she was asleep or not, but he was just too tired.

Chapter 46

Eileen bustled into the Refectory with Jasmine, where Richard and John were sharing a morning break.

'I thought it might be useful to drive down and have a look at Home Farmhouse,' she said. 'I haven't been down there in an age. I would like you to come with us, if you are not too busy.'

They knew Eileen was keeping herself occupied. Chris seemed to have been gone for so long, though it was actually only a few days – they knew she was finding it hard to cope.

'I suppose the Reserve will just have to wait,' John grumbled, getting up. 'You want to go in the trap?'

'That would be perfect. It's a lovely day for it.'

They trotted away along behind Gilbert House, past the turnings to the Reserve and on to the public road, crossing it onto a farm track which wound away between fields, ending in a weedy yard.

The rambling, substantial house stood against a stand of trees, flanked by a range of barns and stables. It was sound and weatherproof enough but had a sad and neglected air. An overgrown garden and small orchard lay behind it.

Several skinny cats melted away into outbuildings and startled crows squawked and flapped away from the trees.

Unlocking the door, they stepped inside, their footsteps echoing on the flagged floor.

'It is criminal that we have done nothing with this place,' Eileen said, 'when you think of all the homeless people there are…'

'The farmers who rent the grazing from us use the barns for storage,' John said, 'and several of the cottages out on the fields have retired farm workers still in them. We have been too busy getting The Gilbert established to even think about this place. What did you have in mind? I can't see many homeless people wanting to live out here!'

'I have no idea!' Eileen said. 'I was hoping you two might have some thoughts. Do you think you and Sophie would like to set up home here, Richard?'

Richard laughed. 'I think it would be Sophie's idea of hell....' he began, and stopped, realising how disloyal that sounded.

There was an awkward silence which they covered by moving on through the rooms, reminding themselves what a fine, dry and roomy house it was.

Eileen's phone rang.

'Mrs. Gilbert, it's Magda. That man is here again.'

They didn't stop to do more than lock up, and the pony was startled and more than a little indignant at being expected to trot all the way home. As they went, Eileen reflected that she had set out to create a small but loving and benevolent movement. She had no lust for power, no illusions that she could change the world, but merely a wish to do good, as far as one person could when given the chance. It seemed to her, at that moment, that some people were so consumed with envy and bitterness that they were not able to tolerate even so small a gesture.

Daniel was waiting for them, lounging on a sofa in the Refectory, with his feet up on a coffee table.

'I ordered coffee but your staff seem to have better things to do than bring it. You really should keep them in line, you know,' he said.

John moved towards him but Eileen raised her hand, which shook only a little.

'You will leave my house, Daniel,' she said with dignity. 'You are not welcome here, now or at any time.'

He swung his legs down and rose lazily.

'I like it here. I could get used to this life. "With all my wordly goods I thee endow," eh Eileen? What's yours is mine. And don't claim we are divorced, because we know that's not true, don't we?'

'Mrs. Gilbert's fortune was acquired long after your separation. It is a non-matrimonial asset. No court would award you a penny of it,' Richard said.

'But Eileen will, won't you, Eileen? She knows she has to keep me sweet. Why don't you tell them our little secrets, Eileen? I am sure they would love to hear them.'

'They already know all about you, Daniel. There are no secrets here, not anymore.'

For the first time, Daniel looked uncertain, but then regained his composure.

'Or maybe the newspapers?' he wondered, his voice light.

'Quentin Rivers tried that one. It didn't get him very far,' John snapped.

'Or that nice Inspector Letwynd, Eileen? Shall I tell him all about us?'

'You can tell him whatever you like, Croft,' John said. 'Do you really think your nasty little tales would *hold water,* would *float Letwynd's boat*?' He laughed harshly. 'He'd soon have your measure, he's a smart man. Now bugger off and find yourself a *river* to fall in.'

Daniel looked startled.

'Leave now, or I will call the police myself,' Eileen said.

'You and I will have another little chat, Eileen. Just you and me and perhaps Jack. I will look forward to it,' he said, but his voice had lost its certainty.

'We will not. There is nothing for you here.'

'We'll see,' he replied and strolled out.

Eileen sank down onto the settee, her heart pounding.

'Well done.' Jasmine said.

'I think it might be time to get an injunction to stop him bothering you, Eileen,' Richard said. 'I'll look into it.'

Chapter 47

Richard knocked and entered Eileen's office.

'We have received an official communication,' he began.

Eileen raised her eyebrows. 'Indeed? And what might be the nature of this official communication?'

Grinning, Richard said, 'We have had a letter from our MP. He wants to visit The Gilbert. He informs us that he will be accompanied by a Minister from the Department of Health and Social Care.'

'Does he now?' Eileen said, leaning back in her chair. 'I'm not fond of politicians, I have to admit. What could they possibly want with us? Surely they can't be in need of charity?'

'Perhaps they want you to help clear the National Debt.'

Eileen chortled. 'Seriously though, Richard. What are they after?'

'Only one way to find out!' Richard said. 'I will reply when I have a spare moment.'

If the politicians expected The Gilbert to be impressed by their presence, they were probably a little disappointed. Her people, having been forewarned of the visit, were friendly enough as they were given a cursory tour, but didn't pause in their work. When the Minister attempted to peer over Gemma's shoulder in the workroom, she snapped her laptop shut and waited patiently until the Minister retired.

Eventually they reached the Refectory for lunch, where they were treated with the same open courtesy as any visitor would be. Eileen noticed that the Minister was taking careful note of everything he saw, asking probing questions at every opportunity, most of which were answered in the same rather vague tone that Richard had used with the manager candidates.

Having eaten, they retired to Eileen's office.

'Eileen…I may call you Eileen….?' the MP began

'I prefer Mrs. Gilbert, Mr. Wallace,' Eileen replied coolly.

'Er, yes of course…. Mrs. Gilbert…. we are impressed by your beautiful home,' the MP finished lamely.

Eileen nodded acknowledgement of the compliment. She assumed that eventually the politicians would get around to revealing the purpose of their visit, but her patience was wearing thin.

'We do not, as a rule, do guided tours,' she said. 'I am hoping that you are not here merely out of curiosity. This is a workplace, we are busy.'

The MP looked a little embarrassed, but the Minister was unfazed. He leant back in his chair, steepling his fingers and regarding Eileen over his spectacles.

'This Government believes in the importance of the role of the Third Sector in delivering quality services for our country. The articles in The World were brought to our attention. Your operational model has caught the attention of the Prime Minister!' he said rather dramatically, pausing for effect.

Eileen and Richard did not react, merely waited.

'We are considering inviting The Gilbert Foundation to tender for contracts to roll out your model nationally.' He waited again for a reaction. When none came, he moved seamlessly on.

'Of course, we would need to undertake a detailed analysis of all aspects of your model, to determine which would fit with our vision for Britain, before making a decision, and would require your cooperation as our people carry this out. However, before I recommend the undertaking of such an analysis, I need to have a clearer understanding of the main tenets of your operation to establish their sustainability'

The MP took a glorified clipboard from his briefcase and a gold pen from his pocket.

'What is your annual budget?' the Minister asked.

Eileen smiled and shook her head.

'I would happy to explain our ethos and operational methods in more detail, Minister, if you are interested, but such financial information would remain confidential until I was satisfied that you were serious in your desire to embrace the Gilbert model in all its aspects.'

The Minister sighed pointedly. 'I understand the nature of commercially sensitive information, of course, and respect that such detail may need wait until our negotiations were more advanced. Perhaps you could tell me what proportion of your expenditure goes on overheads – such as staffing, the public facilities, and premises – and what proportion on your beneficiaries.'

'Why do you separate the two aspects?' Eileen asked.

The Minister hesitated, baffled by the question.

'It is important to understand the staffing costs and overheads to beneficiary ratio, so that we can analyse how cost effective the operation is.'

'Why don't you include the employees and the public who use the facilities among the beneficiaries?' Eileen asked, her expression ingenuous.

Richard smiled quietly to himself.

'Employees are paid to carry out their duties, Mrs. Gilbert. A workplace is not a charity.'

He stopped, realising that what he had said did not actually make much sense here.

'Employees are not the beneficiaries of a charity,' he amended. 'They carry out their duties and are financially rewarded accordingly. Perhaps we could move on to the premises. I understand that this is your home and, of course, wish it to reflect your status and afford you all possible comforts. You accept, I am sure, that this standard is not necessary in every workplace.'

'Why not?' Eileen asked. 'Though I accept that it may not be necessary for a workplace to be in quite such grand premises, you have to remember that employees spend a third of their lives at work. Our experience is that people have much higher morale, and hence productivity, in congenial surroundings and with good terms and conditions.'

The Minister chose not to reply, merely shaking his head. His people would do the cost analysis – he was really only here to dangle the possibility of much sought-after contracts before these people. He was accustomed to an air of excited anticipation and cooperation on such visits.

'What exactly is the purpose of the Reserve and Park in relation to your work with your beneficiaries?'

'Some of our beneficiaries are in fields related to the environment or community projects.'

'I understand that, but the facilities are not *necessary*, surely? You have staff with the expertise to work with such beneficiaries, that is sufficient.'

Eileen sighed.

'We could find nothing on your website to indicate a proper application process for potential beneficiaries,' he said.

'We don't have one,' Eileen replied. 'If people approach us, we work with them to establish their needs. Otherwise, we approach them to offer our services.'

'You offer help to people who have not even asked for it?' the MP asked. 'That is extraordinary!'

'I like to think so,' Eileen said, and stood up. 'Thank you for your visit, Mr. Wallace, Minister. Having worked for many years for both Government and charitable care providers, I suspect that the Gilbert Foundation's model will not prove to be to your taste. If you should decide to embrace the notion that all people deserve the best, then feel free to return.'

She led them out and saw them off the premises.

'Don't you think you might have been a little hasty?' Richard asked.

'I was nowhere near hasty enough.'

Chapter 48

Sophie spread the Lads' art works out around the apartment and walked round studying them with excitement.

'With their back stories, this could be something like the Seasick Steve or Cat Named Bob phenomenon, if we get the marketing right,' she muttered. 'If we could just convince our buyers that they were looking at the next Banksy, this could really take off.'

She heard Richard let himself in the door.

'Were you serious about this?' she asked him, her arm sweeping around the room.

'I thought you said it wasn't a good idea,' Richard replied, startled by her change of tone.

'Well, it would have to be done properly, of course,' she replied airily. 'We could make them anonymous, like Banksy. That would get the buyers attention without exposing the artists to a lot of intrusive publicity. So, what did you mean about "our money", Richard?'

'I meant that any savings we have belong to us both, I suppose. As you said, you supported me while I pursued my career, so you have a stake in my past earnings.'

Sophie sighed with satisfaction.

'Then I think we should buy into Crispin and Anna's gallery and put on an exhibition of these works. With the right kind of publicity, we could start the next Big Thing.'

But Richard had also been thinking about the issue.

'I said that I hadn't thought it through and, now that I have, I am concerned about conflict of interest. The Gilbert can't be seen to profit from the people it supports. That was what Alkenby tried to imply about the Standby homes.'

'The Gilbert wouldn't profit!' Sophie retorted. 'It would be our money, not hers.'

'But I am the Director of The Gilbert and it would be my money, and they are The Gilbert's beneficiaries. It doesn't feel right.'

'Perhaps we should ask the artists, Richard. They might not be so squeamish about where their good fortune comes from! And if it takes off, you wouldn't need to go on working for The Gilbert.'

Richard turned away, closing his eyes. After a few moments, he turned back.

'Sophie, I am not going to leave The Gilbert.'

'Well, I am!' Sophie said. 'I'm going to take my share of our joint assets and buy into the gallery. Then I'm going to make these artists rich and famous. I won't make their lives a little bit easier like The Gilbert has – I will transform them. The Gilbert's charity will be nothing to what I will be offering them! They will be rich in their own right, not pathetic charity cases! And you needn't worry your ethical head about exploitation, Richard. I will see to it that they are properly represented and rewarded, and they will thank me for it!'

She began to gather the pictures up, but Richard grabbed her wrist.

'These were a gift to The Gilbert, Sophie.'

Sophie flung them into the air.

'Keep them!' she hissed. 'There will be plenty more where they came from. Let go of me!'

Richard sat in silence as she rang down to reception for a taxi to be ordered and packed a case. When she was done, she said,

'Please arrange for the rest of my things to be sent on to the London flat. I trust that you will also send me a substantial amount of money.'

The taxi sounded its horn and Sophie left without a backward glance. He heard the sound of the lift fade away but sat on, staring at the floor.

There was a tap on his door. As if waking from a deep sleep, he rose unsteadily and opened it.

'Sorry to barge in. I saw Sophie leave,' John said. 'Thought you might need a friend. Tell me to bugger off if you like.'

Richard smiled weakly. 'You are a good man, John, and very welcome. The whisky is in that cupboard.'

*

Word soon spread that Sophie had gone and Richard found himself treated like an invalid in need of building up. Somehow everyone seemed to sense that her departure was permanent and feared that his heart was broken. Richard himself couldn't decide if it was or not. It certainly didn't have the devastating impact that it had the first time, but he was bleakly saddened by the sense of failure that occasionally overwhelmed him.

Eileen reassured him that he mustn't worry about the Lads, as long as they were made aware that The Gilbert was not involved. It was, after all, their choice to make – they were adults and Richard must accept what Sophie had said about ensuring they were properly represented and rewarded. The Gilbert would quietly keep an eye on them, as it did with so many other champions.

'And who knows,' Eileen said, 'maybe they really will become rich and famous and be forever grateful to Sophie.'

Chapter 49

John answered the knock on his door and took Harry through to the kitchen. Harry looked awkward and uncomfortable, so John busied himself with filling the kettle and putting it on the range.

Eventually Harry said, 'I thought I ought to tell you first that I am leaving The Gilbert.'

'I am sorry to hear that, Harry. I wish you wouldn't.'

Harry shook his head,

'I came here to be near Annie. She won't have me back – I have tried, believe me, but she won't even talk about it. I don't want to stay round here without her.'

'Why won't she talk to you, Harry? What did you do to upset her so much?'

'I don't know, she won't say.'

John took a chance. 'Did she find out about you and Jennie Green?'

Harry looked appalled and jumped to his feet.

'Sit down, Harry. I'm not stupid and neither is Annie.'

Harry looked near to tears. John poured the tea, plonked a mug on the table in front of Harry and sat down opposite him.

'Well?' he asked.

'She didn't know, John. Honestly, she didn't!'

'Oh, I think she did,' John replied.

He sat back and waited. Harry sat looking down and twiddling with his mug. Suddenly he took a deep breath, and, like a dam bursting, he told it all, his words tumbling over themselves in his haste to be rid of them.

'So, you actually saw the person who probably killed her? Hells bells, Harry, why didn't you tell the police?'

'But I didn't see them! All I saw was some headlights in the dark! I have no idea who it was!'

John acknowledged the truth of this with a nod.

'But at least it would have told them that it wasn't somebody she arranged to meet there, Harry. That it might be someone she didn't know. I don't know what difference that would make, but it could, you know.'

'They wouldn't believe me. They would think I did it!'

'And did you Harry?' John asked

Harry looked him straight in the eye. 'I didn't, John.'

John held his gaze for a long moment before nodding.

'Fair enough, but you have to tell the police, Harry. If you don't, then I have to. You'll be OK if you just tell them all of it. I think you should tell Richard, then he can represent you.'

Harry looked horrified. 'I can't, John!'

'Yes, you can. We'll do it now, then I'll ring Hallam.'

He took out his phone and tapped Richard's number.

'Harry and I would like a chat, Richard. Can you come down?'

Harry began to shake as they waited, but once he started to tell Richard, he felt the adrenaline drain away and a great relief steal over him. Richard listened closely, without interrupting.

As Harry fell silent, his eyes searching Richard's face for reassurance, Richard said,

'Tell it to the police exactly as you have to me, Harry, and then answer their questions honestly. Don't go into detail about what you and Jennie got up to, that is not relevant. Concentrate on the evening she died. I'll be with you and will keep you straight, OK? If you are innocent – and I do believe that you are – I'll be with you every step of the way. Ring Hallam, John, let's get this over with.'

Hallam was intrigued to be told that John Hardy had rung and particularly requested that it was she and Atkins who came to hear the information The Gilbert had for them. She briefly wondered if it was quite professional, considering her hoped-for relationship with John, but realised that was taking professional ethics a little far, even for her.

It was not John, however, who greeted them and took them quietly into one of the mews apartments, but Richard. Harry was waiting for them, rigid with anxiety.

Hallam listened as quietly as Richard had, as Harry haltingly told her of his affair with Jennie Green and the events of the evening of her death. He hung his head in shame as he recounted how he had run away and left Jennie to her fate.

'Are you quite sure you didn't recognise the vehicle, Harry?' Hallam asked.

He shook his head.

'Can you think back and picture the scene?' she continued. 'Would you say the headlights were low or high off the ground?'

Harry closed his eyes and was silent for a while

'Quite high, I think…. like an SUV or a four-by-four…not low like a saloon car. And I think it was a dark colour.'

'Good, well done,' Hallam said, 'that narrows it down. What did it sound like?'

'It was really windy and raining, I couldn't hear it.'

'Never mind,' Hallam said. 'Think carefully. When you were going out of the car park, did you look back? Did you see the vehicle side on?'

Harry screwed up his eyes and concentrated. 'I did, I had forgotten. It was just a glimpse as it disappeared behind the workshop. Yes, it was quite high and biggish, I think. I didn't see the driver, though. It was too dark.'

'That is really helpful, Harry. Well done. At least we have an idea of the vehicle, now.'

'Does Annie have an SUV, Harry?'

Harry stared at her in horror.

'No, she's got one of those little mini cars. You can't be thinking it was Annie? She didn't know about me and Jennie. Why would she come to the Reserve? No! You're wrong! She was at the hospital!'

'Calm down, Harry, we have to explore every possibility.'

'Are you going to arrest me?' Harry asked.

'No, Harry. We could, for obstructing the police, but that is not up to me. You will need to sign a statement and we will no doubt want to speak to you again.'

When they had gone, Harry started to shake. Richard took him across the yard and handed him over to John.

'Nobody except Mrs. Gilbert will know about this, Harry, unless you tell them,' Richard reassured him.

'If you are going to stand a chance with Annie,' John told him bluntly, 'you're going to have to come clean with her.'

Harry knew he was right, but he had done enough confessing for one day.

When he did grind up the courage to go and see her, Annie agreed to listen to his confession, but her response was scathing,

'Did you really think I didn't know? I'm not bloody stupid. I bet you feel better now, but it doesn't make any difference. If you think it's going to make it right, you've got another thing coming.'

'I am leaving The Gilbert, Annie, I thought you ought to know. I'll be going back to Prudhoe, to my parents' place for now. I can't stay here without you.'

'And this concerns me how?' Annie snapped, and showed him the door.

Harry was now desperate to be gone. He dreaded people's regret and surprise, and their efforts to persuade him to stay. Most of all, he dreaded that they would throw some sort of leaving do. He was packed and gone within the week, leaving John completely knocked off balance, having to tell his bewildered colleagues that Harry had felt he couldn't stay without Annie.

*

Dean knew he lacked social skills – that had been made plain to him from a very young age. He saw that others made friends but had never been able to fathom exactly how they did it. He longed to be accepted, to be part of it, whatever 'it' was. He went over and over Eileen's generous gesture to him at the press conference and wanted only to show her that his loyalty and devotion to her and The Gilbert was now absolute. He had no idea how long it would be considered appropriate to wait before he approached John Hardy, so he hung back until after the monthly meeting and then took his chance.

'I wondered…' he began, 'I don't know how it works, but I thought I would just ask…'

John waited patiently.

'It's just, well, I wondered what my chances would be of getting Harry's job.'

John had been half expecting this.

'We haven't made any decisions about replacing him yet,' he said. 'When we do, you would be welcome to apply, of course.'

Dean beamed. 'I will! Will you let me know when it comes up, John?'

John looked at Dean's face and realised what it would mean to him.

'I can't promise anything, Dean. There could be a lot of applicants. Some of the other volunteers might want to go for it.'

Dean tried not to look downcast. 'Of course, yes, of course… I see…'

'I'll let you know, Dean,' John said, patting his arm.

'Thanks, John, I appreciate it.'

John watched him go, his expression thoughtful.

Chapter 50

'Richard? Chris here.'

'How's Jack?'

'It was rough at first, Richard, but he is getting stronger by the day. In fact, I don't think I have ever seen him looking so well. He has his mother's mettle, that's for sure. He is ready to talk to you about the police. He can't face a busy place like The Gilbert – can you come here? And he wants you to bring Eileen. I thought it best if you tell her, somewhere quiet. You can tell her that he was going to reply to her letter that I forwarded but then he saw the coverage of Jennie Green's murder on the Gilbert Estate. You can imagine how that spooked him. I'll text you the address. Just let me know when you will be arriving.'

Richard made his way to Eileen's apartment. She knew he had news as soon as she opened the door. As he told her, he watched her face light up and tears slide down her cheeks unchecked.

'They are in Scotland, Eileen, way out on the north west coast. It's some sort of hippy community, I think. Self - sufficiency, arts and crafts, smallholding, that sort of thing.'

'I'll get packed,' she said.

*

The narrow road wound endlessly through stands of pine, over craggy tops, down into valleys and up again. They had left the last village behind miles ago. At last, they breasted another rocky summit and looked down to an old sandy flood plain, a river winding across to dunes and the sea beyond, the setting sun dazzling them. Dotted below they could see crofts – long, low, single-storey cottages painted brilliant white, with fenced allotments. Shaggy ponies, sheep and a few highland cattle grazed the wiry grass between them. At the bottom was a wooden building with 'café' and 'shop' painted in white on the roof, surrounded by a stony parking area.

'That's it,' Richard said.

Eileen stretched as she got out of the car, cramped from the long miles. A bitter wind snatched at her and she shivered.

Chris emerged from the building and Eileen hugged him, her heart jumping in her chest.

'Come in,' he said.

The big cafe was full of tables with pretty, faded tartan cloths, and mismatched chairs. It was empty. She watched as Chris made tea and sliced rich fruit cake, pulled cling film from a plate of sandwiches.

'I will take you across when you have had your tea. He will have seen you arrive. Take it slowly Eileen…give him time.'

She couldn't eat, but she sipped her tea, glad of its refreshing heat.

'OK? Ready?'

Eileen nodded and they followed Chris across to the nearest croft. It was dark inside and as her eyes adjusted, she saw him. He stood near the window – he will have watched them walk across. Uncertain, she waited. He seemed to cross the room in slow motion, stopping in front of her. She gave a little cry and lifted her arms in entreaty. He stepped into them, his face dropping into her neck as they clung together.

Richard and Chris slipped out and wandered in the gloaming.

'This is a quite a place, Chris, but what on earth do they live on?'

'You would be surprised how many people find their way here and visit the café and shop. There are sea eagles and golden eagles, and all sorts of rare wildlife to see. Bird watchers, hikers, cyclists, tourists out for a drive. There is a jetty on the river mouth, beyond the dunes – the wildlife boat trips stop off for a cuppa and souvenirs.

The people make crafts for the shop. They run craft workshops. They have their animals, they fish, they grow some veg, though the soil is very sandy. Some of them go to the city for the winter months, when they are not needed here, to earn some cash. There has been a community here since the 1930's.'

'Really?'

'Communes and self-sufficiency didn't start and end with the Sixties, Richard. The Estate thought they were all mad but were happy to let the abandoned crofts to them for next to nothing. Sadly, that is all changing. As they fall vacant the Estate is selling them off, effectively cashing in on the work of generations of occupants. It is the way of things now. Crofts that no-one wanted are now sought after for second homes or holiday lets. It's undermining the survival of the whole community, though – soon there won't be enough permanent residents left to work the communal allotments and animals, and facilities like the café and shop.'

The men's eyes met.

'I know exactly what you're thinking.' Richard said, laughing. 'The Gilbert changes your way of looking at things, doesn't it? Where once you just saw a problem, now you see a chance to make a difference.'

They wandered back.

'Jack is going to come back with us for a visit.' Eileen said, her face glowing.

'That is good news,' Chris said, searching Jack's face.

'It's time,' Jack said softly to him. 'There's no hurry – they are going to stay for a bit, see how we do things here, and then we will all travel back together. I'll take them across to the guest croft to settle in, then I will cook you all a meal. Tomorrow I would like my friends to meet my mother.'

Eileen was anxious about meeting Jack's people. Wouldn't they wonder where had she been these last years, why had she never been before?

They were a tough, hardy bunch.

'Mother, eh? We didnae even know ye had a mother, Jackie,' a weather-beaten older woman in shorts and enormous boots stated baldly, looking Eileen up and down.

Jack merely smiled. 'I was lost but now I am found.'

When they went, Eileen left the four-by-four vehicle they had driven up in – the community might find it useful.

'You just can't stop yourself, can you?' Richard laughed.

'It was Jack's idea,' she said stoutly. 'Nothing to do with me. If we can't blow a few minds without you sticking your two pennorth in it's a pretty poor do, eh Jack?'

*

They arrived at The Gilbert late in the night and sank gratefully into their beds, sleeping on into the day. No-one disturbed them, though they were all eager to meet this mysterious son. They had strict instructions from Jasmine that there was to be no welcoming committee, no fuss.

Trays of breakfast were left outside the door and taken away again, cold, to be replaced with fresh. At last, word spread that the trays had been taken in. Eileen and her guest must be awake, so they could all stop tiptoeing around.

Jack stood in the dormer window, staring out at the gardens, six years of Eileen's letters to him scattered across the table. She came up behind him.

'Ready for a look round?' she asked.

He nodded and they made their way down the staircase and out onto the patio. Jack climbed slowly up the hill to the little summerhouse and finally turned to look at the house, tears standing in his eyes.

'It's exactly right. How on earth did you find it?'

'It was waiting for us, Jack, waiting to be found.'

Jack's step quickened as he headed for the French doors. He pulled one open and stepped inside.

'Wow!' he said, suddenly laughing like a child. 'Look at my refectory, just look at it!' And he was away, scurrying from room to room, exclaiming with delight. He bounded up the great staircase, strode along the corridors, flung open doors. He hurried back down, outside into the courtyard, paused to stare all around. He ran up the snicket between the cottages and took in the barns and the ponies. He flew back down and across the courtyard and hauled open the conservatory veranda. Eileen, puffing along behind him, unlocked a cottage door and he went through, slid open the back door and stepped out onto the balcony. He stopped dead and stared down the valley.

He turned to Eileen. 'It's all here, isn't it? Every last feature. You remembered it all…'

She nodded and he gently folded her into his arms.

'Thank you,' he said softly.

*

The days wound slowly by as Jack was introduced to the Gilbert's people and became familiar with the house. He approached James with some reluctance, but it gradually faded as he was proudly shown the kitchen and cellars. Jack found it impossible to resist James' welcome into the kingdom that should have been his, and was drawn back again and again.

He was also welcomed into the workroom and began to feel less like visiting royalty as the Project Workers drew him in, explaining their role and taking him through some of their projects. He withdrew a little, though, as Gemma described with pride the homeless projects she was involved in, but then he sat himself down by her and said quietly, 'I was homeless for a long time…'

Gemma touched his hand. 'That must have been horrible. We spend a lot of time on homeless projects – it's one of Mrs. Gilbert's priorities.'

Jack nodded wordlessly, squeezed her shoulder and moved on.

Back outside, he took gulps of fresh air and headed for the stables. The ponies trotted across the paddock to see what he might have for them.

'You familiar with ponies?' John asked, coming up behind him.

'Yes, we get about on them where I live.'

'You want to explore the estate? Shall I take you?'

'That would be great, thanks.'

'Tell me about this place you live, then,' John said, as they trotted along the back road.

As Jack described the settlement, he realised how much it meant to him.

'It sounds like you are settled there, happy. Will you come and live here, d'you think?'

'I don't know, John. I have a good life there, and people who've come to mean a lot to me.'

John nodded. 'I know what you mean. I feel the same way about The Gilbert.'

*

After a week or so, Jack went to find Richard.

'I've got to go and talk to the police, haven't I? You said they might not charge me with anything...'

'I would be surprised if they do – you were just a kid, trying to protect yourself and your mother from a grown man. You didn't set out to hurt him. There were no witnesses. But I can't guarantee it, Jack. Whatever happens though, you will be able to stop looking over your shoulder for the first time in your adult life.'

'OK, let's get it over with. You'll be with me, won't you?'

'Of course. I'll ring them. Eileen will need to come – they will want a statement from her too.'

*

'Eileen and Jack Gilbert are here, guv, with Richard Aubrey.'

'We'll see the lad first. Put him in interview room 3.'

'Now then lad, what have you got to tell me?' Letwynd asked Jack.

Jack took a deep breath then slowly and carefully recounted the events of that grim night, six years ago. Occasionally he stopped to steady himself. Letwynd waited patiently, Hallam wrote quietly.

When he was done, Letwynd studied him thoughtfully.

'Where have you been since, Jack?'

'I was homeless for a long time, moving around. I ended up in Scotland, in a commune. No-one knew where I was.'

'Not your mother?'

'No.'

'What brought you back, Jack?'

'My mother hired a private detective. He found me.'

'That's more than we managed to do, lad. How well did you know Jennie Green?' he asked, suddenly changing course and watching Jack closely.

'I only met her once, at a fundraising do. I heard her name a lot though, when my mother and Daniel were talking about her work. I knew she was giving my mother a hard time. Not that he was sympathetic. He treated her like shit, putting her down and slapping her about. I don't know why she put up with it. Kids see and hear things they're not meant to, when the grown-ups think they are away in their bedrooms.'

'How long have you been at The Gilbert?'

'Ten days.'

'Your first visit?'

'Yes.'

'And you haven't seen Jennie Green since?'

'No.'

'What about Daniel Croft?'

Jack shuddered. 'No, and I hope I never have to see him ever again.'

'I think that's enough for now, Jack. We may need to talk to you again. Thank you for coming to see us. It was a brave thing to do. Well done.'

Richard settled Jack in a coffee shop and went back to be with Eileen while she gave her statement.

Wrung out, Jack and Eileen were glad to get back to her apartment at The Gilbert.

*

'Interesting,' Letwynd said to Hallam.

'Their accounts pretty much tally with one another.'

'Well, they would. They've had ten days to get them straight.'

'Don't you believe them?'

'Actually, I do,' Letwynd replied. 'But now it looks even worse for Eileen Gilbert. I would want to kill Jennie Green if she and Croft had done that to my family.'

'But they didn't have to come and tell us, guv. Jack could have stayed under the radar in Scotland forever. Officially, he doesn't exist and they must know that. No tax record, no driving licence, nothing. We'd probably never have found him. Are we going to charge him with anything, guv?'

'What would be the point of that, Hallam? Waste of public money. If we did, Richard Aubrey would tear the case to bits anyway.'

*

'I think it's time for me to go home, Mum. There's a lot of work to do to get ready for the winter. They'll be needing me.'

Eileen winced at his use of the word 'home.'

'I will see you soon though, won't I?'

'Why don't you come up for Christmas? It's always a good time, you'd like it, we have fun. I could come back with you after, for a longer visit. Quite a few people go off to the city from January for a month or two, to earn a bit of money. There's not much needs doing and no tourists.'

'I would love to, Jack, thank you.'

'Would you mind if I invite Chris, too? He's never been up for Christmas – it was always his busiest time at work.'

'Jack, Chris has been the nearest you have ever had to a father. He was there for you when I was not. I have no right to mind, and I wouldn't even if I did have the right. Do you want a car to go back in?'

Jack laughed. 'I don't have a licence, mum. Oh, I can drive alright but not legally!'

'Shall I drive you up?'

'No, put me on a train, they will pick me up at the other end. We do it all the time. And we've got that flashy four-by-four now, haven't we!'

Chapter 51

Eileen Gilbert didn't do Christmas. She had always said that she considered it to be grossly over-rated – there was enough loneliness about without rubbing people's noses in it. Gift giving, parties and feasts should be part of everyday life, not a once-a-year ritual. Lonely and homeless people needed attention every day, not just on December the Twenty-fifth.

Out of respect for those that did, however, she always closed The Gilbert for a week over Christmas and New Year.

Spending Christmas Day with the Right Hons had become the tradition for Richard, Eileen, John, George and Susan, who always arrived bearing an enormous, perfectly roasted turkey and a pudding as big as a baby's head.

This year, however, Eileen announced at the Wednesday staff meeting,

'Chris and I are going to spend Christmas with Jack. He will be coming back with us for a long visit and I thought I would throw a party, early in January. It will be a good way of saying thank you to everyone who has worked so hard through this last difficult year. I have already mentioned the idea to James, and we are going to get Chris's wedding crew back to take the pressure off him. I want him to be able to enjoy it too! Perhaps we could start drawing up a guest list.'

*

Dean stared at his invitation from The Gilbert. An Epiphany Party? He hadn't been to a party since he was a child. And what was an Epiphany? He placed it reverently on his mantelpiece, pushing aside the clutter and wiping off the dust with his sleeve, to give it pride of place.

*

Hallam knocked and entered Letwynd's Office.

'I have had an invitation from The Gilbert…no, that is not quite right…I have had an invitation from John Hardy to attend a party at The Gilbert…' she stumbled to a close, her face pink.

Letwynd raised an eyebrow and put down his pen.

'What you do in your private life isn't really any concern of mine, assuming it doesn't bring the Force into disrepute, of course,' he replied, a small smile lifting his mouth. 'Look, if we had a shred of evidence that John Hardy was a person of interest in the Jennie Green case, I would take a different view, but we don't. If he turns out to be our man, I will eat my truncheon, with curry sauce. And I will deny we ever had this conversation.'

Hallam beamed and Letwynd watched her leave with something like regret, his eyes straying to the picture of his wife and kids on his desk.

She had been a lot like Hallam when they had met when they were training. Pretty as they come. Keen as mustard for the job, but she had given it up to raise four children and be there when he could get home. When had he last come home when he was supposed to? He couldn't remember. He glanced at the clock on the wall. It was an hour past his finishing time and he hadn't even noticed. He closed the file on his desk. Why not today? He packed his work away and set off home, his step firm.

Chapter 52

October was a mellow month, as if the weather gods had exhausted themselves in the September storms and gales. John and his team spent every daylight hour preparing the Reserve and Park for their winter slumber. Fences were repaired and treated, hedgehog houses were furnished with bedding, nest boxes emptied and cleaned. George busied in the gardens, clearing leaves and giving the lawns their last cut.

Richard often slipped across to spend the evening with John. They would doze in front of the fire, occasionally conversing but often comfortably silent, the radio murmuring quietly in the background, the dogs crashed out on the rug.

They discussed replacing Harry. It was obvious that he would not now return, and they needed to replace him before the spring. What should they do about Dean? He had a knack of upsetting people, but he could not be faulted in his devotion to The Gilbert. He would, presumably, not need to live in Harry's cottage, having his own place down in the town. They knew that he stayed in the Reserve late into the night, patrolling in case the murderer returned. He could not be dissuaded from it and they had given up trying.

It was late one night towards the end of October when Richard and John, who had both dozed off in the warmth from the fire, were roused by Floss and Milly growling and pacing at the door to the hall. Tilda prodded her wet nose against Richard's hand, whining her distress.

John opened the door and Floss and Milly raced to the back room, standing up at the window and barking.

'Hush!' John ordered. 'Quiet!'

He peered out into the darkness. There was nothing to be seen. They crept upstairs to the back bedroom, leaving the light off, the dogs dancing silently around their legs, and looked out of the window.

'There!' Richard whispered, pointing towards the barn.

'Hells bells!' John muttered as he caught a glimpse of a dark figure in the faint moonlight. 'Looks like we have company.'

They hurried back downstairs, and John fetched two shotguns and loaded them. Richard shook his head,

'I couldn't hit a bus,' he said. 'I don't even know which end is which.'

'Take it,' John growled. 'Just wave it about, scare the bugger. OK, I am going to let the dogs out,' he said, picking up an enormous torch. 'Just don't shoot 'em, eh?'

He slid the bolts back and quietly opened the door.

'Rats!' he muttered, and the dogs flew out, barking furiously while Tilda prudently slipped away under the table.

They disappeared into the darkness. John and Richard galloped after them, the torch beam swinging wildly, following the shouts and curses. These were not guard dogs – it was not in their nature to attack but they nipped and darted about, snarling and barking at the intruder's heels as they fled away towards the hill. The figure paused and Richard and John heard a high yelp as a dog was kicked. Then there was a streak of light which arced into the dark sky, trailing smoke as it went. It landed in the open hay barn and a bloom of flame burst in the darkness, blinding them.

Blinking away the flashes in their eyes, they saw the fire run rapidly across the dry bales, smoke and sparks spitting into the night air.

'Shit!' John said. 'Call the fire brigade!'

He set off in pursuit of the intruder as Richard fumbled for his phone. Lights went on in George's house and his back door was flung open.

They heard a shotgun blast into the sky and John roar,

'Stop right there or I will blow your bloody head off!'

He reappeared a few moments later, his shotgun prodding a dark figure towards the cottages.

In the light of the mushrooming inferno, they recognised Daniel Croft, his face a mess of fear and defiance. John shoved him into the old coal house and slammed the bolt across.

Lights were going on all over The Gilbert. Figures appeared against the leaping firelight, helping George to unreel the garden hoses, beating at the flames with anything to hand.

'The ponies!' John shouted, running.

He yanked open the stable doors and the ponies crashed out, their eyes white with terror as they thundered away up the paddock, screaming with fear and galloping in circles in the darkness, desperate to escape.

Jo ran out into her garden, clutching Paul.

'Here, give him to me,' Susan called. 'I'll take him to Shari's'

'Go with Granny Sue, Paul – you'll be safe with her. Help look after Tanya – she will be really scared.'

Paul gulped back his terror and reached out to Susan who ran through her cottage and across the yard, the little boy clutched against her, his arms tight around her neck.

Chris and Jasmine, panting from running, yanked towels off Jo's washing line and joined the beaters.

Richard became aware that Dean was at his side, furiously stamping on sparks, and slapping at the flames with his coat. He seemed not to notice as Richard beat his head when embers landed in his hair.

Grimly they fought on until a great wrenching groan tore through the night as the barn roof sagged and tilted. Richard yanked Dean away.

'Too late!' he shouted. 'Come away!'

People scattered as the barn caved in on itself, sending flames and sparks high into the dark sky. Not satisfied, the fire raced on towards the stable block and the garage barn, flicking and jumping from roof to roof.

Fire engines, sirens shrieking, dashed into the carpark, disgorging men and hoses, closely followed by two police cars.

'Get back,' they commanded. 'All of you, get back!'

The people fell back before the policeman's advance, collecting together in silence as the firefighters, silhouetted against the orange and red inferno, fought on. Nobody except James moved or spoke until the last flickering fire spot sputtered out – he slipped quietly away towards the house. Jo, Jasmine and Amy, their arms around each other, sobbed quietly while Eileen stood stock still, her expression grim.

As silence fell, broken only by the hissing of steam and the occasional crash of falling beams, hammering and terrified screaming could be heard. The firemen looked around for the source. John beckoned to the policemen.

'Take him away before I bloody kill him,' he said, unbolting the coal house door.

Croft fell out at their feet, sobbing hysterically, his arms over his head against the kicking he was sure would come.

*

They collected in the Refectory, a sorry, dirty, singed group, some in nightclothes, the children dozing in their mother's arms.

James brought out big bowls of soup and platters of bread.

Eileen stared at him. 'Where has this come from, for goodness sake?'

James grinned, the smile creasing the grime on his face.

'It's tomorrow's,' he said. 'Good job I'd already made it.'

Eileen found herself at the centre of the group, the people drawing close as if for comfort.

'It could have been the house if you had not spotted him,' Eileen said.

'Possibly,' Richard said, 'but I think he was just trying to frighten you – show you what he could do if you didn't pay up.'

'Where did you spring from, Dean?' John asked.

'I was just leaving the Reserve when I saw the flames. Good job I had my bike with me.'

'Thank you, Dean,' Eileen said kindly, 'Will you stay here with us tonight, in one of the mews apartments? You will be wanting a shower and some clean clothes. I am sure we can find something to fit you and we can give you a good big breakfast in the morning.'

Dean looked around at the sooty, streaked faces and realised that, apart from the young woman with a child on her lap, he knew all of these people by name, and they were all smiling at him.

'I'd like that very much, thank you.'

'You are more than welcome,' Eileen replied.

Chapter 53

Dawn showed the extent of the devastation. The two great barns and the stable block were smoking ruins, the roofs and all the timbers gone. All of the vehicles were scorched wrecks. The ponies were huddled in the far corner of the paddock, still jumpy with fear. John had been with them since first light, soothing and comforting them.

The firefighters were damping down the embers, combing the area, writing their reports.

Dean couldn't think where he was for a moment as he woke in the clean, sweet smelling bed. He swung his legs out and went to the window. If it were not for the pall of steam and filthy smoke hanging over the cottages opposite, he could doubt that last night had really happened. For now, he could bear to see no more.

Pushing his feet into the slippers by the door and lifting the dressing gown from its hook, he made his way down to the kitchen. He could not resist looking in the cupboards and fridge as he waited for the kettle to boil, examining the bewildering selection of teas and coffees. Almond milk? What on earth is almond milk?

He settled for tea. You couldn't' go wrong with Yorkshire Tea. His mother always used to make tea in a pot and put the milk in a jug. He took them and a mug from the cupboard and the tray from the side. He lifted the lid from a matching pot to find sugar, and rooted in a drawer for a spoon. There were two croissants in a box on the side which he carefully tipped onto a plate. Putting everything on the tray he carried it across to the table. Sliding open the big patio doors he stepped out onto the balcony. The acrid reek of the fire caught in his throat, but his attention was caught by the view right down to the beck. He shaded his eyes against the low autumn dawn and looked across to his precious Reserve. How would it feel to wake up every morning and look out at it knowing he was a Ranger, that he really belonged there?

Going back in he carefully carried the tray to the table outside, settling himself to read the paper he had found on his doormat, but his eyes strayed again and again to the view and he let the paper drop and just sat, looking.

Rustling to the side caught his attention and he swivelled to look at the trellis, searching for the bird or whatever was disturbing the clematis. He jumped when his eyes met the wide, brown pair regarding him with fearful curiosity through the leaves. The eyes studied him for a long moment and then disappeared.

Dean was unsettled. He tried to return to his reverie but found his attention drawn back to the trellis, though the eyes did not reappear. Quickly finishing his tea, he collected everything up and returned to the kitchen. Having carefully washed up and put away, he climbed the stairs. He would have another shower, scalding hot with lots of that sweet smelling, foaming gel. He had only a bath at home – the sooty filth swirling away last night had been a pleasure to watch. There was a new toothbrush and several big fluffy towels to complete the luxury. He pulled on the odd, mismatched selection of clothes and regarded himself in the mirror.

'You dress like a blind thief,' his mother would have said.

With regret, he let himself out of the apartment, closing the door carefully behind him. He saw the eyes, now set in a pretty little round face, regarding him from the window next door. He had never had a lot to do with children. He could clearly remember being one himself, but they were not good memories. An awkward, lonely boy, only his mother and big sister had been able to love him. His peers either mocked or ignored him. He could not remember his father at all.

He closed the conservatory door behind him just as a car pulled up in the yard. Laura and Jim emerged, and Laura actually hugged him.

'Oh, you poor thing! It must have been awful!' she exclaimed.

'It was pretty bad,' Dean muttered, his body rigid with embarrassment from the contact. 'I'll take you round.'

Laura stared, disbelieving at the scene.

'May I take pictures?' she asked Eileen, who nodded her assent.

'Had your breakfast, Dean?' John called,

'I've got to get to work,' Dean replied.

'Go on, it won't take a minute. You can't go to work on empty!' John shouted back.

John was right – he had time.

The Refectory was full of firefighters, but James immediately came to welcome Dean and bring him an enormous platter.

'Get that down you,' he said. 'You need your calories after last night!'

Laura and Jim were not the only ones. Bad news knows all the fast roads and several journalists returned. This time, there would be no dirt dished on their pages, only sympathy that The Gilbert had suffered yet another blow.

*

The Gilbert's people had slept where they could that night. Everyone stank of the fire, however much they showered. The firefighters declared the cottages structurally sound – the conversion had been well done, so they had withstood the heat, but they too reeked of the inferno. Greasy soot lay over everything. The courtyard was slick with it, but the mews apartments seemed to have been protected from the worst by the cottages.

Hallam and Atkins were the next to arrive.

The backs of the cottages were blackened and scorched, and the smoke seemed to have permeated every room, so Richard and John took them into the house.

They listened carefully as the men described the events of the previous night.

Hallam said quietly to Richard:

'We haven't formally interviewed Croft yet – he needs a solicitor with him. He says he wants it to be you. He seems confident that Mrs. Gilbert will pay your fees.'

Richard stared at her in disbelief.

'I have never knowingly defended a guilty person, I made it a rule. I would not have hesitated for a fifteen-year-old boy trying to protect himself and his mother, but I am certainly not going to break it for Croft.'

'I didn't think so. I can't imagine why he would think you would help him.'

'Can't you?' Richard said. 'He still believes he can blackmail Eileen with what Jack did that night, Hallam. He has been here several times, trying to do just that. She sent him away with a flea in his ear the last time. And I'm guessing he doesn't know that she and Jack have already told you all there is to know.'

Hallam nodded her understanding.

'Croft doesn't own a four-by-four, or anything like it, nor can we find that he ever has done.'

Richard nodded and replied, 'So it seems unlikely that he is our killer. If only it was just the baddies that committed crimes, but you and I know that the most innocent people can do the most terrible things if the circumstances are there.'

'And they can be the most difficult to catch because nobody suspects them,' Hallam agreed.

The insurers were commendably quick off the mark, though the cynic in Eileen did wonder if they might have been less so if she had not been wealthy and in the public eye. They agreed that the fire had not only destroyed the farm buildings but also rendered the cottages virtually uninhabitable and gave the go-ahead for damage limitation work to begin. Eileen and Richard were kept busy bringing back the contractors and workmen who had turned Cheppingham Manor into Gilbert House.

John moved in with Richard, Jo, Amy and Paul into the mews. The Right Hons carried off George and Susan, who agreed to go only on the understanding that they would be back every day to help with the clean-up.

'The most useful thing you can be doing is getting the vehicles replaced,' Eileen told George.

'The Right Hons still own a car, though I usually chauffeur it for them,' George replied. 'We could use that to go and look in some showrooms.'

Chapter 54

'Is that Constable Hallam? It's Annie Lovidge here.'

'Hello, Annie, what can I do for you?'

'That man who set fire to The Gilbert...Daniel Croft. I just saw his picture in the Argos. I've seen him in Cheppingham before, several times, back in the summer.'

'We'll come and see you, Annie. Now, if that's alright.'

'Yeah, sure.'

'We're on our way.'

Annie let them in, grinned and said, 'I'll put the kettle on, I know you like a cuppa.'

When they were settled, Hallam asked,

'Are you sure it was him?'

'It took me a while to place him, but then I remembered. He kept trying to chat me up in The Beckside, wouldn't take no for an answer. "I've got a villa in Spain. You'd love it. I'd give you a really good time." Load of rubbish, of course, he must have thought I was born yesterday. And there was one night, late, when I was walking Simon's dog on the meadow, it was just getting dark, and he came out of the side gate of the Reserve –frightened the life out of me in the gloom. He gave me the creeps, I don't know why. His sort are ten-a-penny and they don't usually bother me – I'm used to it, working at The Beckside.'

'Annie, can you remember exactly when it was?'

'You've got me there. It must have been the summer holidays, though, because the kids were playing rounders all day every day. They were still at it, even though it was getting dark. The dog ran off with their ball. I couldn't get it off her till she dropped it to bark at Croft. He kicked her and swore at me.'

'Did you ever see him with anybody else?'

'No, that's it, there's nothing more to tell you. He came several times, though. Once the weather broke, I didn't see him again. Is it true what they said in the paper – that he's Eileen Gilbert's ex-husband?'

Hallam nodded. 'Thank you, Annie, that is all really helpful. If you think of anything else, you will let me know, won't you?'

'Course. I know it didn't work out with me and Harry, but I was happy living up at The Gilbert. They're good people. I miss it.'

*

Letwynd and the team chewed over this new information.

'Right,' Letwynd said. 'Let's get the timeline clear.'

He began to scrawl on a white board.

'Jennie Green came for interview in early June. She and Rivers worked up that Argos article which came out at beginning of July. This named Eileen Gilbert but there was no photo.

Jennie met up with Harry at the reserve workshop through June, July and August. During this time Annie Lovidge saw Daniel Croft hanging around. Jennie was murdered in early September.

Rivers article for the national paper, The Quire, came out in mid-September. This named Eileen Gilbert and featured a photograph of her.

Croft appeared at The Gilbert almost immediately afterwards. So, Croft was in Cheppingham before Eileen's photo was published,' he concluded and stepped back to study the board.

'We know that Croft comes and goes from Spain every so often. He must have seen that first article in the Argos somehow, and come to check it out, just like I said,' Hallam said.

'But why didn't he go up to the house, if he had sussed that it was his ex who owned The Gilbert? He was quick enough to get up there after the second article came out, looking for his share of her money. Why was he prowling about the estate? What are we missing?' Letwynd replied.

'Perhaps he was stalking her.' Hallam said.

Letwynd stared at her for a long time, then his face slowly lit up.

'He was stalking alright, but it wasn't Eileen Gilbert. We've been looking at it back to front! Fetch him up to the interview room, get that duty solicitor back in.'

*

'It wasn't Eileen who was obsessed with Jennie Green was it, Daniel?' Letwyn asked, noting with satisfaction the fear that flitted across Croft's face.

'Did Jennie know you were watching her, Daniel? How many times did you spy on her over the years, eh? Did she promise to run off to Spain with you, way back then? Let you down, did she? She was good at that, by all accounts – using people then dumping them. How did you know Jennie was in Cheppingham eh? Let me guess – you saw that tweet she put up.'

Croft stared at him in dismay, then looked away. 'No comment,' he said, his voice shaking. The solicitor tried to object, but Letwyn ploughed on, ignoring him.

'You'll tell us all about it in the end, Daniel. Stewing over her in your villa, getting more and more bitter. All that anger bottled up for years, you'll let it out, and it will be a relief, you'll see. You must have thought it was such an unlucky coincidence when you saw that article in The Quire and realised that your ex-wife owned the estate where you had killed Jennie. But it wasn't a coincidence at all, Daniel, it was Eileen who brought Jennie there. If you hadn't got greedy and tried to get your cut of Eileen's money, you could have disappeared off back to Spain and we would never have even linked you to it, let alone caught you. Did you see her shagging that young lad, just like she used to shag you? What did you think you were doing, following her up there in your hire car, that stormy night? Plan to give them a fright, did you? You did that alright. You must have seen that lad run away, and then you had her on her own! What did you plan to do? Sweep her away to your villa? I bet she didn't even remember your name!

Daniel's face crumpled.

Letwynd sighed with satisfaction as he charged Daniel Croft with the murder of Jennie Green.

Chapter 55

JCBs rolled into the carpark, scraping and scooping the gooey black mess of the hay barn into wagons as icy rain turned it into a quagmire. The remaining structures collapsed, flinging dirt and soot into the air as they were cleared.

John and Eileen surveyed the carnage with dismay.

'We need to get the ponies away,' John said. 'I'm getting a pre-fabricated stable block put up on the pasture beyond the garden. I don't think we are going to be able to put most of this right till the spring,' he added gloomily, and Eileen was forced to agree.

Having rescued their most treasured possessions, the inhabitants of the cottages watched as every stick of furniture, stinking carpet and soot-streaked duvet was flung into skips in the courtyard.

Great tarpaulins were spread over the floors of the house in an attempt to protect them from the filthy black muck being tracked in by the army of workers, as James worked to sustain them with an unending supply of hot food.

It seemed as if they would never get rid of the black, toxic muck and, in the end, it was decided that the only way was to dig out the top few feet of the entire area and replace it. The car park and the concrete floors of the outbuildings were smashed up and carried away. They did the same in the paddock and ton after ton of soil and hardcore trundled out of the drive. Only then did some hope of cleanliness return.

It was Christmas before the last of the debris was cleared away and it would have taken much longer if every farmer and contractor in the district had not mucked in to get it done.

'Before you go to Scotland,' Richard said to Eileen, 'what do you want to do about Dean, and the Rangers job?'

'What does John think? It must be his decision, not mine.'

'John thinks Dean has earned it. He has sounded out the other volunteers and none seem to particularly want to go for it – they prefer to come and go when it suits them. A couple of them actually said that Dean is the obvious choice! His devotion to the Reserve is without question.'

'Well, that's good enough for me,' Eileen said. 'And John's the one who will have to work with him!' she added with a laugh.

The Gilbert emptied as Christmas approached. Jo and Amy went home to their parents as usual and they took Shari with them –Tanya and Paul wanted to spend Christmas together, so it was the obvious answer. Richard wondered if he would get an invitation from Sophie but was not really surprised when it didn't come. For the first time since he had come to The Gilbert, he thought of spending some time with his old friends, but ruefully realised that he had no London base anymore and the hotels would no doubt be booked solid. Sophie seemed to have a knack of displacing him from his home.

'Fancy a trip to London?' he asked John.

'No thanks. I went there once, that was enough,' was John's retort.

The rest went off to visit friends and family but were soon drawn back – a few days away were enough to fulfil obligations. The Gilbert was home, their colleagues were family. The little group gradually expanded as the travellers returned to while away the quiet evenings in the soft light of the Refectory lamps. Even Marnie Hallam and Dean Magson found their way to them, drawn by the undemanding sincerity of the invitations from their friends, and the simple acceptance they found.

*

John decided that these quiet days were an ideal time to teach Dean to ride a pony and drive a golf buggy.

Dean was proud of his easy progress with the buggy, but he regarded the ponies with near terror.

'Spend some time with them, Dean. Fill your pockets with pony nuts, talk to them, groom them, fill their hay racks. They will soon get to know you. Talk firmly to them, tell them what you are going to do and then do it. Don't hesitate.'

'Can they understand me, then?' Dean asked.

'You'd be surprised,' John replied, 'but even if they don't, they understand your tone of voice. They feel safe if you are confident.'

The ponies watched with interest as Dean approach the new stable block. He went from stable door to stable door, tentatively offering them pony nuts on the palm of his hand as John had taught him. They snickered and shook their manes, their ears flicking back and forth. Dean made reassuring noises, as much for himself as them and patted their faces, trying not to jump when they flung their heads up.

'Right,' John said. 'Watch me put the bridle on, then we'll bring her out.'

Dean watched intently, muttering a running commentary quietly to himself, committing every step to memory and did the same as John saddled up.

'Lead her up and down, Dean. Her name's Hazel. Go on, she won't bite.'

Dean did as he was told, and the pony quietly followed him across the field. As he turned to return, he met Hazel's benevolent gaze and stood, captivated. The pony snorted gently in his face then dropped her head, offering her ears to be caressed. As he touched them, Dean found that the ears were warm and as soft as velvet. When he paused, Hazel nudged him gently and Dean began to smile. He stroked the pony's firm neck, felt its heat against his face. She leant on him and Dean's smile broadened.

John watched in wonder as Dean and the pony bonded.

'Well I'm damned,' he muttered as Dean led her back, his face glowing.

'How do you feel about getting up on her, then, Dean?'

Dean swallowed hard and squared his shoulders.

'I'll give it a go. Will you be holding her?'

'Don't you worry, I promise not to let go,' John said, laughing.

Dean clutched the saddle, his knuckles white, as John led Hazel up and down, but slowly he began to relax, and by the end of the session, he was brave enough to just rest his hands on it.

*

Richard watched with interest as John spent hour after hour patiently riding the estate, leading Hazel and Dean. He and Tilda joined him, and John decided Richard might as well learn too. He led the way, riding bareback as usual, the two learners following behind, the dogs trotting around the ponies' legs.

Marnie Hallam was the next to join the party, so John had to go on foot, now leading three learners.

They tramped the estate, working up an appetite for their evening meal, spent companionably in the Refectory. Dean, as usual, insisted on dealing with the ponies and their tack, loving the feel of their breath on his face and the smell of their twitching hides.

*

The Gilbert slowly returned to life as December gave way to January and preparations for the party began in earnest. Every inch was cleaned and tidied and polished. The tarpaulin sheeting had gone, and the floors were buffed to brilliance. Chris's wedding team arrived with vans full of decorations and had to be stopped from covering the chairs with ruched, white satin coats. Gradually the activity reached fever pitch until, by the time Eileen returned, the beautiful old house was ready to receive its most important guests: Jack and his band of neighbours who had decided they might as well come and see this Gilbert that they had heard so much about.

Last minute preparations began. The Refectory walls had been hung with delicate evergreen swags. A thousand tiny silver stars were suspended on invisibly fine wire from the ceiling and walls, reflecting the light. Snowy linen cloths were laid on the tables which were ranged around the walls to leave the centre clear for dancing. Glasses were polished, and champagne was chilled. Delicious aromas floated from the kitchen and the dumb waiter creaked and whirred as it brought up fresh ingredients and took down trays of the cold courses to be carefully garnished and laid in the fridges and cold rooms. The hot courses were timed to be finished just as they were needed, by some unwritten magical process. The small army of cooks and chefs created a complex dance as they moved around the kitchen, long experience enabling them to thread in and out and around without colliding, as if remotely controlled.

People began to arrive, murmuring and gasping at the softly lit beauty of the room.

The Refectory was full by the time Eileen opened the door at the foot of her stairs, and the spontaneous applause that greeted their arrival brought tears to her eyes.

A huge banner hung across the room: "*Welcome Home!*" it cried.

The more she looked, the more she saw. The Right Hons with their Park Committee; Dean proudly sporting his new Ranger T-shirt and surrounded by the volunteers; Marnie Hallam, with John's arm around her, and his miraculously clean dogs at their feet; Laura taking photos for the Argos; Shari dwarfed by an enormous chef's apron; Jasmine; Chris, they were all there.

Richard came forward and hugged her. 'Welcome home, Eileen. We have missed you.'

Turning to Jack and his friends he said, 'Welcome back to The Gilbert – your second home!'

Jack saw the welcoming faces all around them in the stunning room. He put his arm around Eileen and drew her close. 'Mum, they love you. I love you. You created all this, and I am so proud of you.'

End.

Printed in Great Britain
by Amazon

63209259R00169